MW01707916

THE CHURCH in the wildwood

Alanna Rusnak

Cover design by Alanna Rusnak
Photography by Sergi Zolkin

THE CHURCH IN THE WILDWOOD

Alanna Rusnak

2017

First Printing: 2017
ALANNA RUSNAK PUBLISHING

ISBN: 978-0-9921255-5-4

Alanna Rusnak Publishing
282906 Normanby/Bentinck Townline
Durham, Ontario, Canada, N0G 1R0

Contact publisher for Library and Archives Canada catalogue information.

www.alannarusnak.com

for Scott

we didn't build a church
but what we did build
is quite lovely

"You are not supposed to like things. Only to understand."

"Today is only one day in all the days that will ever be. But what will happen in all the other days that ever come can depend on what you do today."

Ernest Hemingway
For Whom The Bell Tolls

prologue

Saturday, July 9, 1977

WHEN IRIS CARVER DIED, he felt her leaving like cool silk. She whispered past him as she left, tickling the nape of his neck with a ghostly touch; slipping through his fingers and floating down the hall until she was nothing but a shadow bowing into the cracks of the painted wainscotting.

Joseph had wandered from the hospital in a daze of misery and now, standing in the home she had held together with her heart, he sensed her absence in cool breaths of memory and goodbye.

Anger and pain fought an internal duel as he studied himself in the bathroom mirror. He saw her in his own reflection—in the way his eyes held secrets and his expression hung between innocence and too much world knowledge—and for a moment he forgot to breathe.

He let his head fall forward. It hit the glass just hard enough to rend a crack through from the top right corner to the very middle where, when he looked again, his face was split and foreign, wearing the scar of her passing.

It was both her heart and her magic that had held their house together and it made sense, in his grief-stricken mind, that it would begin to fall apart the moment her spirit left.

He looked at himself—at the shades of grief shadowing the hollows beneath his eyes; at his wild, orphaned hair; at his heart spilling raw down his cheeks—and he hated what he saw.

"Who are you?" he asked, watching his lips move but unable to answer himself.

He fingered the old nail he wore strung around his neck with a strip of leather. The word 'RELIC' was carved into its rusty surface. It reflected backwards in the cracked mirror. "Killer," he mouthed to his distorted likeness.

But he didn't dare say the word aloud.

chapter one

Sunday, June 19, 1977

THE BELL RANG EVERY MORNING. Joseph felt its resonate judgement as it echoed across the short mile from town, reduced to something that became more of a feeling in his chest—there in that secret place where he timidly clung to empty dreams of escaping the sheltered life holding him captive.

On Sunday mornings its chime carried more heaviness, adding an additional three rings to its prideful worship as it called the faithful to the old stone church on the hill.

He learned long ago to keep quiet. It did no good to call out for his mother. It wouldn't make any difference and she wouldn't come any earlier. He would be alone from dusk until dawn, sentenced to solitary darkness until the final peal of morning was shucked from the rind of night.

It was what he had known since he was very young.

On nights that felt particularly lonely, he would shut himself into his closet. The complete darkness made it easy to sleep and the door provided one more layer of protection from the late night Saturday sounds of his mother's employment.

The floor was hard but so was he, and he would lie flat on his back, his feet pressed straight against the far wall, the top of his head firm against the other. He would lie like he saw his father lie that ugly day so long ago, when they placed his cold body in a box and fed him to the earth.

He lay still as death, his hands resting over his heart. He liked to feel it beat through his undershirt; the way its tempo could define him as vital though he felt little more than alive. He would click his tongue against his front teeth in rhythm with his pulse and pretend it was music in the house that held no melody beyond the songs of his mother.

"Say your prayers," she would say, locking his bedroom door and dropping the key into her apron pocket with the swish of metal against fabric. "Protect your purity."

"Yes, Momma."

"It's my job to protect your body," she had once told him. "It is God's to protect your soul. That's why you must pray. Every night you must ask God to forgive your greatest sin."

For fifteen years he tried to understand what she meant when she said these things. For fifteen years he heard the story of his great sin; how he killed his twin sister right before birth; how he flipped himself over her and twisted a cord around her throat like a demon; how he took every one of her breaths for himself, taking on the sin of a woman by being born without innocence.

"You bear the mark of her," she had told him. "You carry the curse of her blood within you and so you must repent. God is hardest on the worst of us—the murderers and rapists—and you are both because you stole her life *and* her virtue."

He never questioned her and he didn't question his own guilt though he never actually felt guilty. He thought perhaps his mother still mourned his baby sister and this was how she knew to survive—by heaping her grief onto his young shoulders so he might bear it for her.

His lost twin was the ghost who rested like an angel on his shoulder, whispering to him in the darkness, jumping out of reach just as he would get close enough to grab hold. She was the piece that left him incomplete.

He couldn't imagine the grief his mother must feel. He couldn't imagine the hole that missing life had left. He only knew the loss of a sister he didn't know, a sister he had no real memory of beyond a distant feeling. He couldn't begin to grasp the pain wrapped up in the loss of a daughter.

Poor Momma. Poor lost Momma. As fragile as her name.

She had once shown him her namesake, turning the deep purple bloom in her slender fingers, showing him its unique shape and hooded, perplexing beauty. "I am named for this," she told him. "An iris is one of God's greatest mysteries. It is strange and precious and that is what my mother used to say of me."

Strange indeed.

As a young boy he hadn't understood the noises groaning through their house on nights long after the sun had set and the bedroom key had fallen into her pocket. He never used to understand the engines that rumbled up the driveway and the muted moans and frantic breaths leaking through the cracks around his locked door. He didn't understand why the bath water would be running as the engine left, permeating the air with the scent of Momma's homemade soap. He never used to know his mother put food on the table by letting men release their needs inside her tiny frame, all while his own needs were locked inside his bedroom with him. He never used to know the ways of a man with a woman, or the politics of sexuality, or that if one engine came they could eat pork but if there were two they could eat beef.

He learned most of what he needed to know from books. Momma taught him to read before he was four years old. She taught him his letters and basic math skills and told him he had no need of traditional schooling because she could give him all he needed to know to run the land. She said school was as much a dangerous cult as any organized religion.

The only books they owned were Bibles, a faded blue hymnal, and his father's tragically abused paperback copy of *For Whom The Bell Tolls*—the cover feeling like worn denim, colours sun-baked and fingerprinted to a pale shadow of its origin, pages dog-eared, passages underlined and starred with dull pencil lines.

"Why did he love it so much?" Joseph once asked.

"He said he felt Hemingway's heart," Momma told him. "He said he could smell the blood on the pages as he read it. I think he saw a little of himself there. Kindreds of the shattered souls. Your father was only happy when his heart was broken."

Joseph tried to read it once or twice but had no context with which to relate, so he'd flipped through and dwelt on the highlighted pieces, thinking this was the only way he could know his father intimately and feeling horribly torn by the emptiness the marked words heralded.

He'd taken to sleeping with it under his pillow as a way to reclaim what had been stolen from him.

It didn't work. But it did make him uncomfortable and his

sleep fitful. He felt this was a fair price to pay for the loss of a father.

Lack of personally owned literature did little to inhibit his education. At least once a week, they would take the old Chevette to town with Momma's purse full of her late night earnings. She would leave him at the library 'to find his own curriculum' while she went to the supermarket with her freshly washed lavender hair.

At first he spent time in the children's section, poring over picture books and stories about knights and dragons, but as he grew older and more curious he migrated upstairs to the science and sociology sections. Most recently he had been studying escape artists and professional thieves. He found an entire book on lock-picking and set to studying it with fevered fascination.

He never told Momma the things he learned. He never confessed the hours he tucked himself deep in the stacks with a copy of *Madame Bovary,* or how he'd sneak the latest *Cosmopolitan* magazine from the periodicals desk and read it from behind a propped up hardcover about The Great War. He knew what was happening every time he heard those strange and awful sounds pervading their old house when she thought he was sleeping. He never spoke a word of it. He knew his knowing would kill her.

Such an odd feeling it was, the loss of respect for his own mother. He loved her—he knew that fully—but he didn't know her, not really. She was a stranger. He thought, perhaps, she was a little like Alice, lost in a world of her own imaginings and he was appointed the wise one on the other side, shaking her awake, trying to pull her out of her strange wonderland.

Except he wasn't sure he wanted to wake her. She lived her life with a beautiful innocence and a large part of him wanted to leave her in her ignorance and escape on his own.

But to do that he needed a way to get beyond his locked bedroom door.

HE FOUND THE NAIL WHEN HE WAS THIRTEEN. On a restless night his hands explored the closet wall and discovered its head. It protruded only a fraction but he felt a surge of euphoria at its revelation, knowing its meaning the moment his finger found it.

Freedom.

Whitewashed cedar clad the closet walls and each night, as he scratched at the wood surrounding the nailhead, fresh hints of the sweet perfume invaded his nostrils with a promise of something better.

He could bring no tools with him. Momma only allowed him to wear his white undershirt and blue cotton boxer shorts. He wasn't sure why he needed the nail or how it might help him, but his desire had given him a sense of purpose through the long hours he spent locked in his little bedroom each night.

He lifted his finger to his mouth and sucked away the fresh blood gathering along his cuticle from a small cut gained in his final efforts against the nail. He shifted slightly and felt the unfamiliar push of metal against his skin where he had tucked it, finally free after nearly two years, into the elastic waist of his shorts. He felt strangely ecstatic as he waited silently for his mother to come.

The final peal of the bell began just as he heard her soft footsteps outside his door.

"For whom does the bell toll?" she asked—words rich in nostalgia, clinging awkwardly to the memory of a dead husband in much the same way Joseph slept upon the memory of a dead father.

The last note faded away as softly as her voice, always lingering he thought, between madness and mourning. He could already smell her hair through the small crack beneath the door.

"It tolls for sinners," he answered her with the expected response, sitting up in his bed and turning his body toward the sound of her voice. "It tolls for me."

He heard the key in the lock and waited until the door opened before he stood.

"Good morning, Joseph," his mother said, opening her arms to him.

"Good morning, Momma." He walked into her embrace, not resisting as she pressed his head against her shoulder and pushed her fingers through his hair. He could smell her homemade rosemary and lemongrass deodorant and he found it comforting despite any concerns he secretly harboured regarding her integrity.

"Did you sleep well?" she asked.

He nodded against her and she pulled back from him, reaching out to place a stray strand of hair. "You're so tall now," she said. "You're taller than me. Come, I'm making oatmeal." She took his hand and turned on bare feet, leading him to the stairs.

He pulled his hand back, hesitating. "I would like to get dressed first," he said. "I'm too old to run around the house like this, Momma."

She looked puzzled, pulling out the skirt of her long, white nightgown. "Aren't I much older than you?" She spun in a circle, light laughter floating from her lips.

She was so pretty, her pale skin dotted lightly with freckles and long hair that had gleams of red and gold when the sun hit it right. She seemed young and free-spirited. Looking at her standing at the top of the stairs, bathed in a stream of light from the dormer window and laughing like she didn't have a secret, Joseph felt lonelier than he'd ever felt before.

"Please, Momma." His hand rested against his waist, feeling the nail which no longer felt secure now that he stood before her.

She studied his face with a look of pained softness. He'd taken all the good bits of her and all the handsome bits of his father, Paisley, and been built into a stunning boy. His features were soft and his eyes had a sad little tilt to them, making him seem forever melancholy, even when he smiled. His skin was smooth and pale like hers but his hair was dark and messy like Paisley's, and she heard his father's voice echoing in him now that he talked with the timbre of a man. "Fine, fine," she said with a wave of her hand. "Meet me in the kitchen. Tea?"

"Yes, please."

He waited until he heard her feet on the stairs before slipping the nail from his waistband and tucking it between the pages of the Bible on his worn side table. He dressed quickly and went downstairs where the kettle already whistled.

He settled himself at the table as she poured the tea, cupping his fingers around the mug to frighten away the early morning chill.

"You've hurt yourself," his mother said. She set down the teapot, touching his finger where blood had dried around his nail like a waning crescent moon.

Joseph pulled his hand back and waved her off with the other. "Chopping wood yesterday," he lied. "I got a sliver stuck under my nail."

She raised an eyebrow but settled into her seat before

reaching across to grasp his wrist. “Say our Psalm for us, Joseph.”

He bowed his head, scratching at a scar on his arm that had been there as long as he remembered, and spoke their morning verses to his tea cup.

She nudged his bowl when he finished. “Eat your oatmeal,” she said. “We leave for the clearing soon. And stop that scratching. It's a wonder it healed enough to even scar what with how you never seem to be able to leave it alone.”

Joseph licked his finger and rubbed it over the spot, erasing the lines his nails had left behind, leaving the raised, white scar shining like a beacon from his reddened skin, itching still with the memory of something he couldn't quite grasp.

Monday, October 14, 1968

REVEREND SAMUEL GREENE pressed his little car ahead, the highway passing beneath him with desperation.

“Children raised in the city are a little less human,” Iris had told him two days before when he tried to convince her to take his name and move into the parsonage. “They obsess over the world instead of getting lost in creation.” She spoke her words like scripture, with the faintest whisper of mystery. She couldn’t speak without him getting lost in her—in the cadence of her voice and the melody of her worldview. She was magic. She was a labyrinth in which he happily lost his way. She was his north star and his saving grace.

She was his greatest sin.

The deserted resort lay a mile west off the highway and as Samuel pulled up he could just make out the worn sign hanging crookedly from an iron frame. 'Harridan Bluffs Golf & Ski Resort, est. 1923' it bragged, though despite its former glory it had no right to boast in its eroding state. A heavy chain blocked the overgrown entrance and vandals had spray painted a red X across 'resort' and written 'HELL' and 'MAY ROTH ROT!' below.

Samuel climbed from his car and unhooked the old chain, laying it in the overgrowth before navigating the winding laneway.

The remnants of a guardhouse and heavy gate sat just beyond the first curve. Dense weeds obstructed his path but the car pushed through easily even as his heart beat wildly and his palms grew sweaty against the steering wheel.

He thought of her here, of her bare feet against this grass, of the truths she had discovered and the fear she learned to live with on this land. *What of children raised in a place devoid of childhood? Would they not be even less human than those raised in the city?* He thought so, though no one had ever made him feel more human than Iris Carver.

Faded signs claimed there were golf greens on either side of him, but the land was wild. It had been decades since a golf ball was hit across this acreage.

There had been a time when Harridan Bluffs was the height of fashionable destinations. There were still old men in Fallmoore who told stories of the golden years—of the glamorous New Year's Eve parties and how they almost won the bid to host a Canadian Open championship. The resort hung on during the Depression, becoming a hotspot for the wealthy who needed to pretend their affluence put them above the woes of the world, but when the war started the resort began to lose ground. As more men were called away to fight, things became leaner and leaner until finally they couldn't keep the doors open any longer. Women weren't playing golf, nor were they willing to leave their families in the dead of winter to make use of the slopes. It sat empty for almost ten years before a mysterious buyer bought it up for cash. Folks speculated it would be restored to its prewar glory but nothing came of it. Gates went up near the end of the driveway and as the years went by, people slowly let it slip away until it became just another old story.

Samuel pulled the car to a stop in front of the imposing structure. He stretched his fingers and rubbed his thumb along his palm to work away the cramp caused by gripping the wheel so tightly. It did little to settle him. He knew he wasn't here to find anything good. He knew the truth would hurt him.

He didn't care.

Taking a calming breath, he grabbed a flashlight from the glove compartment and climbed out of the car.

The stillness shocked him more than anything. The lush landscape absorbed the highway sounds and the eerie silence left him feeling like the last survivor on a lonely planet, nothing but the ruins of a painful past to give evidence to the life that once was.

A cricket chirped and a tickle of a breeze lit across the driveway, brushing its fingers across the back of his neck, sending a cool dribble of nervous sweat down his back. He shivered and raised his eyes to a flag so tattered he couldn't tell the emblem or the colour it had once displayed. A chipmunk scurried across his path and he jumped, knocking himself back against the car. He laughed at himself—a pathetic giggle that was more like a restrained sob. With a hand against his racing heart he took in the outer facade.

The building stood three stories tall, paint peeling around all the windows, some of which were boarded up with wood, abused and grey from exposure to the elements. The ground was scattered with trash and ugly words were spray-painted around the outer walls, their vulgarity making his body flush with embarrassed heat.

The courts had ordered the building levelled; the land cleaned up and sold so all profits could go to the victims of the crimes that happened within those walls. It was a nice idea but the baggage that came with the property seemed a sore selling point and Samuel wondered if it would ever actually happen.

Torn police tape hung at the main entrance. He pushed it aside and tried the door, but it wouldn't budge. He picked his way through garbage around to the side where he found a boarded window which had already been pried open by other trespassers before him. He climbed inside and clicked on his flashlight.

Samuel stood in a large space, its ceiling open the full three stories where a glass roof would have bathed the room in natural light had it not been so late in the day. The second floor mezzanine was dotted with doors leading into rooms. The third floor had windows gazing out from more rooms in the upper level. Everywhere he looked, ruin gazed back at him. He navigated around the overturned chairs and tables to the back. A small stage set up with a lectern reminded him of his own church except that, there on the back wall where a cross might have been, hung a framed painting of John Peter Roth, the self-proclaimed prophet of Harridan Bluffs. Long scars marred the stained canvas, looking like someone might have taken a large kitchen knife to the image—an exercise in hate or revenge.

Samuel froze, his flashlight gleaming in Roth's eyes, making it almost seem like he looked back at him. He shivered in its presence, feeling sick. The idea of that man putting his hands on those little girls…

He turned from the self-important likeness, bending in half with hands pressed to his knees as he waited for the waves of nausea to pass. Cold fingers of dread danced along his nape, causing him to feel both chilled and overheated. He knew that face was forever frozen to the inside of his eyelids, and never again would he be able to look at his Iris without knowing the face she'd stared into too many times during her youth.

Saliva collected at the back of his throat and he thought he might vomit. Instead, he willed his breathing to calm and he spit into the dust before pulling himself away to explore the surrounding area.

A large kitchen sat to one side and an office to the other. A hotel reception counter stood back by the main entrance and large stairways left and right of the main doors led to the lodgings.

His heart grew heavier with each room he searched. When he reached the upper level it became clear the children had stayed there. Ragged dolls lay tossed on some of the beds that weren't overturned and he found a small metal firetruck with a missing wheel.

The bed in the last room drew him like a magnet, its cheerfully flowered bedspread belying the horrible truth of those walls. He felt his heart in his chest as he sat on it, not caring about the years of dust or the musty scent of animals. He pushed aside the dirty pillow to see the headboard, staring at the name carved deeply into the wood like he didn't really believe it was there, not wanting to accept this painful evidence that proved her story true.

It was easy to call something ancient history when you

yourself are far removed from its reality, but to be in the place of its horrendous happening and to see the evidence bringing truth to that story was powerfully moving.

He traced the letters of her name, carved with the same knife she tried to cut Roth with on her wedding night. I.R.I.S. He blinked against tears as he pictured her, innocent, frightened and so young when Roth used that same carving knife to mark her for himself on the night he took her as his wife.

chapter two

Sunday, June 19, 1977

THE LAND WAS JOSEPH'S FATHER'S. It had been his father's father's father's. It stretched from the edge of Benwaw County to the southern border of Fallmoore, split by the old railway line. Aside from all the farmable land there were acres and acres covered in forest that gave way to swamp that turned back into forest again. In the very centre, one hundred yards from the railway path, sat a small clearing, and in that small clearing stood a circle of black stones. This was their sanctuary.

The old Carver hunting cabin stood on the edge of the glade, its weather-beaten logs the colour of fog, the hinges on the door stained orange with rust.

"Why can't we have our service inside?" Joseph once asked.

"Because God doesn't live within walls," his mother replied.

She believed if God existed in all things then they had no need of conventional buildings and people to house their faith. God created the world to be the mirror unto himself and there was no better place for communion than upon the same soil from which he formed man.

Her dress was white, like she had been blessed with a purity he knew was a lie, and it looked angelic against the forest floor as they sat crossed-legged inside the stone circle. She straightened the fabric of her skirt and reached for his hands, a small smile on her face as she savoured the place lying closest to her heart.

Handmade wind-chimes littered the surrounding trees. They were made of old bottles, broken glass, and pieces of metal. They sparkled when the sunlight shone right, singing their tinny song whenever the breeze moved. "So there is always a melody of worship in this place," she told him.

Joseph's favourite moment was when his mother would start singing. Her rich voice filled the clearing, disturbing the birds who took to flight in a whoosh of flapping wings.

"Ring out, wild bells, to the wild sky,
The flying cloud, the frosty light
The year is dying in the night;
Ring out, wild bells, and let him die."

It was somber and beautiful, and the way her voice hung on the minor notes made the hairs rise on his arms no matter how often he heard her sing it. Verse after verse he would study her face as she tilted it back to catch the sun through the trees. Little motes would dance in the dust just above her nose and they seemed like tiny angels trying to kiss her as she sang.

Her eyes wouldn't open until the last note had faded, and she would smile like she'd been touched by heaven before cracking the spine of her worn Bible to read aloud. As far as he could remember, they had read the entire thing, cover to cover, twice. They were now on their third time through.

"The man who first taught me these stories was not a good man," she once told him. "He hurt me in ways that time doesn't heal."

"Then why share these stories with me if they came from a bad man?" Joseph asked.

"They aren't *his* stories," she replied. "You know the phrase, 'Don't kill the messenger'?"

He nodded.

"Had I punished him for what he did I would have never learned the beauty in these pages…the poetry and mystery. He hurt me. Yes. But he also gave me a great gift."

His mother read with an air of awe, like she couldn't wait to find out what might happen, like she didn't already know the stories inside out.

He would let his mind drift, perfectly focused on her face so she believed in his devotion while he wandered away. *What would it be like to go to school? To explore the world beyond the only town he knew? To kiss a girl?*

It had been a few years earlier when he first saw boys and girls doing what boys and girls do. There had been whispers and laughter behind the anthropology shelf in the library. He moved aside a heavy text to investigate and saw a girl pressed against the stacks, her pretty white blouse raised just enough to reveal the soft line of her waist. A boy had his hands around her neck, thumbs resting just in front of her ears, the left one stroking her right cheek, his mouth right on hers. Soft sighs emanated from them and they sounded a little like Saturday night. He was so enthralled by what he saw that he didn't hear the librarian come up behind him. "What are you doing?" she demanded in a harsh whisper.

He jumped forward, startled, knocking books off the shelf on the other side. The boy and girl tore themselves apart and the girl's surprised eyes found his, locking for a moment before she said, "It's that Carver kid," with an air of disgust.

That Carver kid. That's all anyone knew of him. The strange boy who didn't go to school, who lived out in the country, who spent time at the library, who didn't play baseball or go to the movies at the little theatre near the top of the hill, who didn't have a friend in the world but his strange hippie mother.

That Carver kid.

"Say a prayer for your daddy now," his mother prompted, resting her Bible on a blanket of pine needles and folding her hands into a teepee at her chin.

Joseph blinked himself out of his daydreaming. "Yes, Momma," he said obediently, clearing his throat and matching her posture. "Lord God," he began, praying the same practised prayer he always prayed. "Kindly have mercy toward the soul of my father; forgive him any sins committed on this earth and allow me to see him again in the joy of heaven. Through Christ, Our Lord. Amen."

"Amen," his mother said, taking his hands and kissing his fingers. "Let's pick flowers for his grave."

His father wasn't really buried in those woods. He rested at the Carver plot in the Fallmoore Presbyterian Cemetery with the rest of his family, but after he died, Momma had gathered all his things and dug them into the ground here. She said a grave is a place of mourning and of letting go. It didn't matter where you put the body; it mattered where you said goodbye. A rough-hewn cross marked the place above his plaid button-downs and herringbone paddy cap. *'Paisley'* had been carved in the crosspiece with a knife.

"He was so heart-struck to learn your sister was dead," she said. "He just couldn't take it. He was a gentle soul, Paisley was. So broken and angry. Couldn't even look at you. Wouldn't hold you either. He said it hurt him too much to look at you and remember your sister..." She recited the story with a strange reverence.

Joseph lay a wild snapdragon at the base of the cross, ignoring her.

"This is where I want to be buried too, Joseph. You'll see to that, won't you? Someday? I want to lay where I am closest to God. I want to be easy to find when he comes to take me back to Paisley."

"Of course, Momma."

She became suddenly agitated, walking over to the big oak tree where the ground had been obviously disturbed. Leaves were kicked and long scuff marks marred the dirt. Small stacks of twigs and branches were piled over by the old hunting cabin. "Town kids," she said, picking up some of the brush and throwing it back into the woods. "Help me, Joseph."

"What is it, Momma?" he asked, tossing a small load.

"Kids come out here sometimes. Telling ghost stories in the woods, I think."

"Why?" Joseph asked.

"Children raised in the city are a little less human. I've always told you that, haven't I?"

"Yes."

"They have no respect for our sacred places." She didn't

stop until the pile was completely gone, its branches scattered back into the woods. “What day is it?” she asked.

“June 19. In two days it'll be the longest day of the year,” he said, foolishly thinking she might congratulate him for being so bright.

She nodded and wiped her brow. “That’s when they’ll come,” she said. “Let’s go home, Joseph. Let’s go home where we’ll be safe.”

“From town kids?” he asked, stumbling after her down the path to their house. “You think they’d hurt us?”

“They’re a little less human, Joseph.”

Saturday, January 1, 1955

ON THE FIRST OF EVERY YEAR, they held hands and formed a circle, men and women, boys and girls. Roth stood on a stool in the centre, the hub of a humming wheel, reading the words of Lord Tennyson as a blessing over their new beginning.

“Ring out the old, ring in the new
Ring happy bells, across the snow…”

It always confused Iris. There were no bells at Harridan Bluffs and the poem was the only piece of literature that didn’t come from the pages of a Bible.

“Why does it matter?” she once asked.

“We are nothing without traditions,” she was told.

The answer wasn’t satisfying but she didn’t dwell on it because in truth, she adored the verses—they moved her somehow—tugging on an internal chord.

When she lay in bed at night, weighted with a sadness she could neither account for nor understand, she'd whisper those words into the darkness, camping on *'Ring out the grief that saps the mind'*, repeating it until sleep closed her eyes to the empty truth of her existence.

"What are you doing?" her friend Rose would ask from the bed beside her.

"I'm praying," she'd answer, knowing in her heart that if the moment ever came and she really heard the ringing of the bells, it would be the moment she found the freedom of a life beyond the traditions of Harridan Bluffs.

November 12, 1962

My darling daughter,

I wanted only to hold you in my arms. I thought I had earned that as your father, but they told me you were already gone. I wanted to bury you so I could plant flowers on your grave, but they claimed there was no body. Your brother is strong and wild and his face grows red as he mourns for you. I watch him and even in his sleep he is reaching out for you and tightening his fists in anger when he cannot find you.

Your mother did not wish for a daughter. She believes that females are cursed. I dreamed of a daughter and feel those hopes dashed like waves against rocks.

I think I loved you before I even knew of you.

Eternally yours,

Father

There is no one thing that's true. It's all true. E.H.

chapter three

Tuesday, June 21, 1977

TWELVE OF THEM WALKED along the old railroad, leaves blanketing the retired ties and crunching beneath their sneakers. The moon was just a sliver, a little hook of a fingernail hanging in the sky like it had been forgotten there. It offered no real light.

A 'No Trespassing' sign hung prominently across the gate by the main road but they all slipped beneath it to disappear into the darkness beyond. Words were not going to stop them.

Since the tragedy, the strange circle in the trees had been raised to local legend, offering a site for ghost stories and a place where town kids deemed worthy were brought to hear the tale of Paisley Carver's chilling death.

The older boys led the way. Neal and Cam Darvey had planned the whole thing and they chose the path, along with their cousin Isaac, while the others followed. Grace stayed right at Sherwin's side and held a flashlight in her hand.

She glanced down at Sherwin's feet as he navigated the treacherous trail. Her light cast enough of a glow that she could see a hole in the end of his running shoe. His laces were so frayed they looked like doll's hair.

"Your feet cold?" she asked him. The early summer air was slightly cool and damp, and from the chill she felt through her own well-built soles she guessed his socks were already wet.

"No," he said. "Why? Are yours?"

"I'm okay."

Sherwin never complained about the low means of his family, about how they had to shop at The Salvation Army Thrift Store on Douglas Street or how they were on the church list for the Feed-A-Family Turkey Drive every Christmas. He always seemed content.

Grace studied him out of the corner of her eye—the strong line of his jaw and the thick wave of his dark hair. She smiled softly to herself and slipped her hand into his.

"You guys coming to the movies Friday?" Cam called back to them.

"Farrah Fawcett," Neal added. "They're finally showing *Logan's Run*."

"Not sure," Sherwin said.

"Oh, Farrah," Cam hooted and the other boys joined him like wolves howling at the moon.

They were walking farther and farther from the main road.

"I'm not sure we should be doing this," Grace whispered.

"Come on, Gracie," Sherwin said, bumping her playfully with his shoulder. "It'll be fun."

Jackson ran up from behind and grabbed Grace at the waist.

She screamed and jumped forward.

The boys in front spun around and as a trio hissed, "Shhhhhhhh."

Grace shoved Jackson. "Not funny!"

"But you're so cute when you're mad," Jackson teased, hopping out of the way of her hand as she reached to shove him again.

"Take it easy, Jackson," Sherwin said. "It was hard enough getting her to come with us. Don't make her change her mind now."

"Whatever, lame-o!" Jackson said and he ran to catch up with Neal.

"Why tonight?" Grace asked. "Of all the nights? Why summer solstice?"

Jackson turned and kept walking backwards, his flashlight up at his chin, "Because it's spooooooky," he said, laughing. "It's when the witches like to play."

"It's stupid," Grace said, kicking at a dead leaf.

"Better than hanging out with your mom, isn't it?" Sherwin asked.

"She had a shift at the hospital tonight. She thinks I'm at an end of school party."

"You are!" Sherwin winked. "Or you will be soon, anyway."

Up ahead the boys had stopped and were pointing their flashlights into the trees. "It's this way," Cam said and he stepped off the path.

TIME SLOWED TO A CRAWL the moment Joseph heard the lock turn and the key fall into his mother's dress pocket. He lay back on his bed, fully dressed, hands laced behind his head, staring up at a ceiling that had nothing to say to him.

He listened to the shuffle of his mother changing into her nightgown and the sound of her bedsprings moaning as she crawled beneath the blankets. This meant she was not expecting a visitor. Relief flooded him.

He lay still, clicking his tongue against the roof of his mouth while the sky changed from murky twilight to full night. As darkness reached the final corner, he sat up on the side of the bed, flipped on his lamp, and pulled the nail from between the pages of his Bible. He spun it in his fingers several times before approaching the door on his tiptoes.

The ancient floorboards groaned beneath him as he crouched at the keyhole. His body made too much shadow to see more than the dark shape of the hole, yawning at him from its place on the old door. Using an unwound wire coat hanger as a tension hook he pushed the nail into the keyhole, feeling the resistance of the locking mechanism inside.

He lost track of time as he fought with it. His legs protested against his crouched position but he ignored the pain and stayed focused on his task. The more he tried, the more he understood what he had to do to make it give, recalling all the reading he had done on escape artists and professional thievery to outsmart the old lock workings.

When it finally released, Joseph collapsed on the wooden floor, his arm over his face while he stretched out his legs and waited the long minutes it took for his blood to start circulating properly again. He gritted his teeth against the sharp tingles coursing from his feet to his thighs. When they passed, he put back the nail, turned off his lamp, and slipped quietly down the stairs. He grabbed his jacket and hat from the coat tree, pulling the door closed so gently its click was hardly noticeable.

He zipped his jacket as he walked out past the garden and

disappeared into the woods, pulling his collar up around his neck and the grey cap down securely over his ears.

The night felt cool for late June. His breath shot out ahead of him as he navigated the forest floor in the darkness, walking along the path to the clearing. He dug his hands into his pockets to keep the cold away from his fingers, though he wasn't certain if the chill was from the air or his own nervousness.

He wasn't exactly sure what had compelled him to make this journey but the thought of kids on their land made him curious and acutely aware of how alone they were. It was just himself and Momma and her invisible, nighttime visitors.

Every story he had ever read was somehow about having friends. Even the ones that weren't nice. Other people had people in their lives. He had his mother. Even she had other people. Momma said she was all he needed and friends would only bring him trouble. He wasn't sure anymore if she was right.

The worn path opened up in front of him even though the darkness didn't. He and Momma walked the same way every Sunday when they came to have the services she claimed meant they were paying proper respect to God and to his dead father. Each step was hauntingly familiar. He knew his way with or without light.

Guilt plagued him as he thought of her waking to find his bedroom empty. *"But I wanted to see what the less than human humans were doing,"* he imagined himself saying. *"I don't want you to keep me away from the world anymore."* She would be so hurt and feel so betrayed.

He prayed she wouldn't wake up.

THE WOODS WERE DENSE and the darkness felt heavy as

the town-kids left the railway path and descended into the full cover of trees. Flashlight beams cut through in an eerie bouncing rhythm that was oddly comforting. Twelve different sets of footsteps broke the forest stillness.

Grace was relieved when they came out of the trees into a clearing. "What is this?" she asked, waving her flashlight over the circle of black stones in the centre of the glade.

"This is where it happened," Cam said, coming up beside her with an armload of small branches. "There be blood on this soil." He laughed and dropped the twigs in the middle of the stones. Some of the other boys did the same until they had a pile large enough to keep them warm and lend some light.

"I thought you already had wood gathered," Jenna commented.

Cam shrugged. "We did, but someone moved it. Maybe they're watching us now."

"Shut it!" Jenna said, pushing him and laughing, though she did pause to take a quick look around for prying eyes.

Wind-chimes played a haunting soundtrack in the background as the boys set up the branches in the centre of the stones.

Neal pulled a plastic bag from his coat and, one by one, lifted out twelve white taper candles. When they each held one, he took a lighter and lit his own, passing his flame until all twelve wicks were fluttering against the night breeze. "Youngest lights the fire," he said. "Grace, you're up."

Grace looked to Sherwin. He winked and nodded his head in encouragement. She knelt by the pile of sticks and held her candle against a flyer for Ernie's Hardware Store until it caught, the flickering light bouncing off the strange glass wind-chimes that seemed to hang from every tree. "Why are there twelve stones?" she asked as she moved back into the circle.

Jenna pulled a card from her back pocket and placed it in Grace's hand. "Because of The Hanged Man," she said.

In the light of the fire Grace could see the image of a blond man, hung upside down by a foot that was lashed to a tree branch. The roman numeral for twelve was at the top of the card. "What is this?" Grace asked, uncomfortable.

"It's a Tarot card," Jenna shrugged. "I got them at the discount store. I thought it was funny."

"Hilarious," Grace said.

"Who has the cups?" Cam asked.

Isaac pulled out a sleeve of small paper cups. "Got 'em!" He separated the stack and passed them out.

Neal fished a small bottle of schnapps from his jacket. "It was all I could find at home," he said sheepishly as he poured a swallow into each cup.

"Say the thing," Morgan begged, practically giddy as she sniffed at the liquid in her cup.

Neal grinned, tossing aside the empty bottle and raising his cup. They all matched his motion and he gestured wide with his candle as he spoke. "*Oh come to the church in the wildwood, to the trees where the wildflowers bloom, where the parting hymn will be chanted, we will weep by the side of the tomb.*"

"Amen," the kids called out in chorus.

"Amen," said Neal, tipping back his drink and taking it in one swallow.

Grace took a little taste and made a face.

"Don't be a baby," Cam said, putting his finger on the bottom of her cup and tipping it back so she would drink the rest.

Grace swallowed, sputtering a little and wiping her mouth

with the back of her hand.

Neal held his candle so it cast heavy shadows on his face. "Twelve stones for the twelve apostles of the truth," he said in a low whisper. "Take your seat and hear the tale." He threw his head back and laughed wickedly.

Morgan and Jenna giggled and ran to a stone while Grace grabbed hold of Sherwin and leaned in to his ear. "I don't want to be here. I want to go home."

"Gracie, it's all just in fun. Come on." He swung an arm around her shoulder and pulled her against him. "Loosen up a bit. You're way too serious." He kissed her temple and she smiled in spite of herself.

"Okay," she said. "But only for a little while."

"Deal," Sherwin said, winking at her and pulling her back to a stone, taking the one right beside her.

JOSEPH SMELLED THE FIRE BEFORE HE SAW IT. The trespassers were doing a poor job of keeping quiet and he would have found his way to them even if he hadn't known the path so well. Laughter and silly noises floated on the air. It all made him very sad.

Friends would only bring him trouble, that's what Momma always said. And girls? Girls would turn his world on its end.

He never told her that was exactly what he wanted—that for once he wanted to feel his world flip upside down. He wanted to know what it meant to be truly alive. To live for something beyond himself. To have adventure and chaos. To feel the ecstasy of love and the pain of a broken heart. Ever since that moment in the library when he watched the boy put his mouth over the girl's, he thought about wanting it. He pined for a life beyond the calm control of his mother. He wanted a life of his own.

He eased up beside the big oak tree and peered out at the scene before him. He knew his mother would be furious if she saw the desecration they were making of her land, but he felt a warm stirring of joy in his belly at the sight of it all.

The old shovel leaned against the tree like it always did. Momma said it was a tool for goodbyes and so it should remain at the place of the farewell. The rusted head cut into the dirt at the roots of the oak and the wooden handle was cracked and grey. He felt its age as he wrapped his fingers around the old shaft.

When the story began he slid down the back of the tree until his bottom landed on the ground, the shovel resting across his lap. He leaned his head back, closed his eyes, and listened, feeling more alive in the stillness of the moment than he had in all of his fifteen years.

Unlike the teenagers in the clearing, he had never heard this tale before. At least not like this.

chapter four

Tuesday, June 21, 1977

"IT WAS A DARK AND STORMY NIGHT," Neal began. Laughter and feigned spooky noises filled the clearing before everyone settled to listen to the story they had all heard a thousand times before. "Iris was the prettiest girl anywhere around Fallmoore. People say she could have whatever she wanted just by looking at a man. People say you should never look her straight in the eye. People say she's a witch and this is her hallowed ground." He paused, moving his hand in a wide arc to take in the whole clearing. "No one knows where she came from," he continued. "Paisley Carver picked her up hitchhiking one evening on his way home from Harridan Point. Her hair had a little red in it and her eyes had a little green and he was never the same after meeting her. He brought her back to his land and he married her that summer. She was only seventeen. She was always barefoot when anybody saw her, and she always wore these white dresses you could see through to the shadow of her legs when the sun shone right. She wouldn't talk to the ladies in town. She thought women were unclean or something. When Paisley got her pregnant he was so proud, bragging around town to all his buddies who were jealous because his wife was younger and prettier than all their wives put together. He was a kind man and he did whatever she asked him to do. He waited on her like a queen. When the doctor heard two heartbeats inside his Iris he was thrilled to learn his family was going to double, and Iris set to work sewing two white baptismal gowns. But slowly Iris grew sullen and though he continued to care for her she became cold and cruel. When it came time for the babies to be born, Iris sent Paisley away. He waited outside the doors and soon heard the sound of two babies crying. But then it suddenly turned to one. He burst through the doors to find a naked baby boy lying on a scale with no sign of the second child. He held the boy against himself and turned to look at his wife who was as white and angry as a ghost. Blood covered the floor. 'Your daughter is dead,' she said. The doctors pushed him out of the way, wheeled Iris to surgery to deal with the bleeding, and left him standing with a wailing baby, a dead daughter, and a broken heart."

"Was the daughter really dead?" Grace asked, caught up in the story.

"No one really knows," Jenna said. "Some people think she just threw the girl away. There's no birth record for a daughter. At least not that anyone's seen."

"So how do they even know?" Grace asked, scratching at her arm.

"Paisley knew. He knew there was supposed to be twins," Jenna told her. "He bragged about it."

“Can I get back to the story, Ms. Interruptus?” Neal whined.

“Sorry,” Grace mumbled, settling back against her stone. The fire crackled in the centre.

“Poor Paisley was heartbroken,” Neal continued. “He began to see Iris for the witch she really was. He couldn’t bear to hold his son and he became obsessed with finding out the truth about his daughter, but it was as if she hadn’t existed. As days went on he felt weaker and weaker. He thought maybe she cursed him, but he couldn’t prove it. But Iris? Well, she was as happy as she’d ever been, caring for her little boy and ignoring Paisley as he grew more and more desperate in his search for the truth. She soon grew tired of him and, saying she had a way to bring him peace, she led him here to this very spot. There was a hole in the ground and in it she had placed a doll Paisley had bought himself to remember his lost daughter by. ‘You must bury your grief, Paisley,’ she told him. ‘Your daughter is dead. You must move past it.’ And she picked up a handful of dirt and dropped it into her cruel excavation.

“‘But she isn’t,’ Paisley argued. ‘I feel it in my heart.’

“‘Your heart is wrong, darling,’ Iris insisted, and she set a shovel in front of him and backed up towards that tree,” Neal paused to point behind him at the imposing structure of an ancient oak. “And there, hanging from a branch, was a noose.”

“‘Bury your daughter, Paisley,’ Iris said to him, backing away into the shadows. ‘Bury your daughter and come home to me, or bury your daughter and join her. Follow your heart, my darling.’ Then she disappeared, leaving Paisley to weep over an open grave.

“The next morning Iris returned to this clearing to find his body hanging right there. The rope *creeeaaaak creeeaaaak creeeaaaking* and the branches groaning and the grave firmly filled."

Grace shivered and stared into the fire. She knew the story —everyone knew the story—but being at the actual site caused cold fingers of apprehension to trace their way along her spine.

JOSEPH HAD BEEN YOUNG when his father died and his recollections were thin at best. There were cloudy images of standing on tiptoe to see into the coffin. He remembered a blue scarf wrapped around his father's throat and tucked neatly into his suit jacket. He couldn't remember feeling sad.

He let his fingers wander over the bark as the boy spoke of the very tree he sat against. He imagined the trouble it would have been to climb up into those branches; the way his father must have sweat; how he had surely been blinded by tears. He could picture him, finally standing on the thickest branch, reaching down to pull up the noose that waited for him and setting it around his neck, pulling it tight enough to scratch his skin. Joseph felt the same fear Paisley must have felt as he stood there, seeing the last thing he would ever see, saying one last prayer or calling out one last word. Was it his lost sister's name? Joseph thought that was what he would have said if he'd known it—the final truth that sent him to his death. It seemed appropriate.

He wondered what it felt like to die.

He wondered what it felt like to live.

"THEY SAY THE GHOST OF PAISLEY CARVER haunts this land," Cam said. "They say he never stopped looking for his daughter. They say he lies in wait for a girl to come and then he grabs her and keeps her locked in a tower. They say he is a daughter collector."

Grace was so distracted by what Cam said, she didn't notice Neal had left his spot by the fire until she felt arms come around her and pull her back towards the dark shadow of the woods.

She screamed so loudly it hurt her throat and she thrashed her legs so hard they kicked pine needles into the fire, sending up a fireworks display of sparks.

"Whoa, whoa, whoa, calm down, Grace," Neal said, laughing, dropping her and jumping out of the way of her flailing fists. "It was a joke."

Everyone laughed except Sherwin. He rushed to her side and helped her stand. Her body trembled and she fought against the angry tears burning behind her eyes.

"Not cool, Neal," Sherwin said, lowering himself so he could see straight into Grace's eyes, brushing some pine needles from her hair.

"Whatever, man," said Neal. "We were just having some fun."

A branch cracked and they all spun towards the hanging tree.

"What was that?" Jenna whispered.

"Nothing," said Cam. "Just a raccoon or something."

Another crack.

"Guys…?" said Morgan.

A form appeared at the base of the tree. The dark shape of someone in a paddy cap, holding a shovel.

Three long seconds of silence hovered over the group like an ominous fog before a loud cacophony of screaming and swearing filled the clearing. Candles fell to the ground, their flames snuffed against the earth, wax leaking across the dirt like white blood as the kids rushed to get away.

Everyone ran. Everyone except Grace. Instead of seeking escape, a strange calm fell over her and she stepped forward, oblivious to the chaos around her.

JOSEPH FELT DRAWN TO THE GIRL by the fire and he slowly moved from the shadows into the flickering light, setting down the shovel and showing her his hands so she would know he had no intention of hurting anyone.

Her eyes were wide, glowing from the reflected flame, and her short golden hair and small features gave her a look of perfect innocence, reminding him a little of his mother and a little of the artwork in an old version of Peter Pan he once read at the library.

He wanted to freeze himself in that moment, caught in her gaze, caught in those eyes that held a promise he couldn't quite grasp.

Friendship?

He only knew she was somehow redeeming this place of death with her presence, though he didn't understand how.

"COME ON, GRACE!" Sherwin insisted. She waved him off. She could feel his panic but all of her own was gone.

The shadowy figure had nearly reached the fire, standing just a little taller than she did. As the light of the flames touched his face, she saw he was just a boy, no older than herself, wearing an open jacket over a grey collared shirt and suspenders with dark trousers.

TIME SLOWED SO EACH BREATH seemed a new day, as if the longer they stood in silent contemplation, the more they seemed to know each other. Joseph felt naked in her gaze but he was not ashamed.

He felt *known.*

And it felt like heaven.

Her eyes held a strange pity but there was something more, something that made him want to know *her*, something that made him more aware of his own loneliness than he'd ever been before.

He felt a sob building in his throat.

An older boy suddenly ran forward and grabbed her from behind. "Run, Grace, now!" She stumbled back, something fluttering from her hand as she did, looking back at him over her shoulder as she disappeared into the woods.

Joseph felt a hot tear slip down his cheek and he bent to pick up the paper that had fallen in the dirt, looking down to see a picture of a man hanging from a tree.

Emotions burned through his body in a confusing rush. He felt broken and angry and terrified and discarded. And something else. Something new. Something, he wondered, that was possibly like love. He closed his eyes and tried to settle his spirit, seeing her face floating before his closed lids.

He felt *found.*

Sighing, he wandered over to the wooden cross marking Paisley's forest grave. He set the hanged man's card against the wood, pushing its bottom edge a little ways into the dirt. "What did she do to you?" he asked the inverted man on the card, thinking of his mother and father and the story he wanted to fully know but also avoid entirely.

A scream punctuated the night. He glanced across the

clearing in the direction the kids had disappeared as a sharp pain stabbed through his leg. He gasped as it shot up towards his thigh and he buckled to his knees, grasping his ankle, confused and frightened.

He heard yelling and the sound of branches being broken underfoot.

"I think I twisted it." The female voice floated to him from somewhere beyond his sightline. "Help me."

He heard some grunting, more snapping twigs and a weak whimper that seemed laced with tears before all went silent again, but for the wind-chimes that haunted the clearing.

He looked back to Paisley's cross, rubbing his ankle. "Are you here?" he whispered. "She hurt you and so you're here?"

He received no answer.

Joseph picked himself up, kicked dirt onto the campfire to put out the flame, and limped through the woods to the house, his heart heavy; the image of the girl by the fire tugging at some long lost thread in his mind.

From Iris' Journal

October 30, 1964

It is possible to hate someone and love them in the same breath. I think if Paisley stood before me right now I would kill him for what he has done to both me and our son.

When I found his secrets in the clearing, I could do nothing but let them stay buried, and then reclaim the land over them for better things.

I plan to meet God there. There where Paisley met God.

I made a circle of twelve stones around his secret. Twelve doesn't mean anything to me except that it's the age I was stolen from myself. It's since twelve that I've been trying to steal myself back. One stone for each good year and now I will spend every prayer I have within me within them, trying to break through to heaven.

I hate Paisley.
I love Paisley.
Joseph is my world.

I want nothing more than to be ten years old again...

chapter five

Thursday, August 17, 1954

MARKING A FIRST DEcade on earth meant much more than the nine years that came before. Iris didn't know what a tenth birthday meant outside the walls of Harridan Bluffs but there was no happier day for a Harridan girl than the day she turned ten.

Every girl looked forward to The Promise Ceremony. Sister Lily would do their hair. Sister Mary would take their picture. Sister Margaret would bake their favourite fruit into a pie.

Turning ten opened the door to the journey of becoming a woman, and it was the first day the girls were allowed to wear a dress with lace along the bodice and seaming that showed the beginnings of their grownup shape.

Iris sat very still as Lily wove a white ribbon through her long tresses. "Such a pretty one," she said. "I think perhaps there will be a fight for your attentions."

Iris hadn't understood what she meant then and had posed proudly for her portrait, sitting on a wooden stool beside the large framed likeness of The Prophet on the platform in the sanctuary.

She went with Sister Mary to the darkroom where she watched her mix things from different jugs, slowly bringing her likeness to light in a shallow tray.

When the photograph dried, Iris pasted it into The Promise Book herself, displaying her careful penmanship below where she wrote her name with a feather pen: *Iris, Daughter of Zion.*

She thought the book was lovely and they allowed her to turn back the pages to see all the other daughters before her, their pretty photographs and their names, written as carefully as she had written her own.

The earliest entries had another name and date written below the images. "What do these mean?" she asked.

"That's their assignment," Sister Mary told her. "That's who won the plea to marry her. Just as you'll be chosen from this book one day too."

"Oh," Iris said, thinking it romantic a man would one day see her face within those pages and make a proclamation that he wished to love her. At ten years old she really couldn't understand any chance she had at true romance had been reduced to something of a hand-bound Sears catalogue.

IRIS HAD BEEN YOUNG WHEN her father passed away. She had no memory of him beyond the faded photograph that graced the mantle in the small apartment above the bakery; full army uniform, handsome and proud. She also had no memory of what had initially brought her and her mother to Harridan Bluffs, though retrospect told her it was probably how pretty she looked in her Sunday dress the day 'the man' first invited them.

John Peter Roth baptized her mother into his church one month before he took her as his third wife. She signed over everything they owned, including the two pairs of shoes they each had and the small monthly benefits they received from her husband's life insurance. Blinded by her own grief, she thought she was entering a group of God-fearing people that would help care for her little girl, put food into their hungry bellies and friendship into their lonely hearts.

Iris found Roth strangely handsome, with dark, mesmerizing eyes that cut straight to her soul, black hair peppered with grey, and smart three piece suits tailored to his slim build. She had loved him immediately. There was a spark of the mischievous to him and he was playful when he came into the children's dorm at the end of each day to read to them from the scriptures. They would sit around his feet while one lucky girl snuggled up on his lap as he read from the curling pages of the old book.

Six men lived at The Bluffs including the prophet. They had their own sleeping quarters on the second floor and they each had at least two wives. A few years passed before Iris realized many of the younger wives were the daughters of another man's older wife, but she didn't know enough to question it.

She had very faded memories of life before the complex and never thought to ask her mother why each woman had only one boy baby, why none of the females wore shoes, and why the little girls were not allowed to go outside.

"Why is the door to our dorm locked every night?" she once asked Roth.

"To protect your purity, Iris," he had said.

"And why can't we play with the boys?" she asked after spending an afternoon with her nose pressed against the window, watching a small group of boys kicking a ball in the front yard where the grass wasn't so high.

"It is to protect your purity, Iris," he had told her. "You don't need rough and tumble games to fill your day. Find Rose and play chess."

ROSE WAS JUST OVER A YEAR OLDER than her but they were the dearest of friends. She was a pretty girl, petite and feminine with flaming red hair, and a pale smattering of freckles dotting her ivory face.

The girls all slept on the east side of the third floor. Walls had been knocked down to create a large dormitory with sixteen beds. Iris slept in the bed against the wall, right beneath the large window, and Rose slept in the bed right next to her. They would whisper late into the night, giggle over their plates at dinner time, sit side by side through their lessons, braid each others hair, and handle Tuesday laundry duties together.

But then the changes came to Rose's body. "I've had my first blood, Iris," she had whispered between their beds one night.

Iris understood what this meant for Rose's body, but not that it meant she would be losing her dearest friend to the high demands of womanhood.

They called Rose out from their dormitory very early on a Saturday morning and Iris didn't see her again until Sunday when she walked into the sanctuary. She saw Rose standing at the front of the room wearing a white, shapeless gown that seemed to swallow her. Her hair looked like fire and her eyes were shifty and frightened.

The Prophet had walked up to her and kissed her forehead before turning to his small congregation to make his announcement. "We have a new woman among us!" he cried, and applause broke out around the room, echoing up to the glass ceiling.

"Brother Saul," he called, holding his hand out to one of the men who stood expectantly in the front row.

Saul came forward. Roth took Rose's hand and handed it to Saul. "What God has joined together, let no man tear apart."

Iris saw naked panic written across Rose's face but as she looked around at the other faces in the room she only saw joy. She found her mother, standing with Roth's other wives, a soft, sad smile turning up the corners of her mouth.

Saul lifted Rose's hand and kissed it. There was fire in his eyes as he recited their traditional marriage pledge, "Sing and rejoice, O daughter of Zion: for, lo, I come, and I will dwell in the midst of thee."

"Go and make *new* daughters for us!" Roth proclaimed over them and Saul guided Rose through the crowd, back to the staircase leading up to the men's dormitory. A tear slipped down Rose's cheek as they passed Iris and she made brief, panicked eye contact with her before disappearing up the stairs. Roth carried on into the usual Sunday morning service that had them reciting scripture together and drinking a small sip of wine from a communal cup.

THE NEXT MORNING, Roth gathered the women and girls together and took them outside, their feet bare against the cool dirt. He took a white cloth, a deep, red stain across the middle, and attached it to a rope against the flag pole before raising it up to almost half-mast. Iris recognized it as the gown Rose had been wearing. She searched the small crowd of women for her friend but she was nowhere to be seen. A low hum of panic settled in the pit of her stomach. "Where's Rose?" she asked the girl beside her. "Is that blood?"

"Shhhh," she hushed. "She's where she has been placed."

Roth guided them all to take the hand of the female beside them and together they formed a circle around the flagpole and recited a passage from Proverbs.

"Who can find a virtuous woman for her price is far above rubies. The heart of her husband doth safely trust in her, so that he shall have no need of spoil. She will do him good and not evil all the days of her life…she looketh well to the ways of her household, and eateth not the bread of idleness. Her children arise up and call her blessed; her husband also, and he praiseth her. Many daughters have done virtuously, but thou excellest them all."

WHEN IRIS FINALLY SAW ROSE a week later she was a shell of the girl she had been. Her eyes were dark with heavy circles beneath them and though she made longing eye contact with Iris they couldn't speak because Rose belonged with the women, not the children. She slept in the woman's dorm with the other wives and tended to the babies during the day. Her schooling was over. She had become a wife of Harridan Bluffs.

Iris felt her absence like a gaping hole in her heart.

SHE FOUND THE FIRST NOTE a month later. Her pillow made a crinkling sound when she lay down at night and she reached into the pillowcase to find a folded piece of paper.

Iris,

I wish for nothing more than to be by your side right now. The burden of being a wife is more painful than you can imagine. Don't believe anything they tell you.

I remain your friend always,

Rose

Iris stole a pencil from the classroom the next day and wrote her response on the bottom of the page.

What has he done to you?
I miss you so much.

The truths that came out of their exchanges haunted Iris. The things Rose described were despicable to the mind of a child. Iris looked differently at every woman there but saw nothing of the pain Rose described. She began to live her life in fear and that fear slowly built as she started to recognize the way Roth would stare at her across a room.

She would overhear some of the little girls talking about how they couldn't wait to be selected from the Promise Book and all she wanted was to slap them for being so foolish.

As she fell asleep each night she reminded herself these

girls were born into this life and knew nothing different. Then she would dig through her memory and try to bring into focus that photograph of her father on the old mantle; she was sure that somewhere out there was the memory of a good man who let little girls remain little girls.

chapter six

Wednesday, June 22, 1977

THE COLD MORNING FLOOR WAS A shock to Iris' bare feet when she sat up on the side of her bed. She grabbed a pair of Paisley's old work socks from the bureau, slipping them on before lifting her robe off the hook on the door and knotting it tightly.

She padded down the stairs, pausing at the bottom to stare at a leaf that lay curled on the floor just inside the front door. She bent to pick it up, surprised to find it wet. Rubbing it between her fingers, she tested the lock on the door with her other hand. It was secure. She was certain the floor had been clean when she went to bed the night before. She looked back up the stairs, wondering if Joseph could have possibly been outside, but she could still feel the bedroom key in her nightgown pocket.

She went into the kitchen and set the leaf on the wood stove where it hissed as the moisture touched the hot cast iron. She opened the top trap and set two pieces of wood into the coals left from the previous day to dispel the early morning chill. She filled the kettle, set it on to boil, and climbed back up the stairs to Joseph's room.

He didn't make a sound from behind the door though she knew he would be awake and waiting for her. She let her forehead lean forward to touch the wood, closing her eyes and sighing.

SHE HAD NEVER MEANT TO SUSTAIN THEIR LIVES with the attention of strangers, and she worried that Joseph had wisdom enough to know what went on when his bedroom door was locked each night. It had been a long time since an actual *stranger* had been in her bed but she still depended on near-weekly visits to put food on their table.

Things had been hard following Paisley's death. His suicide had vetoed any chance she had at receiving insurance monies and so she accepted the advances of the town's divorce lawyer after three winter days of having little more than cabbage to eat.

Joseph had cried when she tried to feed him the meagre broth. He cried when she locked his bedroom door for the first time, only to settle when she whispered through the keyhole that he just needed to pray and God would multiply their pitiful cabbage into loaves and fishes.

"But I don't like fishes," Joseph had said, hiccuping through tears and darkness.

"Okay," she told him. "Peanut butter and pickles! You pray."

"Okay, Momma."

"FOR WHOM DOES THE BELL TOLL?" she whispered, her hand pressed against the door as she waited for his practiced response from beyond.

"It tolls for sinners." Joseph's voice cut through the solid-core and she could hear the shuffle as he changed position inside. "It tolls for me."

Every time she expected him to say *'it tolls for you',* and somehow she longed for that because it might finally open the door to true honesty between them. For months now she'd seen it in his eyes, felt his quiet judgement and his wavering trust in her beliefs. She didn't know what it meant except that sometime soon her world would cave in. He wasn't a child any longer. He might choose to hate her. He might choose to condemn her. He might choose to leave her. Her heart ached at the possibilities piling up before her—an impossible mountain that would surely kill her spirit in the end.

She put the key in the lock and turned it before recognizing the regular resistance wasn't there. She paused with her hand on the knob, certain she imagined it, convinced her mind was playing tricks.

She shook her head and opened the door. Joseph stood before her, fully dressed. "Good morning, JoJo," she said, resorting back to his childhood nickname for reasons she couldn't quite understand.

"Good morning, Momma," he said like he always did, but when she looked into his eyes she could see he wasn't the same boy she said goodnight to the day before. Joseph had become a man in the few hours they'd been apart. He seemed hardened somehow. He kissed her cheek but it felt strained, and he smelled faintly of smoke as if he'd been tending a fire in the night. He was so handsome now—tall and strong with dark eyes like a storm. She opened her arms to him.

He walked into her embrace, not resisting as she pressed his head against her shoulder and pushed her fingers through his hair. She breathed in the smoky scent of him, something lingering on the precipice of manhood while still clinging to the sweetness of childhood.

"Did you sleep well?" she asked as he pulled back from her.

His eyes shifted and then focused on her face again. "I did," he said, excusing himself to use the bathroom and brush his teeth.

Iris frowned after him, noticing a slight limp as he crossed the hall. She looked into his room. Everything seemed to be in its right place. His bed was neatly made, his Bible rested squarely on the night table, a tin of homemade deodorant sat on top of his dresser beside the grey paddy cap that used to be his father's.

She had never known him to lie before and she wasn't sure he was lying now, but she felt a heaviness between them she couldn't quite define. There was a separateness—a divide that left her longing for those tender moments of his early days when he would nestle at her breast with nothing but bright adoration in his eyes.

She pulled his door closed and went back down the stairs just as the kettle began to boil.

JOSEPH FIDGETED WITH HIS FINGERS under the table as he recited the morning verses. "He that dwelleth in the secret place of the most High shall abide under the shadow of the Almighty. I will say of the Lord, He is my refuge and my fortress: my God; in Him will I trust…"

"Doesn't it make your heart glad?" Iris asked, dipping a spoonful of honey into her tea.

"Of course, Momma," he said, not lifting his eyes.

"What is it?" she asked, raising the cup to her lips and taking a sip.

"I just…" He paused for a second, unsure. "I just wonder if it loses its meaning when we say it every day the same."

She set down her cup and reached across to grasp his hand, forever marvelling at the strength his fingers now showed, hardened by the land, so much like his father's. "Never, Joseph," she said. "We make the promise stronger by remembering it. There is no other passage in all of scripture that holds more promise than these verses."

"Of course."

"Do you have doubts?"

"No, Momma, no. I have no doubts."

She let go of his hand and smiled as he began to eat his breakfast.

"There's a leaf on top of the wood stove," he said through a mouthful of oatmeal.

She reached over and picked it up, brittle now that it had dried out against the hot surface. She set it on the table between them. "It was on the floor by the door this morning," she said. "It was wet."

Joseph took another bite, staring down at the leaf and not meeting her eyes. "Oh?"

"It was wet," she repeated, "as if someone had just come in from outside. Were you outside in the night, Joseph?"

He raised his gaze to meet hers. "How, Momma?" he asked. "My door was locked."

She nodded, reaching into her pocket and fingering the key. "Of course. Do you love me, Joseph?" she asked, ignoring the poison that emphasized his use of the word 'locked'.

"Of course I love you, Momma." He finished his last swallow of tea, gathered his dishes, and took them to the sink.

"Well, how could it have gotten there?"

He walked back to the table and picked up the leaf, spinning it between his fingers. "Perhaps it was a ghost."

"What do you know of ghosts?"

"Nothing, Momma. Only what haunts you every day that you don't feel compelled enough to share with me."

She sucked in her breath.

Joseph opened the top of the wood stove and dropped the leaf down into the small fire where flames were consuming the wood she had added earlier.

Iris scraped her chair back and carried her own dishes to the sink. She stood with her back to him, her arms tense against the counter.

He stared at her stiff form, the words of the late night story echoing through his head, torn between wanting to comfort her and wanting to hate her. He couldn't bring himself to do either.

"We'll go to town today," she told him. She did not turn around.

"Yes," he said and went to gather his coat.

He had no doubts. He was as sure of this as he was sure of anything.

He was absolutely alone in the world; his mother was a lost soul wearing blinders, and God was nothing but a bedtime story.

From Iris' Journal

December 21, 1964

I am ruined to all the females in the world. We are slaves. We don't belong to ourselves. We belong to the one who claims us.

I was never meant to be the mother to a daughter—but neither was I meant to abandon that which God placed within me. I know that now.

I do look for her sometimes and I see her in shadows. She follows me like a ghost.

I'm quite certain the scar of my choices will be as much a part of me as the scar Roth carved into my thigh.

I miss Paisley. I hate the man he became in the end but I don't blame him.

It was her fault.
It was Paisley's fault.
It was God's fault.

It was nobody's fault.

chapter seven

Wednesday, June 22, 1977

GRACE WAS SPRAWLED ACROSS Sherwin's bed, the latest *Teen* magazine open in front of her as she read about how to have great summer hair and whether Robert Redford really thought looks were everything. Her left foot was wrapped in a tensor bandage. She had only suffered a minor sprain after falling in the woods, but it was tender and her mother told her to keep it elevated.

The record player scratched through *Free Bird* and the lava lamp morphed its contents into a slow-motion dance as *Lynyrd Skynyrd* sang. Rain fell outside the open window, adding to the peaceful soundtrack of the day.

Sherwin pushed through the beaded curtain and held up a black magic marker, a grin across his face. "Found one," he said, plopping down on the brown carpet where large poster boards were sketched out with ‘Home Safe: Race to Save Byton Shelter’.

“You think you’ll get a lot of people signing up?” Grace asked.

Sherwin shrugged as he began to fill in his pencil lines. “A lot of runners doesn’t matter—just so long as we get a lot of sponsors.”

“Hmm,” Grace murmured. “You want help with that?”

Sherwin held up the marker. “Only got one. Sorry.”

He hunched over his project, the sculpted shape of his shoulders and the sinewy grace of his hands distracting her from her magazine. He was long and lean and looked the cliché part of the high school track star.

She was proud of him; proud of this work he was doing to raise awareness; moved by the heartbreak in his eyes when he confessed that his first two years of life had been spent in that shelter with his mother while she tried to rebuild herself following the scars inflicted by a man now spending his days in prison. “There’s always someone who needs help,” he had said. “I might not be here if they hadn’t helped my mom. They probably saved both of our lives. Everyone deserves that chance.”

He’d read about the threat of closure in the Fallmoore Gazette. It was the only time she’d seen him cry. He was determined to do his part and his desire to help was inspiring.

“I talked to Ernie at the Hardware Store,” he said, not looking up from his project. “He said he’d give $30.”

“That’s great!” Grace said.

“And Oliver’s mom? She’s supporting him for $20 but she said if he gets through it without complaining she’ll make it thirty!”

Grace laughed. “Shouldn’t count on it then.”

“Hey, I got all the fundraising stuff in the mail yesterday.” Sherwin crawled over to his desk and pulled down a big envelope with five stamps on it. “It’s got pledge sheets and the forms for the bank when I take in all the money.” He picked up a box from the floor beside his desk. “What’s this?”

Grace sat up on the bed and crossed her legs. She pushed her magazine out of the way and Sherwin sat down in front of her. “A little something for race day,” she told him, wrapping her arms around his neck from behind as he undid the yellow ribbon and lifted the lid.

He sucked in his breath. “Grace…”

“You think they’ll help?” she asked.

He lifted the sneakers from the tissue paper. “Waffle Trainers?”

Grace took one out of his hand and turned it over to show the sole. “So, apparently this was a complete accident—this guy spilled some stuff on his wife’s waffle iron and it made this flexible shock absorbent material and he thought ‘Hey, shoe idea.’”

Sherwin took it back from her and held it like something precious. “They’re beautiful, Grace.” He traced the white Nike swoosh with a long finger. “I can’t take these.”

“Don’t be a dummy!” Grace insisted. “Try them on. You can’t give them back. I won’t take them.”

A silly grin spilled across his face as he loosened the laces and slipped his foot in.

“Well?” Grace pushed.

“Like a glove,” he said.

“No way was I going to let you race in those old things.” She pointed to his worn sneakers laying on the floor by his bed, their soles pulling away from the body of the shoe, looking like a sad puppet.

He put on the other shoe and walked a small circle around the room.

"Will they help?" Grace asked.

"They'll be my saving grace." He cupped her face and planted a thankful kiss on her lips. "What about you?" he said, reaching down and touching her tender ankle. "Will you be able to run?"

"Oh this?" she said, waving it off. "It already feels better, and I've got a few weeks to be one hundred percent, right?"

"Right," he said, grinning and kissing her again.

chapter eight

Wednesday, June 22, 1977

THE CAR COUGHED A GREY CLOUD AS Iris pulled out of the library parking lot. Rain made circles in the puddles as Joseph waited beneath the covered eave for the car to move far enough down the road to put him out of view before he limped up the steep embankment to the south. He pushed through the heavy, low doors of the stone church that shared a parking lot with the library.

He had often thought of entering the old building but Momma's argument of '*God doesn't need walls*' held him back. He hadn't wanted to disrespect her by going someplace she never would; but now, because of a story, he felt himself questioning everything she had ever said to him.

The doors closed behind him with a weighty thunk that echoed across the sanctuary. He felt awed by the space. Wood and glass were everywhere and it smelled dusty though it seemed impeccably clean. He pulled off his wet boots, hating the idea of leaving behind damp footprints, and he stood in his sock feet, ignoring the dull pain in his ankle from the night before, gazing up at the art in the huge window behind the pulpit.

Jesus stared back at him with sad eyes, created out of hundreds of pieces of perfectly placed colours, hands marred with diamond shaped scars as he held a lamb against his chest with one and a shepherd's crook with the other.

As he wandered down the aisle, Joseph ran his hand along a pew, the wood worn smooth from the thousands of hands that had touched it before him. He stopped near the front where massive pipes hung on the east wall.

"They had to rebuild the whole front annex when they brought the organ in."

The voice startled him and he turned to see a man with a dark, well-trimmed beard, no older than forty, standing just behind him with one hand casually in his pocket and the other resting on the pulpit. "They built this church back when people thought music was bad news. They built all the doors too small to bring in anything as sacrilegious as an organ. All that," he pointed to the huge stained-glass window, "that's there because they tore down the original front to fit this organ inside."

Joseph gazed up in wonder. "Was it worth it?"

"You tell me." The man moved behind a small platform and sat. He leaned forward as he pressed his fingers against the organ keys.

A deep minor chord rumbled through the floor and up into Joseph's chest. The hairs on the back of his neck stood on end and a chill went over his entire body. He took a step back and sat in the front pew, letting the notes reverberate through his bones much like the morning bell but with more reverence and presence.

The man grinned at his reaction and played another chord. Joseph spread his arms over the lip of the pew and let his head fall back.

"Yeah," the man called out over the massive sound. "It was worth it."

The note rang out and the silence that followed felt hollow.

"I'm Reverend Samuel Greene," the man said, suddenly in front of him, holding out his hand.

Joseph snapped forward and shook his hand as he stood. "Joseph Carver."

"Carver?" Reverend Greene asked, his eyebrow lifting. "You Iris' boy?"

"Yeah," he said. "I've never been inside a church before."

"Really?" Reverend Greene said, surprised. "How have you managed that?"

"Momma isn't much for traditional things."

"Yes, yes, your mother is in a class of her own, isn't she?"

Joseph ignored him. He couldn't bear to wonder what the sudden softness in the Reverend's voice could mean. "Can I see the bell?" he asked.

"Well, sure you can!" Reverend Greene led him back towards the main doors where they took a wide hallway to a stairwell that curved around a column running all the way to the belfry. "Now, you can't actually go up there," he told him. "There's not much room or a secure place to stand for that matter, but this here is how we ring it." He reached up and pulled a thick rope coiled around a metal hook. "You ever heard the bell where you are?" he asked.

"Every day," Joseph told him. "We're not that far from town." He craned his neck backwards, looking up through the dim opening in the ceiling. “There’s only one?”

“Most people are surprised,” Reverend Greene said. “It’s such a big, rich sound that people assume there must be two or three.”

“It’s smaller than I thought, too,” Joseph admitted.

“We had a bigger one years ago but the wooden supports grew old and weak so they made the decision to switch it out for a smaller one. That was before my time. The original bell is in the Hammond County Museum now. This one isn’t even a traditional church bell because we couldn’t afford it. It’s called a mission bell. It’s smaller and lighter—only about a hundred pounds—but no one has ever really noticed the difference or complained. We’re high enough up here on the hill that the sound carries whether it’s big or small.”

“Can I ring it?”

Reverend Green shook his head. “Sorry, son. Only in the early morning, or after a wedding or funeral.”

“How’s it hung up there?”

“It’s simple really,” the Reverend said. “It’s contained in a metal frame that’s attached to a wooden platform with some heavy-duty bolts. The bell doesn’t actually move when I pull the rope—only the clapper.”

Joseph craned his neck back once again. “I’d really love to ring it!”

Reverend Greene chuckled gently. “Maybe someday,” he said.

JOSEPH RAN STRAIGHT TO THE LIBRARY after retrieving his shoes. With help from the old card catalogue he found a section full of books on old churches and structures, and a detailed account of how they were built. From there he pulled books on architecture and construction methods. By the time his mother came for him he had sketched out three plans for a small church building.

"What in the world are you doing, Joseph?" she asked.

"What if we could build a church, Momma? You know, one of our own, so we're not just sitting in the dirt all the time."

"Our bodies are the only church we'll ever need."

"Momma, I went and saw the church next door and there's a feeling there. It's not like any feeling I've ever had in the woods. Like it's holy or something."

"You're a silly boy," his mother said, closing the books and planting a kiss on his forehead as if he was six years old again. "Holy isn't a feeling, JoJo. It's an attitude."

"I want to build a church," he said again, frustrated, but she only laughed as he angrily gathered his papers and marched out to the car.

IRIS FOLLOWED HIM SLOWLY, disturbed by the stiff line of his back and the resolute way he stomped like he wanted to crush the world with each step.

The thought of him stepping into that church…

A cool wave of nervousness rushed through her.

"Did you speak to anyone while you were there?" she asked, struggling to sound casual as she slid behind the wheel.

"Reverend Greene was there," Joseph replied, arms crossed over his chest as he slumped in his seat. "He's nice. He said he knows you…?"

Iris shut her eyes for a moment, calming her rushing pulse before she turned the key in the ignition. "He's the Reverend," she finally said. “He knows everyone.”

January 16, 1963

Dearest One,

Is it pleasant where you are? Are you warm and loved and held in arms that don't believe you cursed? I am trying to fully live each day but I feel your shadow with me always and I want nothing but to join you. Your brother looks at me with blame in his eyes — like I am the one who sent you away. Your mother coos at him and he forgets for a moment. But only for a moment. He still reaches for you in his sleep.

Part of me wishes I didn't know the truth. A horrible part of me wishes that her lies were honest because at least then I would feel my grief is honest.

I have been robbed. It hurts me to look at her.

Yours,

Father

I suppose if a man has something once, always something of it remains. E.H.

chapter nine

Friday, June 24, 1977

IRIS HATED THE WAY HER FOOTSTEPS echoed across the lonely chamber. They made her much too conspicuous. She wished to move with the grace of a ghost—all whispers and secrets and sighs.

The high ceiling stretched above her and the stained-glass Jesus watched her move down the aisle as she held her cardigan wrapped tightly around herself. "You're not here," she whispered to his image.

"Iris?"

She spun around. Samuel stood at the back of the church, watching her.

"Iris, what are you doing here?" He rushed down the aisle and took her hand, leading her into one of the pews and gesturing for her to sit. "Why are you here?"

Iris tucked her hair behind her ear and looked down at their hands, clasped together on Samuel's thigh. "You met my son," she said.

"I did."

"He wouldn't understand."

"He might."

"Did you say anything to him?"

"Nothing that would make him question you."

"I think he questions everything about me. He says he loves me but I worry that his love is really hate."

"Impossible," Samuel said. "Iris, you've raised a good boy. He's gentle and curious. You should be able to trust him with your heart."

"Do you trust me with yours?" she asked.

"Always," he said, running his thumb around her palm. "And I'll wait forever until you trust me with yours."

A flush rose in her cheeks as he leaned towards her—a hurricane in her chest at the thought of kissing him in his church. She tried to turn her face but he caught it, gently moving it back and setting his lips over hers—as soft as summertime.

"What are you afraid of, Iris?" he murmured against her skin, their foreheads bent together as if in mutual prayer.

"Losing everything," she whispered. "Losing you both."

"Impossible." He kissed her again, his beard rough against her face in a manner that sent shivers through her body. "Absolutely impossible."

The weight of the building pressed against Iris' shoulders in perpetual judgement. She squirmed in her seat, wanting to bolt but desperate to cling to the man who seemed, by his very presence, to be her absolution.

"I hate it here," she said.

"I know." Samuel brushed her hair from her face like he might also be able to brush away her reservations—like he might teach her to find a home within these walls just as he had. "But *I* love it here," he said and he placed his hand over her heart. "And I love it *here*."

Iris blinked back tears. "I know," she whispered, placing her hand over his and falling into his kisses all over again.

Thursday, June 14, 1956

WHEN IRIS' BLOOD CAME she knew her world was ending.

Roth read the children their Bible story, the same light in his eyes as when she first found him handsome, only now it ignited an ember of hate in the pit of her belly.

He smiled at her as he spoke of Joseph and his coat of many colours and, though it was one of her favourite stories, his gaze crept like fingers along her skin and she couldn't shake the disgust his presence bred.

She hung back as the children lined up to kiss his cheek goodnight. He didn't take his eyes off her, even as the other girls leaned up to kiss him. She wanted to stay in her place on the floor. She wanted to dare him to make her approach.

She wanted to know what he would do.

Iris had never seen Roth become angry. He was unnaturally calm—seeming to lack the emotions that make one human—but there, sitting beneath his iron gaze, she saw a spark of something dark behind his eyes and it terrified her.

She slowly rose to join the line.

"You've been chosen, Iris," he said as she raised herself on her toes to reach his cheek with her lips. "This is your last night as a child. Tomorrow you will no longer be the Iris you are today."

As she crawled into bed that night she knew she wouldn't sleep. She reached beneath her mattress, searching until her fingers landed on the blade. She pulled out the knife, the metal flashing briefly when the moon caught along its edge.

She had stolen it from the kitchen and hidden it in her bed after Rose was taken. It was the only thing in her entire world that made her feel like she might have a small bit of control.

Fear ruled her. The knife made her feel brave.

Flipping on her stomach, she moved her pillow out of the way and carved her name deep into the wooden headboard, vowing to never stop being the Iris she was in that moment, vowing to always be strong.

HER MOTHER CAME TO PREPARE HER on Saturday morning, bathing her like a little child and plaiting her hair with flowers while the other women stood quietly and watched. "You are lucky," she said softly as she straightened the long white gown and fastened a ribbon on the end of Iris' braid. "Roth has chosen you so we are to be both mother and daughter *and* sister wives. That's a rare blessing."

"I'm afraid."

"God has ordained it. You have been called to make daughters for Roth." She kissed her forehead. "Don't be frightened. He's a good man. He will be gentle with you."

Iris didn't respond but she searched her mother's face for some hint of doubt and felt a lonely satisfaction when her mother's eyes flitted away from her gaze.

Before she left her room she slipped the knife deep into the pocket on the front of her gown.

From Iris' Journal

December 22, 1964

It was my fault.

chapter ten

Wednesday, June 22, 1977

THE FACE OF THE BOY IN THE WOODS haunted Grace. She couldn't shake his wistful image as he had gazed at her over the fire; how the light danced in his eyes; how their colour seemed very much like her own; how she felt the tears that hung in his eyes burning within her own.

"It was the Carver kid," Cam insisted while they drank Cokes at Donna's diner the next day.

The others joked that it was really the ghost of Paisley.

"What's his name?" Grace asked but no one seemed to remember.

"I want to go back," she'd insisted, angry that they didn't care.

They called her crazy but she couldn't shake her need.

Three days later she found the nerve.

Saturday, June 25, 1977

THE THIN TIRES ON HER OLD BICYCLE protested against the sloppy leftovers of a day-old rainstorm. Darkness began to fall just as she arrived at the end of the long driveway. A mailbox greeted her there, sitting at an odd angle, the Carver name spelled along the side in peel-and-stick letters.

She stashed her bike behind a tree on the west side of the driveway by the fence.

Spring rains had caused the swamps to rise and parts of the driveway remained covered. She took running jumps at these but still managed to plant her left foot square up to her ankle in mud, her sprain throbbing with each landing.

The sight of the house gave her pause. Grace had expected something like her own home—modern and covered in siding—instead, the little cottage sat in the middle of the lawn like something straight out of a Civil War history book. A wooden porch ran the entire front length, complete with a swing hanging from chains. A screen door hung a little crooked and light spilled from large paned windows on either side.

She didn't know why she was there. She felt foolish, sneaking around a stranger's property at night, but she couldn't rid the boy from her thoughts. She swallowed her doubt and walked carefully up the porch stairs, sneaking to the window that looked in on a little kitchen.

The boy sat at a small table, reading from what looked like a Bible. A barefoot woman stood at the sink, her back to the room as the boy read to her. He was dressed much like the time she saw him in the woods and, though separated by a pane of glass, she could hear his voice repeating over and over in her mind, *'I am here. I am here.'*

The woman left the sink and Grace felt dizzy at the sight of her. She had never seen anyone prettier. She had a dainty nose, a little bow of a mouth, and her messy hair was perfect somehow. She watched as Iris approached the table, picked up two dirty tea cups, and kissed the boy on the top of his head before moving back to the sink.

His expression didn't change with the kiss. He continued to read, scratching his arm absentmindedly, his lips moving slightly as his eyes passed over the words. Grace thought he might be the saddest boy in the world.

'I am here. I am here.'

Her hip bumped the swing and it groaned against the chains. The boy's head shot up, catching her eyes through the window.

She froze, holding her breath. His mouth formed an 'O' and she moved to take a step closer until his mother started to turn again.

She ran then, looking over her shoulder just once to see him standing against the glass with his hand pressed flat against it, staring out into the night, trying to find her.

She raced back down the driveway, muddied halfway up both calves but she didn't care enough to avoid the puddles. She fell once, pain shooting up her leg and dirty water getting into her mouth. She spit and wiped her face with a sleeve that only managed to smear dirt, not remove it.

"Stupid, stupid, stupid," she repeated to herself as she raced under the cover of night. She stumbled down into the ditch towards the tree that hid her bike, just as headlights appeared around a bend in the road from the direction of town.

Her heart raced at the risk of being discovered. She wasn't sure how she would explain it.

I was spying on a boy. I can't stop thinking about him. I just wanted to see him again.

Ugh.

Her body felt hot with embarrassment as she lay flat on her belly in the wet grass.

The vehicle slowed, its turn-signal flashing across her hiding place before straightening out in the Carver driveway and moving towards the house. She remained there, motionless until it got to the opposite side of the flooded section, then she crawled from the mud and pushed her bike back onto the dirt road.

It was only as she began pedalling home that she realized the car had looked an awful lot like Reverend Greene's Corolla.

JOSEPH WATCHED THE GIRL DISAPPEAR, limping into the darkness. His breath created a foggy cloud on the glass at the very place where her face had been. He thought of her eyes. He thought of their depth and the curiosity they reflected. He thought how their colour was the very same colour he saw looking back at himself any time he looked in the mirror.

"What is it?" his mother asked, putting a hand on his shoulder, causing him to jump.

"Nothing," he said, turning away from the glass but taking the memory of those curious eyes with him. "Just a raccoon, maybe."

"To bed then," his mother said, following him up the stairs and waiting patiently while he used the bathroom and brushed his teeth. "Goodnight, my love," she said when he emerged.

"Sleep well. May God guide your prayers."

"Yes, Momma." Joseph kissed her on the cheek and moved to back away from her but she clasped her hands on either side of his face.

"I love you more than life," she said, her face cast with strange shadows.

"I know, Momma."

"You are my world."

"Yes."

"Sometimes I don't know if I am dizzy with the spinning or dizzy with the lack of it."

Joseph said nothing. He didn't know what she meant.

"Love is the greatest and the heaviest gift," she whispered, leaning in to kiss his forehead.

"Goodnight, Momma."

Joseph could feel the rumble of a car coming up the driveway and he knew she felt it too by the way her eyes grew wide. She looked nervously over her shoulder towards the top of the stairs.

"Goodnight, JoJo."

He slipped into his bedroom and shut the door, hearing the familiar sound of the key turning in the lock and her bare feet padding down the stairs to answer the front door though there had been no knock.

Joseph stripped down to his undershirt and shorts and lay across his bed, staring at the ceiling. Downstairs his mother giggled. He felt sickness in his belly. He grabbed the nail from his side table and turned it over and over between his fingers as he traced the shadows of his room with squinted eyes.

Bedsprings groaned. Another giggle. Joseph flipped over and buried his face in the pillow, pulling it around his ears to drown the sound liars make, squeezing his eyes shut tight enough to conjure up the image of the girl at the window. He focused on her face. He breathed in her image. He scratched at his arm and thought of her eyes. “I’m here,” he whispered to his empty room, drifting off to sleep with her face on his mind, wondering why she limped on the same side as he did while his mother earned their breakfast on the opposite side of the wall.

Monday, June 28, 1965

SAMUEL GREENE MET IRIS CARVER in the produce section of Harry Johnston’s Supermarket as they both reached for the same apple. Her long hair was braided, its simple plait resting on the side opposite her little boy whom she had strapped to her hip with a long piece of cloth. Golden wisps had come loose to curl around her face and her cheeks had a healthy flush that accentuated her youth. She was a small thing, shorter than him by a foot and she wore a pale yellow dress with delicate flowers embroidered along a hem falling just above her ankles. She couldn’t have been older than twenty.

He picked up the apple, holding it out to her like an offering, but the boy on her hip grabbed it and took a sloppy bite. They both laughed and he saw a dangerous fire in her eyes that mesmerized him. He held out his hand. “Samuel Greene.”

She fit her own small hand into his. “Iris Carver.” She held his gaze. Her voice was unlike anything he had heard before with a playful melody that contradicted the strength he could see in her youthful face.

Her skin was soft and her hand so delicate he thought he could break it with one firm squeeze. He realized he’d been holding it for far too long and let her go, embarrassed. "Carver," he echoed.

"Yes." She took a produce bag and began filling it with apples, inspecting them for bruises before placing them inside. Her son's face was covered in juice and he grinned a goofy smile at Samuel as he took another bite.

"Paisley…?"

"He was my husband," she said simply.

He felt his heart open wide to the beautiful little woman standing before him. He took his own bag and started loading it with apples as well.

He had heard all the nasty rumours surrounding the death of Paisley Carver, the rude whispers of the strange widow and the silly back-handed comments about witchcraft.

He had never met a witch before but he was sure this girl before him couldn't be one.

"I'm so sorry for your loss," he said, tying the ends of his bag together and putting it into the basket on his arm.

She placed her apples in her shopping cart and turned to face him, chewing her bottom lip before she said, "you're the first."

"Hello, Reverend," an older lady called from across the stacks of produce where she was grabbing a ten pound bag of potatoes.

He was loathe to be cheated of the moment but he plastered on a fake smile and responded as expected. "Morning, Helen. Beautiful weather."

"Sure is, I'll see you Sunday," and with that she moved on.

Samuel turned back to Iris but her face had changed and hardened. "Have a nice day, *Reverend*," she said, leaving the aisle without looking back.

From Iris' Journal

February 18, 1965

I dreamt of the prophet again. He came into my bed like a shadow and I nailed him to the ceiling so I could study him. He is uglier than I remember and he smelled of fire and ash. I think he came from hell so I threw a pillow at him and sent him back.

chapter eleven

Monday, June 27, 1977

JOSEPH STRIPPED HIS MOTHER'S bed. He pulled off the quilt and dumped it at the top of the stairs before going back for the sheets and pillow cases. The frame groaned as he pressed his knee into the mattress, reaching across to loosen the sheet. The sound sent a ripple of disgust through him and he breathed through his mouth in case the scent of a *visitor* lingered on the linens.

He couldn't fathom how she did it. How she did *that* and then smiled at him in the morning like she hadn't been defiling his father's bed since the very moment of his death.

He felt Paisley there despite the ugly feelings their marriage bed erupted in him. He felt his father in the grain of the wood and the extra quilts that hung on the blanket rack beside the window. He felt him in the breeze drifting through the open window and the shadow that never really left the north corner.

I would be a ghost, too, he thought. *I wouldn't rest if I knew what went on in my stead...*

He left the bare mattress and continued the chore in his own room. As he pulled back the blanket, a corner hit the side table, flipping his Bible open and knocking the nail loose.

His arms were full of blankets as he registered the sound of the nail hitting the floorboards with a dull *thunk*—he even caught a glimpse as the sun hit the end where it came to rest between two boards, its tip pointing towards the window.

One thing at a time.

He carried his load down the stairs, intending to return to his room after starting the washing machine to put the nail back where it belonged.

Saturday, January 11, 1965

IRIS STOOD AT THE STOVE, her dressing gown cinched tightly at the waist as she waited for the kettle to boil. Headlights glared through the frost on the large kitchen window while a car slowly backed out the awkward driveway, painting her in harsh, judgemental light. She ran a shaky hand across her face as if to wipe away her guilt but she could smell him on her skin. She could smell him all over her. With a desperate moan, she bolted to the sink where she dry-heaved over his whiskey glass.

She jumped when the kettle started whistling, knocking a spoon to the floor. She turned quickly to retrieve it, her nightgown belling out beneath her robe, the grace of her movement belying the inelegance of the choice that brought her to such a desperate moment. Holding one hand across her mouth, she poured the steaming water over the infuser.

She didn't want this. She didn't want any of this. But she didn't know any other way. All she'd known before Paisley was that she was a body for someone else's pleasure. And now that he was gone it had been too easy to accept an invitation back into old habits. She got to keep her shoes this time. She thought that had to count for something. She glanced down at her bare feet and smiled sadly at the irony of her thought.

He wasn't a bad man—the one who had propositioned her and come to her door that night to follow through on his offer. He wasn't a particularly good man either, she supposed. He hadn't been cruel and he'd come through on his end of the deal. She would be able to buy groceries again.

She raised her cup, the amber glass warm in her hands, thinking the hot liquid might calm her nerves enough to go to sleep. She took a sip, closing her eyes as the heat moved down her throat just as a warm drip of his congress trickled down her inner thigh. Her whole body trembled at the intimate reminder of the choice she had made.

A sob grabbed her.

She flung her cup against the wall, collapsing to the floor where she wept as the tea dribbled down the wallpaper and gathered like a crime scene in small puddles against the baseboard.

Her chest heaved as she stared at the mess, thinking it to be like the tears of the wounded—aching in darkness and shadowed by sin. Upstairs she heard Joseph call out for her and begin to cry, but she couldn't bear the thought of looking into his innocent face. She allowed her own tears to match his insistent wailing.

Long moments passed before Iris composed herself enough to pull away from the cabinets where she had collapsed. She crawled on her hands and knees to the broken cup and gathered the amber pieces into a small, sad pile. Reaching behind her, she pulled Paisley's old toolbox from under the sink and found a torn piece of sandpaper.

Joseph's sobs turned to hiccuping whimpers as she picked up each piece and worked the edges with the rough sandpaper, winnowing the sharp sides to a smooth shine. Tears traced a path along her face as she worked, and she prayed a different Psalm over each piece as the brine of her pain landed on her toils.

She wept until she was too dried up for tears—like an orange that had been sucked of all its sweetness until nothing remained but a shrivelled shell.

When she finished sanding all the pieces of glass, she took a spool of fishing line, winding it round and round each piece until she could string them all together. She held it up, surveying the organic way the pieces spun and chinked against each other in a strange kind of living melody.

Her body protested the long hours on the kitchen floor but she didn't even realize until the sun reached her through the window over the sink, catching on the glass, shining through to create a beautiful reflection on the wallpaper beside the refrigerator. *For the clearing*, she thought, *to bring worship to the trees.*

She gathered herself from the floor and splashed her face with cold water before wiping up the spilled tea and ascending the stairs to her son's room.

"JoJo?" she called, rapping softly. "JoJo?" she said again, putting the key in the lock and opening his door.

Joseph was curled up on the small rag rug that sat beside his bed in front of the side table. He looked up at her with red, sleepy eyes, his body still hitching with the sobs she ignored through her own suffering. The room smelled of urine and she could see the stain across his sheet where he'd left his blanket kicked back.

"Oh, JoJo." She gathered the boy against herself, rocking him as he clung to her. "Momma's sorry. Momma's so sorry."

Joseph didn't make a sound but his body slowly relaxed and he was soon patting her back in his own attempt to return comfort to her.

"Look," she finally said, holding up the wind-chime so it caught the morning light through Joseph's window and splashed muted tones across his back. "Look, JoJo…I've made you a coat of many colours."

Joseph smiled and tried to catch the flickering lights in his palm as the town bell started to chime, creating a strange morning lullaby that embraced them both, calming them enough that they could rise and make their way to the bathroom where Iris ran a bath for Joseph. "You'll never have to eat cabbage again, JoJo," Iris told him. "Momma promises."

Monday, June 27, 1977

THE CLOTHESLINE WAS STRUNG from the front porch to a tall pine on the edge of the forest. Joseph had hung the quilts to freshen and the sheets to dry. They looked pretty as a picture, flapping colour against the deep green of the tree line.

Iris set the basket down on the deck and unpinned the first pillow case. She sang as she worked, some b-side Hank Williams gospel piece she remembered from the grainy 8-track player in Paisley's old truck. She had an herb garden in the truck bed now. He would have liked that. It was little more than a rusted-out frame but having it around comforted her because it made the short time they had together seem real.

She still missed him in her own way, but whole days could go by where she didn't even think of him. Guilt followed her like a stubborn shadow, but she carried on, vowing to be bright no matter her history. Joseph still needed her. She had to believe in that.

WHEN PAISLEY PULLED OVER HIS TRUCK to offer her a ride on that day so long ago she had been sure he was an angel. His eyes had been warm as he jumped from his seat. He had rushed around the front of the truck to take her sad little potato sack of meagre belongings and open the door for her. "I just need to be safe," she told him, tucking her legs up beneath her on the bench seat and pulling her dress down to cover her bare feet.

"My place is out in the middle of a forest. It's not much but you'd be safe there." He said it like he knew she'd say "no", like every girl he'd ever talked to had always said "no".

"Okay," she said and he just stared at her like she spoke another language until she reached across and placed her hand on his arm. "Okay," she said again.

"Oh. Oh. Right. Okay then. Good." And he pulled back onto the highway, rubbing his hand along the spot where she'd touched him.

She'd slept in his bed that first night but he didn't lay a hand on her, he just put on fresh sheets and retreated to the sofa by the fireplace while she trembled in the silence of the little house.

She wept the next morning when the distant sound of ringing bells pulled her from a restless sleep. Their call reached into her depths and her heart settled. She knew then she would never leave this place.

Paisley was a simple man but he wasn't stupid. Two weeks later he came back from town with a newspaper and a question. She'd been sitting on a stool in the garden, weeding his tomatoes when he crouched down in front of her, placing the paper on her lap. "Is this where you came from?" He pointed to the dark headline.

POLYGAMIST COMMUNE UNCOVERED AT BANKRUPT SKI RESORT OUTSIDE HARRIDAN POINT. ALLEGED CHILD ABUSE AND UNDERAGE MARRIAGES SUSPECTED.

Iris handed back the paper. "It doesn't matter where I came from, Paisley. It only matters that I'm here." She stood and brushed off her skirt. "Can you live with that?"

Paisley stayed on the ground, reading the article slowly, shaking his head and chewing his lip. He finally looked up at her and reached for her hand. "Would you marry me, Iris?" he asked, his chin trembling.

She knelt back down so they were face to face. "Would you take me as I am?" she asked him. "Will you promise to never talk to me about this again?" She pulled the paper from his hand.

He cupped her face and kissed her forehead. "God as my witness," he promised and the hope in his eyes nearly broke her heart.

"Then yes, Paisley Carver," she said. "I will marry you."

And she had, only three weeks later in the town hall beside the cemetery.

Paisley was always so kind. He treated her like something

precious and she revelled in it because it was all new. Life was simple and easy and she loved him as deep and as hard as any seventeen year old could love a man.

For five months they were deliriously happy.

IRIS WAS PLEASED when she first realized she was pregnant. It wasn't until Paisley said, "I hope it's a girl as beautiful as you," that she began to feel herself pulling away.

Girls were bred for one thing in her experience and she couldn't bear the thought of bringing a female into a world she knew as oppressive and destructive. It didn't matter that she had left that life behind because it was only just behind her. She feared at any moment they would find her and return her to the people she had left, return her to the man who called himself her husband when she was only twelve years old. And if she had a daughter and they discovered her? The thought tore at her heart and made her feel dizzy with sickness. It didn't matter that arrests had been made and the danger was locked away—somehow it was always there, a brutal weight on her young shoulders.

When she discovered she carried twins, she spent long hours praying she would be the mother of two boys. She prayed they would be strong and wise and able to protect her. She prayed God would shield her from the curse of a daughter—or rather, that God would spare a daughter the curse of her past.

When it came time for the babies to be born, Iris fought through thirty-two hours of intense labour, and it was as the doctor was off having a coffee and a cigarette that the first baby came.

The nurse was flustered, having to handle the delivery

herself, and she brought the little bundle up by Iris' head. "It's a girl," she said.

"No."

"Yes, a daughter."

"No, I can't have a daughter."

"But sweetheart…"

"Take it away!"

"But your husband…?"

"Another is coming. He will be pleased with his son."

The nurse touched the baby's face, making a decision that would alter the course of her life. "My shift is ending soon," she said.

"Go," Iris told her, and she gripped the handrails as a new contraction took over her body.

"They'll know you've already had a baby."

"Fix it," Iris said through gritted teeth.

The nurse lay the baby on the scale and rounded to the end of the bed where she helped Iris deliver the first placenta, wrapping it in the padded sheet and shoving it in a trash bag. She wiped blood from Iris' thighs and had her lift her bottom to replace the sheet beneath her.

"Will they know?" Iris asked.

"I don't know."

"Go. I will deal with them."

The nurse lifted the baby. "You're sure?"

"If they ever find me…if they ever knew about her…" Sobs hitched her body and a wave of pain came over her and she cried out. "Take her away. Go."

The nurse rushed away, clutching the baby to her chest.

"It hurts," Iris said as the new shift nurse entered the room.

She took one look and ran back into the hall to call the

doctor.

JOSEPH CAME QUICKLY, but in doing so, caused much damage. Iris lay sobbing and bleeding in the bed when Paisley burst through the door to find his son, naked and wailing, in a bassinet across the room.

"Where's the other one?" he asked, rushing to the baby and lifting him from the crib, hushing the infant and staring at the splash of blood across the floor in horror as the doctors worked to stop the hemorrhaging.

"Gone," Iris had wept. "There is no other!"

IRIS DROPPED THE LAST SHEET into the basket and let her hands fall to her stomach. She could remember how empty she felt after the surgery that removed her womb and how distant Paisley became after that. He had been sick with grief and she couldn't find it in herself to tell him the truth because she was sure he would have gone after the girl and brought her back to them. She couldn't have lived with that.

She told him the early tests must have been wrong. She told him that maybe Joseph had absorbed his twin into himself. That happened sometimes. She'd heard of it.

No matter the story, it turned out Paisley couldn't live without his daughter. For months he lived in a state of perpetual mourning until she was sure she couldn't stand one more second of it.

He killed himself on a Sunday. She didn't find him until Monday morning, swinging from that old oak tree like a twisted pendulum.

March 2, 1964

Beloved,

Your mother believes women are born cursed with blood. She believes your brother has the same curse because she says he killed you. She has a way of spinning her own truth and falling for her own lies and nothing I can say or do might convince her otherwise.

After the birthing she bled to near death and to save her they had to cut away all her invisible inside womanly bits. She says this was her salvation. That she has been purified so that she might purify. She frightens me sometimes. The experiences and burdens she carries from her time at that horrible place have shaped her into a woman of strange beliefs. I don't know how to save her from it.

I am so sorry, dear one, that you were taken from me before you were even really mine. But perhaps it is for the best.

Your mother is a strange, special woman and she believes in strange and special things. Life for you would not have been normal here. Perhaps you've found a home that can afford you dance lessons and Lilli Diamond dresses.

I will never stop missing you,
Father

But in the meantime all the life you have or ever will have is today, tonight, tomorrow, today, tonight, tomorrow, over and over again (I hope)··· E.H.

chapter twelve

Saturday, October 19, 1964

IRIS COULDN'T WRAP HER MIND around what had happened. She couldn't reconcile the man who rescued her on the side of the road with the black bag that flashed harshly each time the sun managed to eke its way through the heavy tree cover.

She thought about him as the kind man he was, the man before the babies and the lying, and she ached for him. She longed for the way he called her darling; the way he rested his hand on the small of her back when she stood at the kitchen sink; the way his kisses made her feel like she deserved him even when her mind tried to convince her otherwise.

Her memories didn't match reality. "You have to be awfully occupied with yourself to do a thing like that," she whispered to him, quoting a passage from his favourite book as he hung on the end of the rope, a tragic marionette.

One of his shoes had fallen off. He'd hung there with only one shoe on, the other foot clad in a sock with a hole. When she found him she'd picked up the shoe from the dirt and dusted it off against her skirt before slipping it over the dirty sock and carefully tying his shoelace. She'd stood staring at his feet for a long time before she finally pulled herself from her stupor enough to make her way back to the house to call the police.

Help came in a flurry of activity. She led the crew through the trees, holding Joseph on her hip while he watched everything with wide eyes, asking over and over, "Papa? Doin'?" She didn't know how to answer him.

One man held onto Paisley just above his feet while the other climbed into the branches to cut the rope with a utility knife. His body fell, knocking back the man holding his feet, dropping to the dirt with the sound of cracking bones and flesh on flesh. His eyes were slightly open, staring at nothing.

"God!" she cried out.

"Not here," someone murmured.

She turned her back on the scene, wandering over to the centre of the clearing where the dirt had been disturbed. She did her best not to draw attention to it. Instead, she positioned herself to hide the freshly turned earth while the men carefully unwound the knotted rope from Paisley's throat before they zipped him up in a black bag as if he were a sandwich. She shuddered at the sound.

An officer came to stand in front of her, his little spiral notebook flipped open for her statement. "They'll be taking him to Byton," he said. "They got the equipment to do a proper autopsy and what-not."

She nodded like she cared but she only felt empty.

"How long was he missing?" he asked, touching the tip of

his pencil to his tongue.

"He didn't come back after dinner last night," she told him. "He went out for firewood and Joseph and I fell asleep. I didn't know he was missing until this morning."

They had to carry the body all the way to the road. The two men in EMT uniforms lifted him with little effort and began to make their way towards the railroad path where they'd parked for easier access.

"Stop," she said as they passed her. She placed her hand on the bag and could feel his feet beneath the thick plastic.

"They'll fix him up good," the officer told her, touching her arm to pull her back. "He'll be in good hands."

She nodded and stepped back.

"We could have someone walk you back up to the house," he offered.

She shook her head and bent to pick up Joseph. "I just want to spend some time here for a while," she said. "In the quiet." She looked towards the tree where the rope lay in a messy coil at the roots. "Will you take that away?"

"Oh hell," he said, pulling off his cap and wiping sweat from his forehead. "So sorry, ma'am. Yeah, we gotta take that into evidence." He waved at an officer having a cigarette across the clearing.

"It's fine," she told him coldly, standing quietly as they finished their business and went on their way.

SHE WAITED UNTIL NO SOUND OF THEM remained on the air before turning her attention to the dirt beneath her feet. She fell to her knees and dug through the loose soil, breaking fingernails and rubbing dirt across her cheeks as she wiped away sweat. She dug until her fingers scraped against a small wooden box. She tugged it from its shallow grave and sat on the ground to study it.

"Momma? Dat?" Joseph said, banging on the top of it like a drum.

"It's Papa's," she told him.

"Mine?"

"No, JoJo,"

"Mine," he said and he flipped it open, peering inside like Christmas morning.

"No, JoJo," she said again, pulling him onto her lap so they could both look.

Inside was a small stack of envelopes tied together with a piece of twine. These were resting upon a beautiful porcelain doll with blond ringlets and sleepy eyes. She wore the white baptismal gown Iris had sewn. One of two she crafted while pregnant.

She fingered the lace hem, remembering the happy hours spent with needle and thread. Picture perfect moments, dazzling with hope and fortune.

"Oh," Iris said, tears springing to her eyes. She raised a hand to her mouth like she might catch the emotions that rushed to the surface.

Joseph leaned back and touched her cheek, his little face pinched with concern. "Momma hurt?"

"Yes, Joseph," she said, pulling him tight against her chest. "Momma hurt."

She gazed down at the doll and the letters. Her finger trembled as she traced the familiar handwriting. Confident and well-formed. '*My Darling Daughter*'.

She thought of his hands and how they had gently loved her.

Why had she squandered such love? She closed her eyes and tried to think of them softly but she could only picture how they hung limp at his sides, fingers curled just enough to seem rested, casual even. Like he was only joking.

The wind shifted and she felt him there—in the way it brushed her skin, how it moaned through the branches, groaning with the echo of that calmly swaying rope.

Paisley had buried his little girl in the only way he knew how.

She pulled off her wedding band and tossed it into the box. She resealed it and began to push the dirt back on top, not willing or ready to face the truth that was surely held within.

“Papa doin’?” Joseph asked.

chapter thirteen

Monday, June 27, 1977

THE OVERLOADED BASKET CAUSED an ache in her back. Iris struggled with its weight as she climbed the stairs. Familiar guilt stabbed her heart as she made the bed she once shared with Paisley but turned to sharing with strangers in order to feed their son.

"We all have to do things to survive," Paisley had once told her. "Some things are beyond our control so we do what we must. There's no sin in that."

She'd tried to explain to him what it had been like, being the fifth wife to a man almost forty years her senior, but he'd pressed her face into his neck and brushed her hair smooth with his fingers. "What's done is done," he said. "He'll never reach you here. You're mine. You're allowed to be happy now." And he'd taken her hand and held her fingers up to his lips, kissing the ring that symbolized their vows—legal vows—a claim the other could never hold over her. "I once promised you that you'd never have to speak of the horrible things that happened there," he'd said. "The only thing that matters now is the future we decide to build together from this point."

She let her hand linger on the headboard Paisley had built with his rough, farming fingers before moving on to Joseph's room with the laundry basket.

He'd left his old jeans tossed over the mattress and she flipped them off the bed to the floor so she could put on the fitted sheet.

Joseph never asked questions about his father, though she was sure he had them. She didn't know if he remembered that day—he'd been so young—but any time she caught him looking at her she wondered if he blamed her.

She gave him a good life. It was simple but it was good. She lived every moment for his protection and every choice she made was for his benefit. He'd only questioned schooling once and seemed to accept that she didn't want the secular influence of the public school system to warp his beliefs.

The nighttime locking ritual had begun to keep him away from her nighttime men, but it had turned into a strange religious rite. It had gone on for so long she began to believe her own lies and she couldn't look at him now without seeing the face of her lost daughter.

How much longer would he stand for being locked away? It was ending soon. The nagging voice of her conscience told her so. He was hatching a plan to leave her; she was nearly sure of it.

She had found the place where he dug out the nail—the hole in the wall and the scars in the wood. She didn't know what this meant but she was convinced it would lead to something that would hurt her. Later, she found the nail tucked into the pages of his Bible, right near the front where Delilah cut Samson's hair. This hurt her feelings more than the secretly hoarded nail, though she couldn't quite identify the reason why. More honestly, she wasn't willing to face how close that story came to her own deceptive narrative.

"I did what I had to do," she told the bedding as she tossed out the quilt so it would land squarely on the sheet.

She could see Joseph through the window, digging potatoes in the garden. His shoulders were broadening sooner than they should have. She wondered if he ever thought about girls. He never asked about friends or seemed to be anything but content with the life she gave him. He did his chores and said his prayers and kissed her cheek every single day. He was a beautiful boy, coming through the awkward stage of puberty with little trouble and she was sure that was only made possible by his separation from real society.

His Bible sat on the nightstand where it always did, its leather cover so cracked and worn it was more grey than black. She lifted it, thinking she'd take another look at the nail, when she saw an image scratched into the wooden night table. It was a simple church, depicted with a square front, pitched roof and high belfry. She set the Bible on his bed and reached out a finger to touch the rudimentary etching. Small flowers lined the front of the church. She let her finger follow the fresh scars in the old wood.

"They're irises," Joseph's voice came from the doorway.

Startled, she jumped back, stumbling over the dirty jeans and spinning her body just enough to see her son before she pitched forward across the floor.

Pain shot through her hand and up her arm and she rolled

onto her back, holding her hand in front of her face, disbelieving. A nail—*the* nail—was driven into her palm at an angle pointing towards her wrist.

Joseph was frozen where he stood. "Momma?"

A tremor took over her body. "Take it out! Take it out," she pleaded as tears began to smart her eyes. "Joseph, please."

He fell to his knees at her side, taking her hand and staring at the nail in horror as blood began to slowly pool at the entry point.

"Please."

He could feel her shaking. "It's almost all the way through."

"JoJo, please!"

He bit his lip and grabbed the end, feeling the gritty texture of the rust and dirt.

He pulled.

Iris screamed.

He dropped the bloody nail to the floor and grabbed a clean sock from the laundry basket beside him, pressing it against the wound.

"Why?" she asked, blinking a tear free as he helped her stand. "Why did you have that nail?"

Guilt drained the colour from Joseph's face. He supported her down the stairs and sat her at the kitchen table while he filled a basin with warm water to soak her hand.

Blood came from the wound in small pink clouds, swirling through the water in beautiful designs, reminding him of the stained glass in Reverend Greene's church.

Iris stared at him, the question still heavy in her eyes.

"It gave me a purpose," he told her simply.

She chewed her lip and took a shuttering breath. "I feel dizzy."

Joseph wet a cloth and lay it across her forehead.

She leaned her head back and closed her eyes while Joseph watched the blood dance in the basin.

Her heartbeat rested in her hand. It pulsed in the warm water, spilling out little bits of her love. She concentrated on the rhythm. Counting. Knowing each beat displaced more life.

When she finally opened her eyes she was surprised to find the water wasn't even red. It was pink but only just slightly. Still she had the thought that she should drink it and replace what had been lost. She didn't understand why it hurt so much if so little blood was being spilled.

Joseph watched a story play across her face. He watched as she fought between pain and questions, her brow furrowing, then lifting, then furrowing again. He felt sickness in a hot knot at the base of his skull. He thought to reach out and brush her hair smooth as she used to do for him when he was young, but instead he caught the cloth as it slipped from her forehead when she sat forward.

"You had no purpose?" she asked quietly.

"I want to build a church," he said.

"You need more than a nail to build a church," she told him, taking back the cloth and dabbing her face, shiny with a thin layer of cold sweat.

"Jesus built his church with just three nails."

She smiled weakly, just a sad little tilt to her pale lips. "You're a good boy, Joseph Carver," she said. "You build your church. If that's what you need."

Joseph found Paisley's old tackle box first-aid kit under the sink and poured peroxide on her wound before patting it dry and wrapping it from a spool of gauze.

"You should go to the hospital, Momma." Joseph took the

basin to the sink, dumping it carelessly so a drop splashed back onto his shirt. He watched as the small pink dot faded into the fabric. “You should let a doctor look at it.”

“I’ll be fine, darling,” she said, waving him off with her other hand. “It was only an accident. Tell me more about your church.”

chapter fourteen

Sunday, June 17, 1956

IRIS SAT BY A WINDOW IN THE WOmen's dorm, mending a pair of Roth's trousers, feeling misplaced and lost now that she no longer belonged in the children's room. She sat on a crochet covered pillow to ease the pain of what he had done to her the night before. Rose had warned her. Rose had said it would be like fire forcing its way inside her. Iris closed her eyes and let out a slow breath, willing her body to be steady as she remembered that flame—the way she'd cried out, the way he'd hushed her, the taste of his leathery fingers as he slapped them over her mouth.

"Come for a walk with me, Sister Iris."

Her mother stood in front of her, looking like a stranger—horribly thin with sad, tired eyes. "Hello, Sister Margaret," Iris said, shifting in her seat and sucking in her breath as discomfort swarmed her body. "I don't want to walk."

She had very little connection with her mother since they became part of life on the compound four years before. Other women and older children had been assigned to her care. From her whispered conversations with Rose she understood this was to cement the feeling of overarching family—that no one was confined to just a mother or just a sister—they were all part of one big unit. Blood was not thicker than the word of The Prophet.

"A walk will do you good," her mother said. "Now that you're a wife you're allowed to go outside without a chaperone. You should take advantage of that. Plus the sun is shining today."

Iris sighed and stood, setting the pants on the pillow and straightening her dress before following her mother down the stairs and out onto the grounds.

She tilted her head back, letting her hair be carried by wind that tasted so sweet she almost laughed out loud. The full effects of the sun kissed her pale skin, sending a rush of euphoria through her body, displacing, for a moment, the pain that lingered. After years of being allowed little more than flagpole ceremonies or open windows through which to feel the breeze, the freedom of the open air was a long awaited reward. The consolation prize for having left behind her childhood.

"It must have come as a shock," her mother said as they wandered an overgrown path behind the building.

"What?" Iris asked.

"Your wedding night."

Iris chewed the inside of her cheek and didn't respond.

"I wanted to talk to you, to prepare you for what was coming but you know how the rules work—blood mothers do not mother their blood daughters—and no one really talks about these things…"

"Rose talked to me," Iris admitted.

"So you knew?"

"Only a little."

"Is there much pain?" her mother asked.

"He was angry with me because I was afraid of him." Iris couldn't look her in the eye. "He made me bleed."

Her mother reached for her as if to offer an embrace but Iris ducked away from her arms, crossing her own over her chest as they walked.

"This way." Her mother led them off the path and into the tall grass, back to a spot by a huge maple tree. She stopped where the grass gave way to Queen Anne's Lace, their broad white heads bowing with the breeze, smelling a little bit wild and little like parsley. She began breaking the heads off the flowers that looked dead—the ones that were curling in on themselves into a vase shape like a small bird's nest. She held one up for Iris. "We need the ones that look like this," she said. "Not all of them. Just a few for now."

Iris joined her in the patch and broke off two heads. "What are we doing, Mother?"

"You're twelve years old, Iris. Roth wants you to have a baby. That's not what you want. Not at twelve years old."

Iris picked another dead flower.

Her mother came over to her and took the heads from her hand, dropping them into her dress pocket. One she kept out, rolling it between a thumb and finger until seeds fell into her palm. "The oil in these seeds will block implantation."

Iris stared at her dumbly, knowing nothing of such things.

"A baby can't grow in you if you take them. It's like medicine. You have to take them every day. A teaspoonful. And not longer than eight hours after he's been with you or they might not work. You have to chew them completely so the oils are released. Here," she held out her hand and a little pile of seeds. "Take them now."

Iris opened her hand and her mother dumped them into her palm.

"All in," she said. "And you can't just swallow them. They'll do nothing that way."

Iris looked down at her hand. They looked like hairy little bugs. "What do they taste like?"

"Awful," her mother said "Like strong mint tea mixed with castor oil. Just do it. You'll get used to it."

Iris dumped them into her mouth, immediately gagging, first at their texture and then at their heavy, oily flavour.

"Chew them completely," her mother said again.

Iris ground them with her teeth, swallowed, and wiped her mouth on her sleeve.

"Every day," her mother said. She reached into her other pocket and pulled out an empty salt shaker. She sat on the ground and began working on another flower head, handing one to Iris to do the same, carefully dropping the seeds into the shaker. "Hide this under your mattress," she told her. "You can come out here and fill it up whenever you need more. We'll figure out a way to store enough before wintertime."

"Why are we here, Mother?" Iris asked. "Why did we come here?"

Her mother raised her eyes up to the sky and blinked rapidly. "Because I had nowhere else to go."

"Are you happy?"

"It isn't a woman's duty to be happy, Iris." She brushed back her hair. "A woman's first duty is to the happiness of her husband."

"Do you really believe that?" Iris dumped a small handful of seeds into the salt shaker.

Her mother didn't answer, she just stared back towards the resort building. "I'll bet this place was really pretty when it was a golf club," she said, her eyes going soft as she imagined the good that once decorated the land. "I'll bet it had beautiful gardens and fountains. I'll bet graceful ladies in fancy hats would sit out on the back terrace with glasses of sherry while their husbands golfed."

"What was my father like?" Iris asked.

"You don't have a father, darling."

"Of course I do," she protested. "Or I did. There was a photo of him. I remember it from when I was little. He had hair parted to the side and a thin nose like mine and he had a little mole just here." She put her finger on her jawline just below her right ear. "Was he a good man?"

Her mother worried her bottom lip for a moment before throwing back her own handful of wild carrot seeds. She chewed without making a face and Iris realized her mother was the only wife who hadn't delivered a baby in the last year. She had carried two in their first while at Harridan Bluffs. The first was a boy named Peter but Iris rarely saw him because he was kept in the boys dorm where a couple of the unchosen Promise Book girls took care of him. She never saw the second—only heard whispers of '*poor Sister Margaret, another boy...*' but he was nowhere to be found. He simply disappeared. She had no way of knowing what became of him. No one talked of such things.

"He believed in aliens," she finally said.

"What?" Iris looked up from the flower head she was deseeding.

Her mother picked a seed from between her teeth as she talked. "He had this old telescope he'd take out to our back porch on clear nights. I'd sit out there with him and listen to him talk about how the world was going to change as soon as people realized how much was out there and how he wanted to be there for the first contact. I always told him he was crazy but he'd just say, 'you'll see,' and he'd grin like he knew something no one else knew." There was a small smile painted across her tired face, her eyes focused on something far away as she remembered. "The night before he left for active duty he took me out on the porch and we danced while he sang some silly tune about living on the moon. He was my very own Fred Astaire."

"You still miss him?" Iris asked.

She seemed to shake herself free of the memories and brought her eyes back to her daughter's face. She reached over and pinched Iris' chin lightly between her thumb and finger. "You *do* have his nose," she said. She sighed and stood, brushing some small pieces of dead weed from the front of her dress before starting to walk back towards the building. "This is our life now, Iris," she said. "You must make peace with it. If we were to leave we would have nothing—we wouldn't even have shoes." She lifted her skirts to show her dirty feet and drive her point home.

"Why, Mother?" Iris asked, acutely aware of her own naked feet and the rough ground beneath them. "Why do you think we're not allowed to have shoes?"

"Oh, Iris, you must stop this. It's for our protection. He cares for us in his own way."

Iris stopped in her tracks. "Does he, Mother?" She pulled up her own skirts high enough to show the fresh, raw cuts on her inner thigh. "Does he love me, Mother? Do you even care what he made me do last night?"

Her mother rushed back and wrapped her arms around her. "I have nothing to give you, Iris. I would give you the world if I could. I would fly you away to the moon just like your father's song. This is what we have been dealt. We make the best of it we can. Do your duty." She pulled back and tucked a strand of hair behind Iris' ear. "You're strange and precious, darling, just like the iris for which you're named. Be strong."

Iris had her face buried in her mother's shoulder. "You should have protected me from this," she said around the lump in her throat. Her eyes smarted with hot tears.

Her mother held her for a moment, petting her hair and hushing her with tender sounds that reminded Iris she was still just a child even though she was expected to behave as a woman.

"I don't know how," her mother finally admitted. Iris could hear the tears in her voice.

"I will *never* have a daughter," Iris promised. "I will *never* bring another girl into this life."

Her mother remained silent, still smoothing her hair.

"Has anyone ever left?" Iris mumbled into her dress.

"Only one that I know of," her mother said, unwinding herself from Iris' arms, taking her hand and leading her to the opposite side of the building near the skeleton of an old ski lift. A small mound of dirt was visible through the weeds and a red cross had been painted on one of the old wooden crossbeams. "They ran her down with the pickup," she said.

"Are you trying to scare me?"

"You should know the truth. Accept it. Make the best of it. This is our life."

"I will leave here someday," Iris told her.

"Then I will lay flowers on your grave," her mother said sadly, putting her arm around her and pulling her close to her side before guiding her back up the path.

A SMALL FOYER MARKED THE MAIN ENTRANCE of the old resort. A chandelier hung from the ceiling, its bulbs burned out so long ago Iris didn't remember ever seeing it lit.

A metal basin stood just to the left of the doors, filled with fresh water every morning. A small stack of towels and a bar of soap sat on a wooden chair beside it.

Iris and her mother took turns washing their feet in the basin and drying them on a towel before they entered the main building. Just before they went through the door, her mother dropped the salt shaker into her dress pocket. It settled against her hip, strangely heavy.

"You've been outside," Roth said, greeting them as they entered the large common room. "What a wonderful treat for you, Iris."

Iris couldn't meet his gaze. She couldn't believe there was a time when she thought him kind and handsome. She stared down at his shiny shoes and hated him for them.

"Is everything all right?" he asked.

"Of course, husband," her mother said, rising on her toes to kiss the prophet on the cheek.

"And you?" he asked Iris.

She fought every instinct in her young body to cringe away from him as he took her in his arms and buried his face in her hair, taking in a huge breath of her scent.

"Mmmmm," he murmured, stepping back from her and

admiring her young form. "Do you not have a kiss for your new husband?"

Iris let her lips brush his cheek, the rough stubble of his whiskers causing her to grit her teeth.

"Look at me, Iris." He grabbed her face, forcing her chin up.

She raised her gaze and stared into his eyes.

"Everything all right?" he asked again.

"Yes, husband."

A slow smile split his face. "You have a lot to learn but I have great hopes for you. Know your place."

"Yes, husband."

"Obey."

"Yes."

"Do you love me?"

"Yes." Even as she said it she imagined sneaking into his bedroom while he slept, picking up his shoes from the floor, beating him until he couldn't make a sound, and then wearing those same shoes as she marched down the driveway and back into the real world beyond.

He reached out and fingered a lock of her hair, rubbing it between his fingers like a seamstress might test fabric. His eyes held a wicked gleam. "You look like Saturday night," he whispered before dropping her hair and moving on to his office on the other side of the common room.

chapter fifteen

Saturday, July 9, 1965

SOMETHING HAD HAPpened in that grocery store. Reverend Samuel had watched the softness in Iris' eyes turn to disdain the moment his attentions were pulled from their friendly exchange to an interrupting parishioner. He felt he'd hurt her and he couldn't live with himself if he didn't at least try to make it right; so, when he first went out to the Carver's land, he told himself it was just to clear his conscience.

A warm feeling came over him the moment she opened the door and he realized he had missed her desperately, though their initial meeting had been little more than five minutes long.

Iris said nothing as she stood there in bare feet, studying him with cautious eyes.

"Mrs. Carver," he said.

She didn't respond.

"I've been bothered by what happened at our first meeting and I wanted to clear the air. I wanted to make sure I didn't hurt you somehow."

She tapped her toe against the floor and studied his face but still she said nothing.

"I enjoyed meeting you, ma'am, and there was more I wanted to say to you by way of condolences. I just felt like we were interrupted, and you were offended, and I just…" he held out his arms and shrugged his shoulders, unsure how he should proceed.

The little boy toddled up with two fingers in his mouth. "Apple man," he said around them, grinning out from behind his mother's legs.

"You want tea?" she asked, running her hand through her son's hair.

"Tea would be lovely," he said, stepping inside and following her to the kitchen, trying not to watch the sway of her hips but unable to look away.

"YOU HAVE TO UNDERSTAND something," she said as she placed the tea cup in front of him and took the chair opposite.

"Yes?"

"You frighten me." She wrapped her fingers around her cup and stared down into her tea, unable to meet his gaze.

"But why?" he asked, lifting his drink to his lips, watching the way the sun from the window brought out little hints of red in her hair.

"I have a hard time trusting people who call themselves spiritual leaders." She ran a fingertip along the rim of her cup and finally raised her eyes to his. "I grew up in Harridan Bluffs," she told him.

"You mean…?"

"The Polygamist commune." She let that hang in the air between them like a cloud of putrid smog.

Samuel had followed the story since it broke three years earlier and though charges had been laid and jail time was being served, he could see the pain of it etched deeply in Iris' face. She wasn't free from the damage it had done. He reached across the table and put his hand on hers before thinking the gesture might be too forward.

She pulled back, grabbed her cup, and went to the sink where she dumped it. Her body was tense, arms straight against the counter as she spoke to the wall. "You don't need to be kind to me. I've been a whore since the day I became a woman. I'm not worth your time, Reverend. I'm sure you're a wonderful man and you only wish me well but God has given me all the goodness I needed with Paisley and Joseph. I might only have half of that goodness left but I'll be damned if I don't give him the best life I can."

Samuel's heart broke for her. He set his cup on the counter and stood behind her, feeling the heat from her body, smelling the faint floweriness of her hair. He was careful not to touch her. "You don't need to punish yourself for something that was done to you, Iris."

She slipped around him and went to the door, holding it open in an obvious rescinding of the earlier invitation inside. "A banker will soon be here to pay me for my company," she said as he slowly made his way to the door and stopped in front of her, unable to find the words for a goodbye in the light of her startling confession.

"That's how I survive out here, Reverend," she continued.

"On the generosity of virile men every Saturday night. Probably men that sit in your congregation come Sunday morning."

Samuel swallowed against a strange pressure in the back of his throat. The idea of any man laying a hand on her caused a hot fury to build in his chest that went far beyond the morals of it all.

"You think God has room in heaven for sluts?" she asked and her lip trembled as tears threatened from her eyes, brimming with wet pain.

Samuel felt his own eyes burning. "It's not your sin if it was forced on you," he said quietly.

"I chose this, Reverend," she said, one tear springing loose and spilling down her flushed cheek. "Do you have a prayer for that?"

He sucked in his breath and caught her spiteful words like a full slap in the face. "Thank you for the tea, Mrs. Carver," he said, dipping his head before he left, knowing something within him had shifted, though what, he couldn't quite put his finger on.

HE RETURNED A WEEK LATER. He couldn't stay away. She had found her way under his skin and he couldn't stop himself from thinking about her.

She opened the door in a dressing gown, her hair falling down around her shoulders like a broken halo. "Reverend," she said, surprised, pulling at the top of her robe to hide the exposed skin beneath.

He held a small stack of bills out to her. "Call the man you're expecting. Tell him he's not welcome here tonight. Tell him you have a fever or a headache."

She stared down at the money, mild shock written across her

face.

"I only want to spend time with you," he explained. "I'm not here for anything else. I want to pay you for your time."

She studied him for a long moment before opening the door wide and gesturing for him to come in. He sat on an old sofa while she made her phone call and he smiled at her nervously when she came back into the room.

"Why?" she asked him, leaning against the doorframe between the kitchen and living room.

"The idea of you doing…that…it makes me crazy. I can't explain it. I just…"

"Are you here to save me?"

"Yes." He couldn't tell if she was asking an honest question or mocking him but he didn't care.

She slowly sank into a chair on the other side of the room and started to cry.

Samuel didn't go to her, he simply watched as fat tears weaved their way among her freckles and marvelled that even raw with emotion she was more beautiful than any woman he'd known before.

When she finally settled enough for conversation, she asked him to tell her about his life and he did, even as tears slowly traced a wet path down her pretty cheek.

BY THE FOURTH VISIT she had taken to sitting beside him on the couch. By the fifth he found himself with his arm resting over the back, fingers playing with her hair. On his sixth visit, as she was telling him about harvesting the garlic, he cupped her face and pressed his lips hard against hers. She hesitated only a moment before reciprocating, combing her fingers through his hair and pulling his body against hers while she hungrily returned his kisses.

As he drove back into town early that Sunday morning he felt like both a new man and like a liar. He quickly showered, put on his suit and tie, grabbed his sermon pages from the desk in the front room and left in time to ring the Sunday bell.

Fallmoore Gazette
October 6, 1961
Gated Community Hiding Abominable Crimes
by Mickey Slater

The property at Harridan Bluffs has long been the topic of speculation and gossip but no one was prepared for what police uncovered when they followed an anonymous tip suggesting a dangerous religious sect was practicing its beliefs inside the gated entrance.

A warrant was secured after a week of surveillance heightened suspicions and the police descended on the Harridan Bluffs property late Thursday afternoon in full riot gear.

Twenty-eight children were successfully removed and placed in protective custody at the shelter in Byton. Of the twenty-eight children, seven were girls who had been forced into marriages with men almost twice their age, two of which are currently in the third trimester of pregnancies.

Five men are being held on multiple counts of abuse and eleven women on charges of child endangerment.

Claiming to be a devout Christian following the will of God, John Peter Roth ran the commune with a firm hand, having five wives and thirteen children.

"The saddest part is that the children don't know any different," said Byton social-worker Annalise Hallman. "This is the only life they've ever known and it will take a lot of time and therapy to teach them that all the adult examples they've looked up to are corrupt. It's going to be a slow, hard adjustment. These poor children have never even owned a pair of shoes."

Police report that only the men within the complex wore shoes. Even the grown women were barefoot and it is speculated this was to prevent any escape attempt.

Mrs. Hallman and local barrister, Theodore Swift, both agree the charges against the women will not stand up. "It's very clear that the women are as much victims of this crime as the children," Swift stated.

"It was horrendous," said Chief of Police, William Baxtor, "it takes a sick individual to think they can reduce a child's existence to little more than forced motherhood."

Bail hearing is set for first thing Monday morning.

chapter sixteen

Saturday, July 2, 1977

RACE DAY DAWNED, WET AND grey. Grace frowned at the drizzle painting a sad, watery scene on the window as she pulled on her t-shirt and shorts. The phone beside her bed rang. “Hello?” she answered.

“Rain or shine,” Sherwin’s voice came through the receiver. “I’m not bowing out.”

“There’d better be no one who bows out!”

“There won’t be,” she assured him. “Don’t worry. People believe in it. Plus it’ll probably clear up by race time anyway.”

“You think?”

“Sure. I’ll meet you at the school?”

“Don’t be late,” he said before hanging up.

Grace pulled on a pair of long socks and the sneakers she bought herself to match the ones she’d gotten Sherwin, before kissing her mother on the cheek and leaving the house.

REVEREND GREENE TRIED TO FOCUS on the papers in front of him but he couldn't make sense of the words, let alone form new ones to add. His spirit was heavy and he couldn't shake the growing sense of urgency building inside him. Cool fingers walked along his spine and no matter how he shifted his position, he couldn't shake them.

It wasn't abnormal to have someone laid on his heart. Many times he'd been roused from sleep, an image on his mind, a person for whom he was being called to intercede for. But this was different. There was a darkness to it—a scraping of his soul—a sense that his world was tilting in a way that would break him.

He tried to focus his mind enough to pray but the prompting was far too intense. He scraped back his chair and grabbed his keys.

A SMALL CROWD HAD ALREADY GATHERED when Grace arrived at the schoolyard. The group was mostly kids, but there were a few adults from the community as well. A couple of parent volunteers were collecting the support money and handing out numbered papers that were to be pinned to each runner's chest. The atmosphere was light. Laughter floated on the air and someone led warm up exercises beside a soccer net on the edge of the field.

Grace handed in her fundraising efforts and fastened a 24 to her shirt before she found Sherwin being interviewed by Mickey Slater, a middle-aged reporter for the Fallmoore Gazette.

She stood back, listening to Sherwin, loving the way his voice became a little high when he got excited. He glanced her way once or twice and winked as he continued talking to the reporter who held out a small black tape recorder.

"What's the prize for the winner?" Mickey asked.

Sherwin laughed. "No prize—it's a fundraiser. Oh, but Mr. Halloway said he'd give a $10 gift certificate to the winner just 'cause he thinks we're doing a good thing."

"You got predictions on the winner?"

Sherwin grinned and tilted his head slightly. "I *am* the school track star."

"Humble too," Grace called out.

Sherwin grinned and waved her over.

"He'd better win," Grace told the reporter, tucking herself under Sherwin's arm. "He's got winning shoes. And I made him promise he wouldn't wait for anyone. This is his race. It was his idea. He's going to be helping a lot of people because of what he's doing here. He deserves to win for that alone."

Sherwin pulled her tight against himself, kissing her head. "Can't lose with someone like this in my corner, can I?"

"Photo?" Mickey asked, sticking his recorder in his pants pocket and lifting the camera he wore around his neck on a leather strap. He backed up from them to get a full shot.

Grace grinned up at Sherwin as the flash went off, overwhelmed with pride and eager to watch him let everyone taste his dust.

THE RAIN SLOWED by the time racers were lining up but the air still felt damp and a thick fog had settled over the whole town. The ten mile route would take them from the schoolyard all the way to the All Day Breakfast diner that sat on the side of the highway halfway to Raylea. The proprietor had promised free drinks and cheap pie for all the participants at the end.

“I mean it, Sherwin,” Grace said as they took their places in the crowd of fifty-two runners. “Don’t wait for me.”

He grinned and kissed her quick on the cheek before he bent to tighten his shoelaces. “I’ll be like lightning,” he promised.

“You’d better," she said, smiling and pushing up her sweat band so her hair was off her forehead. She puffed out her cheeks with a big breath of air, bouncing up and down as she shook her arms to loosen the tension that seemed to be settling in.

Mr. Drew, the gym teacher from a neighbouring school, walked up to the edge of the line and raised the starting pistol. “Runners ready?” he called.

“I’ll see you on the other side,” Grace said, lowering herself into the starting position, swallowing the pre-race nerves that had her heart in her throat. “Break a leg! And save me some apple pie.”

IRIS WOKE WITH A FEVER. She didn’t get out of bed. Joseph carefully unwrapped her hand, cleaned the weeping wound, and rebandaged it. He kept cool cloths on her forehead and sat by her side, reading to her from the Psalms. She took small sips of broth but her jaw trembled and her eyes were frightened.

“Hello?” a voice called from downstairs. “Iris?”

Joseph went to stand but his mother grabbed his arm with a sudden strength she hadn’t had before. Desperation shone in her eyes and she shook her head against the pillow. “No, JoJo,” she said weakly.

Joseph shook off her hand and went downstairs.

"Reverend Greene," Joseph said. "What are you doing here?"

The Reverend turned to face him, startled. He held a hat in his hand and he worried the brim with nervous fingers. "Joseph. Hi. It's good to see you again, son."

"What are you doing here?"

"I came to call on your mother," he said, a blush building from beneath his white button-down up into a flushed purple on his cheeks.

"To *call* on her?" Joseph asked. "You're a little early to call on her, Reverend. It's barely three o'clock."

Reverend Greene cleared his throat. "No. To check on her," he said. "I felt compelled. I come every so often to make sure everything's okay out here. A woman living out here on her own, you know…?"

"*I'm* here," Joseph said.

"Yes, you are." He cleared his throat again and started to back out the door. "I guess I'll be on my way then. If everything's all right here."

"Momma's sick." Joseph choked on the admittance. He didn't want to rely on the help of any man who *called on her* but the thought of missing the opportunity to get her the help she needed won out over his pride. "She got hurt. A cut on her hand. I think it's infected."

Reverend Greene stopped, his hand on the doorframe as he looked back at Joseph. "Should I…?"

Joseph stepped out of the way of the staircase. "I don't know what to do."

Reverend Greene took the stairs two at a time. Joseph followed him, feeling the slow burn of anger building in his chest as he watched him go right to Iris' room.

Iris opened her eyes to see Samuel standing in the doorway and she tried to push herself back against the headboard. “No, Samuel, no…my son.”

Joseph pushed past him into the room. “I’m not stupid, Momma.”

She sighed back against her pillows and raised her good hand to cover her face. Joseph knelt beside her and whispered in her ear. “You do what you must, Momma. There’s no sin in that.”

She swallowed back a sob and Joseph gestured for Reverend Greene to approach the bed.

“What have you done to yourself, Iris?” he asked, touching the cloth on her forehead.

She raised her punctured hand weakly. “I’ve been crucified,” she joked, but she choked on her laughter and wept instead.

“You need a doctor,” Reverend Greene said. “You need medicine.”

“I tried to tell her.” Joseph watched helplessly as the Reverend picked his mother up from the bed and carried her down the stairs to his car.

chapter seventeen

Saturday, June 17, 1967

"HELLO, APPLE MAN," IRIS SAID, leaning against the doorframe and biting her bottom lip as she smiled at him.

When he passed the money into her hands their skin touched briefly and he felt a jolt of electricity. She wore a flowery sundress and a string of wooden beads around her neck and he was mesmerized by the shape of her calves as she slipped over to the desk under the window to stick the bills inside the cover of a book laying there.

He felt shy. He always did in the beginning of their visits. Just as he always thought to himself that this was the week he would resist the call of her company.

It was hopeless. He was as weak as any man before him and it didn't matter that he had studied the scriptures and believed the ten commandments really were a compass by which to live one's life—he could not resist. She was his north star.

He stood in the doorway watching her. Her dress moved about her knees in its own slow dance. Warmth flowed over his body as he raised his eyes to her face.

"You're letting the bugs in, silly." She grabbed his hands, leading him out onto the porch, walking backwards to the two-seater swing hanging on rusty chains.

Samuel sank into the faded upholstery and Iris sat beside him, tucking her legs up underneath herself before she tipped up his chin and kissed him sweetly.

Iris was small but her presence was huge and the moment she came close to him she became his whole world. Kissing her was like finding himself and losing himself all in the same breath. She was firm against him and he couldn't help but yield beneath the pressure of her mouth, tasting her, synchronizing the movement of his own mouth, exploring her face and hair with his hands only to pull her harder against himself like he was starving.

She sighed against him and moved her head back so he could kiss her neck and explore the contours of her throat.

"I'm quite certain I love you, Iris Carver," he said against her skin before he lost his nerve.

She pulled back from him, her hands on either side of his face as she gazed into his eyes, searching his soul, reading him and tracing the arch of his brow, her breaths coming long and deep.

The kiss that followed made him realize he really knew nothing of kissing up until that point and then somehow she was on top of him, one knee on either side, their bodies so closely intertwined that, for the first time, he thought he finally understood the phrase 'making love'.

Her dress was pushed up on her legs and somehow his hands were on her thighs and they were so smooth and warm and—

"Iris," he gasped.

Her lips were on his throat.

"Iris!" He raised his hands up to her face so he could pull her back. He could see her pulse in her throat and he knew his own was keeping time in a hyper, scattered rhythm. "I can't," he said but he wanted nothing more than to lose himself in the curve of her thigh.

Her breath was ragged and she untangled herself from him, pulling the skirt of her dress down and wiping hair from her eyes. "I'm sorry, *Reverend.*" She was wounded, spitting his title like a curse.

"Don't," he said, facing her. "Don't do that."

She looked out over the dark yard where she could just make out the shape of Paisley's old truck. "So what's the deal, Apple Man? You come every week. You pay me. You are kind to me. Now you tell me you love me but you won't *love* me…?"

He took her hand, tracing lazy circles in her palm, thrilling at the touch of her but fighting an internal battle that shone out through his eyes. He chose his words carefully. "I don't give you money for any of this, Iris," he said. "I give you money because of my jealousy. The idea of another man with his hands on you for any reason other than love makes me mad with rage."

She pulled away from him and walked down the porch steps to stand on the grass in front of the garden, her arms wrapped tightly around her middle like she was trying to hold herself together.

He stayed where he was, studying the curve of her neck and the untidy wisps of her hair, cold without her beside him. "I do love you, Iris," he said, not raising his voice for the distance but knowing she could hear him over the late night stillness. "I love you for your strength and I love you for your brokenness. I love you for the way I feel when I'm close to you. I think I've loved you since that first moment in the grocery store. Nothing hurt me more than when you walked away from me. And you walk away from me again because I won't do…that…?"

She didn't turn towards him when she answered. "Paisley loved me and I drove him to his death." She walked farther into the yard to the rusted truck and plucked a sprig of mint from the herb garden in the truck bed. She held it to her nose and let its fragrance linger. "When I take Joseph to the library he looks through fairytale picture books and they're all the same. Some poor romantic fool who sings in the woods gets rescued by a prince who takes her to his castle and gives her pretty gowns and fancy feasts. That's not real life, Samuel. Paisley brought me here. There was no castle or fancy meal. I didn't even have a wedding dress. But he was good to me even when I stopped being good to him." She let the mint linger on her lip so the taste crept into her mouth. "You don't have to rescue me, Apple Man." She put the leaves between her teeth and chewed them. "I've already been rescued."

Samuel studied her from behind, feeling helpless and desperate to have her close to him again. "We're all lost, Iris," he said.

"But most people have a map," she replied as she wandered back towards the porch and sat on the step, her bare feet damp from the dew on the grass.

"No, they don't." He rose from the swing and took the spot beside her on the step. He bumped against her playfully with his shoulder. "Nobody really knows where they're going. We're all just wandering around with our fingers crossed, hoping we'll meet somebody that will make our lostness a little less lonely."

He turned towards her and cupped her face in his hands before kissing her lips very softly. "You can't rush me, Iris. My head has been trained my whole life to fight against this."

"Stop fighting," she pleaded.

"It's not so simple," he told her. "There's my congregation to think about. There's a whole town that holds me to a higher standard and if I betray that trust…"

"Love conquers all," she said quietly. "That's what all those fairytales say."

"Ha!" he laughed softly. "If only that were true."

She leaned towards him and rested her head on his shoulder. "Just once I'd love something to be simple."

He let his cheek rest against her hair, his arm around her small waist as the faint smell of mint hung on the air. "Me too, Iris," he said. "Me too."

Fallmoore Gazette
October, 13, 1961
Judge Denies Bail, Roth To Be Detained Until Trial
by Mickey Slater

Judge Henry Newell denied bail for John Peter Roth, self-proclaimed Prophet of Harridan Bluffs, calling the crimes for which he is accused, despicable.

Roth is facing a laundry list of charges ranging from corruption of a minor to child endangerment to forced confinement after his gated community at Harridan Bluffs was raided by police last week.

Roth will be held in a courthouse holding cell for the entirety of the trial after which he will either go free or be remanded to the city jail.

Roth has declined any contact with the press but his lawyer has said he is ready to fight.

chapter eighteen

Saturday, July 2, 1977

SHERWIN FELT INVINCIBLE as his feet hit the pavement. He wondered how different the experience might be had he been wearing those old, split-toed sneakers that were now somewhere in the town dump. These new ones reminded him of fire as they flew beneath him, their red fabric flaming against the cement as step after step he widened the distance between himself and the main group.

He pictured the faces of the women and children who had been at the shelter when he went to meet with the proprietor and he imagined pounding out their sadness with each step.

Better world. Better world. Better world. Left Right. Left Right. Left Right.

Grace was somewhere behind him. He thought of her in those little running shorts and that ridiculous sweat band that made her hair seem both absurd and adorable.

He could have run with her. He could have stayed with the group, even let her get ahead of him so he would have a favourable view of those shorts from the back, but she would have had none of that. It was one of the things he loved about her. She didn't want him to be any less than who he was.

Grace Belle. Grace Belle. Grace Belle.

He couldn't wait until they met up at the end. He let his mind linger on the kiss she'd give him as a reward for winning his own race. They'd enjoy their pie and then he'd take her to help him choose his prize.

Ten dollars wouldn't go very far at the Hardware store but he had seen some folding lawn chairs that would be nice for the back porch. They didn't have any outdoor furniture—just two milk crates flipped upside down. His mother would really love a lawn chair—she'd sit out there and read when she wasn't running the cash register at the grocery store.

He was free when he ran, unstoppable, like he could do anything. Even in the fog he felt powerful, breaking through it with his strong stride, wondering what kind of pie he would have at the end of it all and how he'd have to be sure and set aside a piece of apple for Grace. With a scoop of vanilla ice cream and a slice of cheddar cheese. Maybe he'd have apple too.

Better world. Better world. Better world.

IRIS WAS HARDLY RESPONSIVE as Samuel strapped her into his Toyota. Joseph climbed into the back and held her head on his lap, shooting daggers of judgement at the back of the Reverend's neck as he slid into the driver's seat and put the car into gear.

"You good?" Samuel asked over his shoulder.

"Fine. Go." Joseph waved him forward.

Samuel switched off the radio and started down the long driveway. "How's her breathing?"

"Shallow," Joseph said. "Just drive."

"She should have gone to the doctor days ago." Samuel slammed his hand against the steering wheel in frustration.

"She said it was just a flu," Joseph protested. "She said she just needed tea and rest."

"She's obviously delirious."

"Listen, Reverend," Joseph said, the hard edge of his voice cutting through the tension inside the vehicle. "I didn't know. I just did what she asked me to do for her. Maybe if you were more than a Saturday night hump you might have been here to help her."

Samuel pursed his lips but he didn't say anything. He couldn't blame Joseph. He couldn't blame anyone that might judge their secret relationship. No one understood. Even after all this time he wasn't sure he understood it himself. He only knew that his world would be destroyed should anything happen to his Iris.

His Iris. He glanced in the rearview at the boy in the back, his face painted in such regret and terror that Samuel wished he could offer a kind word to lessen the pain, but all his attention had to be on driving and keeping *himself* together.

A thin fog hovered just above the road. It wasn't yet night but Samuel had to strain his eyes to pick out the shoulders. A misty rain hit the windshield. His wipers did little more than create grey smears across his vision.

Iris moaned and he looked back, seeing her face pinched in pain as her back arched against a strange seizure that took over her body. Sweat had smeared her hair across her forehead in thick strips. He reached back and squeezed her hand. “I’m here, Iris,” he said. “I’m here.”

May 8, 1967

I took Samuel to the clearing today. He didn't say much beyond thinking it was a pretty place. I wonder if he worries that I dabble in unsightly things there. He once told me there are rumours around town that I am a witch. Ha! If I had any power would I be left hiding in this poor old house?

We held hands as we walked. For a few moments it felt true—like living out a page of an L. M. Montgomery novel.

In the woods I feel human. In his arms I feel like a woman. Both are good but I fear neither are forever.

September, 1961

ROTH CALLED FOR IRIS every Saturday night. He was gentle with her, as if through his tenderness he could atone for the scars he left on her skin five years prior. She didn't think it was anything like what love was supposed to be.

As he moved over her she kept her eyes tightly closed. She imagined sinking a knife into his belly—all the way to the hilt—so far it got stuck. She wanted to be the assassin in the Book of Judges who killed the king while he was in his own castle. She imagined how it would feel to have his hot blood spilling over her. How his body would sag down on top of her. How it would take every bit of strength she had to roll him off but she would do it because she was the strongest person she'd ever known.

Slowly, a plan began to take shape in her mind.

SHE HAD BEEN AROUND ENOUGH pregnant women to know how to fake her symptoms. It wasn't hard to huddle over a toilet and force herself to vomit, to wet her face from the tap so it appeared she was sweating, to crawl back into bed with an overdramatic groan.

The women swarmed around her, calling her blessed, adjusting her pillows, kissing her damp forehead, going on and on about how glad they were it had finally happened for her, and how they knew how heartsick she had been that she hadn't conceived yet.

"I just need to rest," Iris told them, wishing them away.

"Of course, of course," they said. "We'll check on you after the service." And they left the room, buzzing with excitement over another new life joining their family.

She waited ten minutes before slipping from beneath the covers and grabbing the potato sack hidden under her bed. It held her other dress and some underclothes. She didn't own anything else.

Everyone was in the sanctuary when she crept down the stairs. She slipped around to the door beneath the staircase that led directly into the kitchen. A huge pot of soup stewed on the element but there were no other signs of life. She grabbed a slice of bread from the counter and snuck around to the back door that opened onto the vegetable garden.

The makeshift grave by the ski lift was hardly visible anymore but Iris pushed back the weeds to find the old mound of dirt, now half covered with scattered grasses and a few dandelions. She pulled the salt shaker from her dress pocket—the one that had protected her from pregnancy since Roth had claimed her—and she set it down on the grave in a final gesture of goodbye. "I hope I don't come back here," she told the mound. "But if I do, you and I, we will be dirt sisters." She picked one of the dandelion heads and stuck it in her hair. "Wish me luck," she whispered, and then she slipped into the tall grass, following the long line of the driveway towards freedom.

She knew she had less than an hour before she'd be found missing. She didn't know where to go but she didn't care. If her taste of freedom lasted only moments she would die with a smile on her face for having sampled it.

She was surprised when she came out on the road, realizing she hadn't actually believed she'd make it that far. The gravel on the shoulder cut into her bare feet so she hopped up on the edge of the pavement and followed it south.

She had gone at least a mile before she heard a vehicle behind her. She didn't look back. She thought of the grave and continued forward with more resolve. If they wanted to run her down she wouldn't give them the satisfaction of showing them she was afraid.

But, instead of speeding up, she heard the vehicle slowing down. It passed her and pulled over to the side up ahead.

A man climbed out. A stranger with a kind face. "You okay?" he called out to her. "You don't have any shoes! You need a ride somewhere?"

Iris walked right up to him, comforted by the concern in his voice and the softness in his eyes. "I could use a ride," she said, knowing it was only a matter of time before a vehicle came peeling after her.

"I'm Paisley." He took her sad potato sack, flinging it into the bed of the truck before rushing to open the door for her.

Saturday, July 2, 1977

FOG DANCED A FOOT ABOVE THE ROAD, dispersing with each of Sherwin's footfalls only to fill the gap again as he passed. He thought it strange—like running through clouds. Or ghosts. "Boo!" he said out loud, laughing at himself. He looked over his shoulder. There was no sign of any other runners. He had probably put a full mile between them and himself. For a moment he wished for someone to high-five but then was glad there was no one. He looked forward to the bragging rights such a victory would bring.

He thought about pie. He thought about lawn chairs. He thought about Grace and a smile spilled across his face as he imagined putting a bit of ice cream on her nose just so he could kiss it off.

Lights appeared over the crest of a little hill. The road had been quiet for quite some time so he sensed the engine through the soles of his feet before he actually saw the headlamps cutting through the fog. They amplified the haze, spilling through it in a way that made it hard to determine where the car was.

It took Sherwin too long to realize it had drifted to the wrong side, coming directly towards him where he should have been safe. His focus had been stolen by thoughts of his pretty girl and her short shorts. He couldn't judge the driver's intentions appropriately. He veered towards the middle of the road, thinking the car would go by on the opposite side, but the driver started to turn back, realizing they were misplaced.

Sherwin sidestepped but he knew it wasn't enough.

He didn't have time to be afraid.

The impact was hard and fast. Sherwin's leg gave way with a crunch that echoed through his entire body. He was flung sideways, both feet lifting off the ground so he flew back towards the side he had been running on.

He landed with a sickening crack. His head bounced off the pavement as his body skidded seven feet, his cheek dragging along the cement until he came to rest near the gravel shoulder.

Brake lights punctuated the fog as the car came to a shaky stop almost one hundred yards down the road. Sherwin reached a shaking hand towards it in a weak cry for help.

"WHAT *WAS* THAT?" Joseph cried out from the backseat, the impact having flung him forward so his head hit the passenger side headrest.

"I don't know!" Samuel said. He managed to stop the car and they sat quietly in the middle of the road, the engine idling.

His heart raced and he wiped a hand across his brow. He flipped the windshield wipers on again, as if that would help with the fog. "You okay?" he asked.

"What was that?" Joseph asked again.

"I don't know. A deer?" Samuel started to open his door to investigate.

"What are you doing?" Joseph held his mother as another seizure took over her body. "She needs to go. Now!"

Samuel pulled his door shut again. "You're right." He put the car back into drive, racing the rest of the way into town, his mind unable to explore an appropriate response to what had happened when his whole heart was struggling to stay alive in the backseat.

SHERWIN'S HAND FELL BACK to the road as the taillights were swallowed by fog. The sound of the engine disappeared into nothing. He tried to pull himself up but his legs wouldn't work. He stretched down to inspect his knee and just below he felt sticky warmth. Something sharp stuck out from his flesh and he cringed when he touched it though he wasn't yet feeling any pain, only weakness.

He brought his hand back up and stared at the blood, surprised by its thickness and fascinated by the way it made web-like strings as he separated his fingers. Slowly he began to understand that the blood belonged to him, that the something sharp was a broken bone, that whoever did this had disappeared and he was absolutely alone.

His head fell back to the pavement and he rested his cheek there. He smelled rubber and tar and sand and he traced a pattern, his finger leaving a fine line of blood as he attempted to connect the asphalt dots into something that made sense.

Better world. Better world.

He tried to start the mantra again but without his feet keeping rhythm he was only lost.

Fog surrounded him. A sob exploded from his throat as his body caught up with his brain, waking to a pain that threatened to consume him.

chapter nineteen

Saturday, July 2, 1977

GRACE WAS NOT AN ATHLETE. The pavement passed beneath her, her body pushing forward with a grinding reluctance. She fought through it only because she believed in what the race stood for. The pain of a ten mile run was worth the smile of pride she would see on Sherwin's face when he greeted her at the end. She felt the corners of her mouth tug up at the thought.

He was far ahead by the time she was halfway through town. She hadn't seen him since the first corner, which meant he wasn't holding back at all. She was glad.

She kept pace with a group of fifteen as they crossed the street in front of the hospital while a car with a broken headlight waited to turn. Something about the car tugged at a corner of her memory but she was so focused on keeping her breathing even that she couldn't afford to waste her energies on things that didn't matter.

Her lungs were burning by the time she made it to the main road but she forced herself ahead because she knew quitting wasn't an option. She concentrated on the thought of Sherwin's face as she placed one foot in front of the other, determined to see the end.

With her head down and her mind focused, she didn't notice the crowd of runners up ahead until she was almost upon them. Frightened murmurs mingled with the fog, the sound settling uneasily in the pit of her stomach as she approached.

They were huddled together in small groups. Heads were shaking. One girl had tears streaming down her face as a friend consoled her. Jenna grabbed her by the arm when she tried to push her way through. "Don't, Grace," she said, trying to pull her back. "You don't want to see."

"What?" Grace asked, pushing against her. "What is it?"

"It's Sherwin."

Sherwin!

Grace fought her way through the crowd, her heart skipping and her jaw clenched so tightly it began to ache. A few people tried to slow her down, to put their hands on her shoulders and steer her away, but she just shook her head and pushed through.

She saw the blood first, specks sprayed out in a fan pattern from a still mound on the pavement. She recognized the dark splash of thick hair and collapsed to her knees, ignoring the sharp pain that shot up her legs and fighting the desperation that wanted to pour out of her in loud, chaotic sorrow.

Sherwin was lying with his legs on the road and his upper half in the gravel, one cheek raw with road burn, one leg bent at an impossible angle, a shard of bone protruding from torn skin. His eyes were open and glassy with shock. His mouth moved but no sound came out. He stretched a weak hand toward her and she crawled closer, pulling his head onto her lap, her whole body trembling.

"Why isn't anybody doing anything?" she screamed at the ogling crowd.

Oliver came running up to them. "I just went to the Martin place," he panted. "They let me use the phone. An ambulance is on the way."

"Finish," Sherwin said weakly. "Finish the race."

Oliver looked around at the idle racers. "You heard him. You're not helping by standing here," he said. "Sherwin wants you to finish the race."

Nobody moved.

Grace raised her voice. "Don't make it for nothing," she said. "Please."

People slowly dispersed, offering a lot of '*hang in there, buddy,*' and '*help is coming*' and '*be strong*'. Sherwin closed his eyes and fumbled to find Grace's hand, holding onto it and controlling his breathing as runners slowly resumed their race. Soon only a small circle remained huddled around him.

"I owe you some pie," Sherwin said, coughing and grimacing as the movement pushed pain through his body.

"What happened?" Grace asked him, bending over so her lips were close to his ear.

He shook his head, so subtly it was hardly noticeable but for its shift against her thigh. "I don't know," he whispered. "I just saw lights." He closed his eyes again and clung to her, getting blood on her t-shirt and staining the paper pinned to her chest. His head rested in her lap. He could sense her fear and it matched his own.

"I'm sorry," he tried to say, but he didn't actually make a

noise. Grace leaned down close to his face to hear him. "I owe you some pie," he whispered again.

The whirl of a siren cut through the hushed conversations of the kids that remained, causing a few to look up and start pushing others off the road to stand safely on the shoulder.

Grace kept petting Sherwin's hair, fat tears rolling down her cheeks as flashing lights broke through the fog.

Saturday, October 12, 1968

SAMUEL STOOD AT THE BACK of the sanctuary, his hands gripping the scrolled lip of the pew as his eyes wandered over the stained-glass shepherd standing watch over the building. There was no true silence there, though he often found himself alone within the church. The sound of branches scraping the roof or the groan of the old wooden beams reminded him he was never completely on his own.

"How did you do it?" he asked the shepherd, whose sad eyes didn't move. "Women threw themselves at your feet. They kissed you and rubbed their hair against you. How did you do it? How did you resist?"

The window gleamed in the sunlight and the lamb remained nestled against the chest of the man who claimed to be as human as he was God.

"Perhaps there are fights you can't understand," he challenged the empty church. He read the words framed across the bottom of the glass picture, "*Though I walk through the valley, you are with me always.* Then be with me," he prayed. "Make me strong."

He turned and left through the front doors, climbed into his car and made the short trip out to the Carver land.

He had to end things with Iris. He knew he couldn't continue. More time in her presence would cause him to fall away from the values and truths he had cherished his whole life.

For a few moments he felt strong.

Until she opened the door.

She stood before him, bare feet and wild hair, with tender eyes that made him think maybe—just maybe—she could truly love him. Conflicting needs tore at him. His love for the church was powerful. But his desire for this beautiful woman made that all seem distant and irrelevant. The idea of walking away from her ripped at his heart.

She studied him quietly, her face soft, lit gently with light from the porch lamp beside the door.

His jaw clenched and unclenched. There was a battle for his soul and he already knew which side would win. He was weak. But being in her presence filled him with a strength he couldn't quite define.

"Samuel?" she finally said, her voice gentle with concern, cutting through his conflict and pushing back his hesitation.

He crumpled at her feet, wetting them with tears he didn't even know were falling until he felt the dampness on her skin. She remained silent, her hand lost in his hair as he wept and kissed her feet.

Iris waited patiently until he settled and wiped his eyes. She knelt down so she could see his face. "Remember Jesus and the prostitute and how she wept at his feet?" She brushed hair from his forehead and touched his wet cheek.

Samuel nodded but couldn't yet form words.

"Perhaps I am your salvation."

If it had come from anyone else he would have thought he

was being mocked, but she said it with such innocence; he could do nothing but pull her into his arms and bury his face in her neck.

"I came here to say I couldn't see you anymore," he mumbled against her throat.

She pulled him back and gazed long into his eyes. "No you didn't, Samuel." She kissed his eyelids as fresh tears squeezed out from between his lashes.

"I know," he whispered and he let her help him up off the floor, holding his hand as she guided him up the stairs and into her bedroom. "But your son…?" he began.

"He's asleep."

She closed the door with a gentle click—the echoing hit of a hammer to the final nail in the coffin of his virtue.

IRIS STOOD WITH HER BACK to the door. Samuel stood near the foot of the bed, every sense heightened, every atom in his body like a separate being: the rushing of his heart, his pulse in his throat, the tiny hairs on his arms, how her smell burrowed into him in a way that made it his own. He tried to breathe, forgot how, and gasped against a dizzying lack of oxygen.

"I don't know who I am," he said, breathless as she closed the gap between them.

"I do," she said. "You are kind. And sweet. And gentle. And afraid. And it's not good for man to be alone." She unbuttoned his shirt and he made no move to stop her. "I will be your Eve."

Samuel's last thought before she pushed him back on the bed was that Jesus had never met a woman quite like Iris Carver.

chapter twenty

Saturday, July 2, 1977

THE LIGHTING IN THE HOSPITAL HALLway assaulted his senses and Joseph blinked rapidly as his eyes adjusted from the dull day outside. The magazines on the table beside his chair were at least three years old. He sat and stared at the bumper on the wall that prevented stretchers and wheelchairs from damaging the paint. He tapped his foot and clicked his tongue and picked at a hangnail. He could count as many as eight scars along the drywall where the bumper hadn't helped.

A crew was working on his mother. They didn't want him in there. He was helpless.

Reverend Samuel wandered the hallway like a ghost, his face ashen, wringing his hands in front of him. He had purchased a coffee from the vending machine by the cafeteria and it sat on the table beside Joseph, smelling strangely chemical and looking like a paper cup of oil.

"You can go," Joseph said.

Samuel turned pained eyes towards him and shook his head.

"Don't you have a sermon to prepare or something?" Joseph asked. "Shouldn't you be praying or something?"

"I can't leave," he said, picking at the tape on the corner of a poster. "She needs me. Iris needs me."

Joseph crossed his arms and leaned back against the wall, closing his eyes against the pacing image of Samuel. "This is a small town, Reverend," he said without opening his eyes. "People will talk."

"They don't know…"

"Be sure your sin will find you out."

Samuel marched over, grabbed his coffee, and sat beside Joseph. He took a long swallow, making a noise of distaste as the bitter liquid went down his throat. "You sit in judgement of me," he said, taking another sip before abandoning the cup on the table again.

"I do," Joseph said, turning his body away from Samuel.

"Why?"

"You're a man of God, are you not? You lead a church, for Christ's sake," Joseph sat forward and finally looked Samuel in the eyes. "Oh, sorry, did that offend you?"

Samuel reached a hand out but thought better of it and let it rest back on his lap. "Whatever you think was going on…"

"I know *exactly* what was going on." Joseph stood, unable to stay beside the liar who sat there. "I heard everything. She locked me in my room every Saturday night so I could '*pray*'." He made air quotes around 'pray' with his fingers. "I heard *everything*. You were just a paycheque, Reverend Greene. You were just a load of groceries or some gas in her car."

Samuel shook his head, rubbing a hand back over his hair. "No, no," he said. "It wasn't like that. It isn't like that. We love each other."

"What of the others? Does she love them too? The ones that still came after you left? What of them?"

"No, no," he said again, still shaking his head. "She was done with all that. She has been for years."

"You still gave her money, didn't you?"

Samuel didn't respond but the pain written across his face gave Joseph pause. He wasn't helping anything by trying to hurt this man. His mother was still hidden behind a curtain somewhere fighting for her life. Fighting in the hall with the one other human being who might actually care for her was pointless. He sat back down. "It doesn't matter," he said. "None of it matters. I just need her to be okay."

"So do I, son," Samuel said. "So do I."

They sat in silence, an unsettled truce between them as they waited for an update.

Commotion drew them from their thoughts a short time later. There was a rush of activity as an ambulance was unloaded and a stretcher wheeled down the hall by running EMT's. A girl ran after them but, just as Joseph and Reverend Greene had been, she was turned away as the stretcher was taken into a closed room.

She stood rejected, hands hanging at her side, her body hunched like she was mourning. She stared at the door for a long moment before slowly turning. Her feet dragged, one shoelace untied and trailing behind her as she moved towards the line of chairs where Joseph and Samuel sat.

She wore running shorts and a bloodstained t-shirt with a number pinned to it. Her long striped sports socks disappeared into Nike sneakers and her short hair was wild, sticking up over her head, pushed back with a yellow sports band.

She stopped.

Her eyes locked on Joseph's. He was flooded with the memory of the story in the woods—his father's story—and he remembered the girl who'd looked at him over the fire, the girl who had spied on him through his kitchen window. He remembered those haunting eyes.

Her left cheek was smeared with blood. Her presence hit him like a stab to the gut—like all the worry and fear he felt for his mother was suddenly doubled by the pain he saw across her face.

"Grace!" Reverend Greene jumped to his feet to put his hands on her shoulders. "Grace, are you okay?"

She nodded, her wide eyes shifting from her focus on Joseph. Recognition registered across her face. "Sherwin was in an accident," she said, her voice low and shaky. "He got hit. His leg is pretty messed up."

Samuel directed her to the chair beside him and got her to sit down. "I'm sure he'll be fine."

She shook her head and wiped a tear, smearing the blood so it formed a checkmark beside her eye. "I don't think he'll ever run again." A sob hitched her body. She scratched at a mark on her arm, and Joseph was surprised to see a scar nearly identical to his own.

"How did you get that?"

She glanced up, her brow furrowing with confusion before noticing where his gaze was directed. "Chicken pox," she told him. "I was three."

Joseph held out his arm. "I have the same scar," he said. "Strange, right? It itches all the time."

"Mine too," she said, trying to smile but it only looked like it hurt her.

"I'm Joseph."

"Grace."

Joseph was happy she was there. She shifted his focus from Reverend Green and made him feel okay about the sorrow that coursed through him because he saw the same feelings etched across her face. He leaned his head back against the wall and sighed, the act of it relaxing his body, even if his mind wouldn't slow down.

He watched the events of the day play across the back of his eyelids. He felt the movement of the car as they rushed Momma here. The way her sweaty hair had clung to her forehead and his hands. The sound of the hit.

The memory of the impact came back so hard and fast that he jumped forward in his seat, realizing with glaring clarity that, until that moment, he'd forgotten it had even happened.

And he knew exactly what had come in contact with the front end of Reverend Greene's car.

"You okay?" Grace asked, her hand rising from the arm rest as if she wanted to touch him.

Joseph stared at her, unable to form the truth on his tongue "I'm fine," he lied, settling back in his chair, hating himself, hating Samuel, and wishing he could take away every bit of her pain so she might have some peace.

Monday, July 4, 1977

THE GUTTURAL NOISES coming from his mother caused the hairs on the back of Joseph's neck to stand on end. He hugged his arms around himself, pacing at the foot of her bed while she writhed against the disease, tangled in the sheets.

Her body would tense, toes curling inward and spine arching into a C shape while her teeth ground together, a horrible, agonized sound coming out from between them.

The doctor listened to her heart as pain held her in its vicious grip.

"Isn't there anything else you can give her?" Joseph asked.

"I'm sorry, son, she doesn't seem to be responding to anything we've tried. She was vulnerable without vaccinations."

Joseph rubbed his upper arm where a battery of medicines had been pumped into him when the hospital discovered he wasn't immunized.

"It's a dangerous game you were playing," the doctor said, feeling Iris' forehead as the spasm finally settled and she rested back against the sheets, exhausted and sweating. He made a note on her chart and left the room.

Joseph followed him into the hall. "Isn't there anything?" he asked again.

The doctor placed a large hand on his shoulder. "Pray for a miracle," he said. "Tetanus is a terrible way to go." His eyes held a hint of empathy but Joseph felt the words like a slap.

"Is she going to die?"

"All you can do is pray for a miracle." He clicked his pen and walked off down the hall.

JOSEPH WANDERED BACK INTO HER ROOM and sat by the bed. Iris turned her head towards him and wet her lips with the tip of her tongue. "You look like your father, JoJo," she said. "You look like he looked after I broke him."

"No, Momma," Joseph said, taking her hand in his.

"Yes, JoJo." She reached across with her other hand and touched his face. "And now I've broken you too." She stroked his cheek with her thumb before letting her hand fall to rest on her chest. "I've earned this," she whispered. "Only pure hearts deserve happily ever after."

"No, Momma."

"Where's Samuel?" she asked, her voice little more than a breath. "I broke him too, didn't I? And your sister..."

"What, Momma? What about my sister?"

But she had fallen asleep.

June 9, 1964

My Darling,

I've spent so long looking for the truth and so many doors were slammed in my face. Your mother, God bless her, calls me a fool who has lost his mind to his grief. You should see her with your brother—how she coos and plays. I wish I could see it as beautiful. I only see it as an incomplete scene void of you.

Have you heard that the truth will set you free? I wish such sentiments were true for me but now that the truth is right in front of me I feel far more trapped in my grief than I ever was before.

Tell me this, dear one, how does one grieve what is still alive? How do I mourn for you when I know you march around a stranger's kitchen playing dress-up in a stranger's high heel shoes? A stranger you call Momma. A stranger who has no claim to that name.

I found her secrets. I found the diary where she spills her truth and every word of it burned my eyes like fire.

I had to learn how to ask the right questions but even as I stood on that stoop and knocked on that door I don't think I really believed I was going to finally have my answer.

I knew her as soon as she opened the door. She was the nurse that was there on the day you were born. "What have you done with my daughter?" I asked her. Oh, the fear in her eyes at the patter of little feet as you came up behind her. I thought I was looking at your brother but no, I was looking at what I'd lost and realizing that my search was over caused me to fall to my knees.

She said she would call the police. She said I was crazy. I said, "I only want to hold her. Please, just once."

She slammed the door and I heard her lock it and it must have been twenty minutes later a police car came and an officer forced me from the stoop and told me if I ever came back I would be arrested and charged with trespassing.

Truth has not brought me joy or freedom, it has only affirmed my pain.

In life and in death I remain eternally yours,
Father

You never kill anyone you want to kill in a war. E.H.

chapter twenty-one

Saturday, October 12, 1968

THE CEILING WAS WHITEWASHED beadboard, starting at the height of the window and rising towards the centre peak. A small lamp on the bedside table cast long shadows across the plaster walls. White paint had chipped away along the wooden headboard and Samuel lay tucked beneath a heavy white and grey seersucker quilt, one arm behind his head while Iris rested against his shoulder, her finger drawing lazy circles on his chest.

"You can't quit me," she said quietly and he smiled in spite of himself.

"What if this was your life, Iris?" he asked.

"This *is* my life," she responded, propping herself up so her hair fell down around her face as she looked at him.

"I mean me," he clarified. "Every day."

She shook her head and kissed him softly on the lips before

grabbing a robe from the foot of the bed and swirling out of the room. He heard a door close down the hall and soon the flush of a toilet and the running of a tap into the sink.

Samuel ached for her to return. He let his sighs drift up to the ceiling, waiting for them to fall back on him in shades of guilt, but it didn't happen. He marvelled at that, digging himself deeper into the tangle of sheets as he reflected on the change that was happening within him. He'd lived his life as a devoted servant of the Church, so focused on his ministry that he'd never felt the need of a woman before Iris. She changed everything. But she also changed nothing. He was still a man of conviction and ethics. He didn't feel any less valued by the God he'd given his life to. He didn't feel there was anything profane in what had transpired. No, what he felt was more profound than profane, like his love had finally found the physical home it had sought since that destined meeting over the apples.

He had fallen all the way. And he wasn't sorry.

Because falling felt like finally arriving.

IRIS' ROBE HUNG OPEN when she returned. She climbed back up on the bed, crossing her legs like a child—though all Samuel saw was a woman in whose presence he felt drunk with wanting. He sat up and put his hand on her knee. "I have a big empty house beside the church," he began, but she put a finger against his lips to stop him.

"I won't leave this land, Apple Man," she said. "I won't take my son out from under these trees. Children raised in the city are a little less than human, don't you think? They obsess over the world instead of getting lost in creation"

"I need more than Saturday night, Iris," he said, his voice

pained.

"Leave your church," she offered simply. "I will be your church."

He should have been offended but just the smell of her made him crazy with desire. He let his hand run up her leg and she leaned in to kiss him again until his fingers found a rough bump that made him pause. "What's this?" he asked, their faces inches apart.

She pushed his hand away and pulled her robe down to cover her leg but he stopped her and pushed the material aside. A distinct 'R' was carved into the delicate skin of her upper thigh. He traced it with a finger and looked at her with the question written clearly in his eyes.

"The 'R' is for Roth," she said. "John Peter Roth."

He looked from the scar to her face and back again without saying anything. He knew she had a history at Harridan Bluffs but she never spoke of it and he never pushed for her story because he was afraid it would break his heart.

She pushed his hand away again and pulled her robe tightly around herself. "My mother was brought in after my father died. When I came of age I was placed in The Promise Book and groomed to be his wife. I was sealed to him when I was twelve years old."

"Oh, Iris, I didn't have any idea," Samuel said.

She waved him off. "I was afraid of him. An older friend told me what the men did to you when you were sealed to them. I took a knife from the kitchen because I thought I could protect myself but he found it before I even had a chance and he cut me like that so I would know I always belonged to him. He forced himself on me. He…"

Samuel pulled her against his chest, a whole world of

understanding opening up to him. "You don't have to say it," he said. "He has no power over you anymore."

"I ran away when I was seventeen," she continued. "I got away right before the police raid."

He held her until the sky began to lighten, knowing full well she was still running and would never stop—the fear was too engrained into who she was. He slipped away from the house with a burdened heart as the sun rose in the east, painting the sky a brilliant shade of pink, wondering if she would ever be truly his.

IRIS LISTENED TO THE SOUND of Samuel's engine fading away as he drove his car out the driveway and turned towards town. She lay back on her pillow, smelling him in the sheets, already missing him.

Shame, elation, gratitude, and confusion rushed through her in a disconcerting mess of emotion. *Who was she that such a man could love her? Who was she that she could deny such a thing?*

She thought of the other men who were frequent parts of her life. They were nothing like Samuel Greene. They were all just other Roth's, taking what they wanted from her and caring nothing about her beyond her womanhood. She reached beneath the covers and let her fingers wander over the scar like she always did when she felt trapped.

She didn't know how to love Samuel the way he deserved. She only knew what she'd been taught.

Joseph was her priority and so it didn't matter that her heart wanted Samuel with every beat. It didn't matter that he could be the true source of her happily ever after. She couldn't leave the house that had saved her life. She couldn't give up her freedom to be a pastor's wife, and she certainly couldn't sacrifice her son's humanity by moving him into a town that would kill his country spirit and squash the beauty of his innocence.

All she could do was pledge the corner of her heart that didn't already belong to Joseph to this beautiful man who somehow saw her as worthy. She could promise faithfulness and vow to never again allow another man into her bed. And she could wait—forever if she had to—for Samuel to leave his church and join her in the forest.

It all seemed so lovely and romantic but impatience gnawed at her guts.

She turned her face and buried it in the pillow Samuel had laid on, screaming into the cotton cover. The heat of her own confusion blasted back at her and she withdrew to wipe a calming hand over her face, letting out a long, slow breath before climbing from her bed and running a bath so she would be fresh and clean to greet her son a good Sunday morning.

Wednesday, July 6, 1977

A SMALL NEEDLE pumped clear liquid into Iris' arm. It stopped the convulsions but made her weak and sleepy. "I don't want this to be your memory of me," she told Samuel, turning her face away from his kindness.

Samuel took her chin and tried to pull her back. "You are perfect," he said.

"No, Samuel," she said. "I'm not…tell me how you'll remember me."

"I'll remember you perfectly," he said, speaking around the

lump in his throat.

"No, tell me really, what will you remember? Really?"

He drew in a large breath, steadying himself as he caught and held her glassy gaze. "I will remember your hair on my chest—how it tickled my skin but I could never bear to move it because having it there meant you were beside me and those moments were what helped me realize the truth of heaven."

She smiled sadly and waited for him to continue.

"I'll remember how you tasted of summertime no matter the weather and how your laugh was the brightest part of any day I got to spend with you. I'll remember the way your voice could cause chills to climb my back, and how the only thing better than being in front of you was being inside of you, because those were the moments I felt I really knew who I was. I will remember how you are my forever and every thought of you causes my heart to rush and my face to flush, and I would tell a million more lies to have one more moment to tell you I love you…and I will remember wildly loving you because I can never forget what I will carry inside me for the rest of my life."

"You're a poet, Samuel Greene," she whispered, her eyes half closed, her smile sweet.

"And you are my muse, Mrs. Carver."

"Mrs. Greene," she said.

"What?"

"I'm yours, Samuel. All of me. You know that. I shouldn't have been afraid to give it to you. I'm sorry."

He kissed her gently, a hot tear dropping onto her cheek.

"I need to ask something of you," Iris said.

"Anything."

"I need you to leave me."

"What? No, Iris, no, I can't leave you…not now…not ever."

"I need this, Samuel," she said. "I need to know you're leaving with those beautiful words you just said and that they are your truth about us. I need to not watch you waiting for my death. I need you to sit in your memories and be warmed by them. I need you to let me go quietly. I need you to let our goodnight be sweet."

"Iris, I can't..." he begged.

"You can, my love," she said. "I need this. Stay until I fall asleep and then go and remember me how you just described... please."

He fought against his tears but it was a battle he wasn't meant to win. Nodding his head weakly, he climbed into the narrow bed beside her, pulling her head onto his shoulder so her hair spilled across his chest and tickled his neck. He wanted it there forever. "You are everything," he whispered into her hair.

"Thank you," she said, nestling closer to him, her own tears wetting his shirt. "Goodnight, Apple Man," she said, raising her face to receive his final kiss.

It was soft and long and the ending she'd forever longed for.

"Goodnight, Iris," Samuel said, her body relaxing against him as she fell asleep, knowing he would lay there awake, memorizing the feeling of her in his arms until dawn began to break and he slipped away from her forever.

Thursday, July 7, 1977

JOSEPH LOST COUNT of the hours he spent by his mother's side. She drifted between sleeping and weeping and calling out for him or Samuel and though his heart ached for her, he found himself wishing she would just hurry up and die. He hated himself for those thoughts. He had spent a guilt-ridden night in their quiet house at her insistence but he'd come back early. He couldn't stay away.

"Did I ever have chicken pox?" he asked her.

Her eyes were glassy and half-focused when she reached her hand out to him. He pulled his chair closer, its metal legs screeching against the tiles, and took her cold hand in his.

"What a funny question, JoJo," she said. "You were never around other children to be able to catch it. I protected you from those things…but I did so many other things wrong in my life." Her voice was little more than a whisper and slow tears leaked down her face. "You were the one thing I did right. I'm so proud of you, JoJo. You are a good boy—in spite of all my bad choices and the hateful things I've made you believe."

Joseph shook his head but she lifted her other hand to touch his face and still his dispute. "I thought I was doing right by you but all I was doing was lying to staunch my own guilt over the terrible things I've done. Your poor father—you're so much like him, JoJo—he was so good to me and I stole his heart and ripped it apart." Her hand became a pitiful fist beside his cheek and he reached up with his other to bring it back down to the mattress. "You didn't kill your baby sister," she said quietly. "I don't know why I ever said that. I thought it would make it better. I was protecting her and hurting you."

"It doesn't matter, Momma." Joseph said. He thought back to the story he heard in the woods, of the little girl who had disappeared and how he always knew in the depths of his heart he had never been responsible for what became of her.

His mother wouldn't be hushed. "It matters more than anything in the world," she said. "I'm dying, JoJo. What's to become of you?"

"I'll be fine, Momma. I'm strong." He paused for a moment before he added, "and you'll be fine."

She smiled sadly. "I love you," she said, making a weak attempt to squeeze his hand. "Build your church for me, JoJo. Keep me inside its walls. Promise me, Joseph."

"I promise, Momma."

"Go to the clearing. In the centre of the stones. Look beneath the ground there, okay? There is something there for you. Some answers."

"Okay," Joseph said, remembering again the haunting story he overheard in the woods.

"Don't make a relic of me," she begged. "Don't hang onto me like this. Remember me in sunlight."

"Okay."

"Do good things, JoJo. Be a good man and don't cry for me. I haven't earned it."

Joseph rose and leaned over her, putting his lips near her ear and speaking with gentleness, reciting one of the Bible verses she had so often said to him over the years as an expression of her love. "I have set you as a seal upon my heart and a seal upon my arm," he whispered.

A sob hitched her body violently and she turned her lips to his ear. "For love is strong as death and its jealousy is cruel as the grave."

She wept the kind of tears that possess a body and make it impossible to do anything else. She became her own mourning and Joseph could only watch, the empty space in his heart growing ever wider with each heart-wrenching tear that fell.

He fidgeted with the nail that had brought them all this trouble. The rust made it rough, most of it still stained with his mother's blood because he couldn't bring himself to wash it off.

He scratched at it with the tip of a pen that had been left on her little side table. RELIC. He might have promised not to remember her like that but he would be damned if he forgot what had led them there.

If he had only gone back to his room and picked up the nail as he had intended...

Flakes of rust fell onto his jeans and he imagined himself breathing them in through his nose, sucking them into his bloodstream so he could join her as payment for his sin that put her there.

He brushed them onto the floor instead.

Later that evening Iris slipped into a coma as he slept fitfully in the chair beside her bed.

October 17, 1964

My Treasure,

I chose a doll I thought might look a little bit like you. When I lifted her from the shelf she winked and I'm sure the shopkeeper thought I was crazy as I stood there weeping. I'm sure she's telling stories to all her girlfriends of the foolish man who bought a dolly to replace his poor daughter. "I need to bury more than an empty box," I told her as she rung up my purchase. "I need something to say goodbye to."

Every piece of my heart longs to be where you are — to touch your hair and hear your laugh and see love in your eyes — but you are lost to me.

You are forever lost.

I dressed the doll in the white gown your mother sewed. She made it with such care, singing as she stitched. She made it with such love only to dash that like china on a dirt road.

I don't know how she could possibly have a song left to sing but sing she does from her perch of beauty and dammit but don't I still find myself wanting her.

I can't go on.

I am forever lost.

I pray, one day, you are found.

I will wait for you in heaven,
Father

I am thee and thou art me and all of one is the other. E.H.

chapter twenty-two

Saturday, July 9, 1977

BETTY BELLE STILL HAD NIGHTmares of the day Paisley Carver arrived on her doorstep. She had lived in fear from that moment until she read the news of his suicide in the paper. A part of her mourned his death because in the depth of her heart she thought maybe she was partially to blame. Her daughter wasn't really her daughter.

Iris Carver was just a child herself when she pushed those babies out that early morning in the hospital. Just a child, but her eyes held a fire that Betty had found terrifying.

The church bell had been ringing as that little baby made her first cry and Iris had covered her ears against its pealing. At the mention of a girl, Iris had become angry and she'd turned her face away, refusing to accept the girl as her own, looking only to the son who was sure to come minutes later.

The poor baby was sobbing with the hiccuping cry of a newborn and Iris pushed her to make the child disappear. Betty had to decide in a heartbeat what to do. Options rushed through her head as she worked to clean Iris from the mess of the first birth. *It's her right*, she tried to tell herself. *It's her body. She can choose the fate of her own child.*

But what of the father?

She knew Paisley waited outside in the hall.

What if she told him? Surely he wanted the child. What if revealing Iris' request ruined their marriage? Could she live with that?

She looked again to the child, picking her up to cradle against her breast. *I could drop her at the door. They would say she is a Harridan baby.*

There had always been speculation about what went on at Harridan Bluffs but no one really knew for sure. It was considered a self-contained commune—some sort of religious hippie cult—but they were left alone because no one actually knew what happened beyond the gates.

The babies started showing up within the first year of the property purchase and continued at a rate of two to three per year. Always boys. Always wrapped in tea towels, tucked into a small cardboard box, and left just outside the main doors of the hospital as a rusty green pickup drove away. The poor things would be only hours old when they were abandoned.

It was a long time before anyone connected the children with Harridan Bluffs, but one of the doctors lived in Harridan Point and ended up following the green truck all the way to the hospital one day. They called them Harridan babies from that point on and feelings of distrust around the complex grew—eventually leading to the arrest and conviction of the men involved.

But it's a girl, she reminded herself. *And Harridan Bluffs has been shut down.*

"Go!" Iris said from the bed.

She looked into those newborn eyes, compassion and terror coursing through her in a rush of heat and motivation.

"You're sure?"

"Go!"

She ran. She bundled up that precious baby, grabbed a set of registration papers from the main office, stole a can of infant formula and a bottle from the obstetrics supply room, and she ran. She packed up her small apartment, called about a place two towns over, and by the next evening she was unpacking her three drinking glasses into the kitchen cupboard of a basement apartment in Raylea while the baby slept in a laundry basket.

She forged the doctor's signature and mailed the birth registration the next day, after which she tendered her resignation from the hospital with a single phone call.

It was easy to begin again. No one questioned the story that she had been widowed and left alone with her poor fatherless baby. The upstairs landlady was an older woman who was more than thrilled to care for her daughter while she made rent money waiting tables at a breakfast diner.

The day Paisley Carver found her she had almost forgotten the story that had brought her to that point.

"What have you done with my daughter?" he asked her.

The fear that fell over her was numbing and she'd bitten her tongue to keep from screaming when her daughter came toddling up beside her to peer around her legs at the man at the door. "I know nothing about your daughter," she told him, speaking around her fear.

"You're a liar," he said. "I remember you. I remember you so clearly. You were there that day." He pointed to the little girl and he bent down to look straight into her daughter's face. "And I know you, little one." He looked back up at her. "She looks so much like her brother."

She told him she would call the police. She closed the door in his face and turned the lock, holding her sweet girl tightly while she dialled the phone and waited for the cruiser to arrive.

For five days after she waited for the knock on the door. Waited for the investigation to start. Waited for her heart to be torn away from her.

But it never came. Instead, the news of Paisley's hanging brought her the freedom she had longed for over the prior two years.

Four years later she kissed her landlady goodbye and returned to Fallmoore when she learned of a new permanent nursing position.

The Carver's rarely crossed her mind. They were a strange topic of gossip around town; the circumstances around Paisley's death were always a matter of speculation but she was never implicated as part of the story and the mention of the Carver name didn't stir the same fear it once did. All the questions had died with Paisley. She was just a single woman with an only child.

She heard talk about the woman with tetanus but it wasn't until she made her rounds that she realized the woman was Iris Carver. Cold tendrils of fear gripped her as she stopped outside the door. *What if Iris recognized her?* She shook her head. That was silly. It had been too long for those emotional moments in the birthing room to have engraved a face into Iris' memory.

Betty straightened her uniform and entered the room.

WHEN IRIS FOCUSED on the back of her eyelids she saw only blackness. When she focused on her memories she became overwhelmed by the colours and sounds and wished it all away. It was only in the stillness that she felt any real peace.

People came and went. She knew they thought she was already dead—or so close they'd given up hope and were only waiting for the machines to agree with them.

She could sense the presence of her son most times, his quiet breathing filled the space with a comforting rhythm that sustained and lulled her. She had said all she needed to say before slipping into this strange sleep state. Joseph would find Paisley's buried secrets and do what he wanted with the truth.

She had accepted the reality of her own mortality. She wished for it but now, resting there on the edge of the abyss, she felt momentary panic. *What if heaven wasn't real? Or what if it was and Paisley was there? How would she face him?*

She sensed another presence in the room, quickly confirmed as she felt her pillows being adjusted and her pulse being taken.

Joseph's voice cut through the stillness. He sounded far away. "The doctor says it's just a matter of time now."

"She's resting," came a woman's voice. *The nurse?*

"She slipped into a coma last night and she's not coming out of it," Joseph said.

I love you, JoJo, she screamed from inside her head.

"She's not suffering," the nurse said

"Right," Joseph said. "She's not." He sounded so tired. Iris wanted to pull him into the bed beside her like she did when he was little, to rest his messy head on her chest, to brush his hair with her fingers and sing him the song of the bells.

BETTY GAZED AT THE BOY, shocked at the sight of him. She saw her daughter all over his face. He stared down on his mother with a heaviness that spoke to her own maternal instincts. His voice was so loaded with grief that she wanted to comfort him with a kind word or a gentle touch but she couldn't move.

The boy slowly drifted back into the hallway.

Betty looked down into Iris' sleeping face. She hadn't changed much over the fifteen years since the birth. She was still small and frail and dreadfully pretty even with her hair plastered in sweaty streaks across her forehead.

Betty leaned down and whispered in Iris' ear, her hushed voice dripping with both pity and anger. "I was there the day that boy was born," she said. "I saved his sister that day. I raised her. She is a kind and beautiful girl and is living a happy, fulfilling life." As she spoke the words, Betty's chest tightened with emotion even as the fifteen-year-old burden of her secret seemed to lift from her shoulders. "You tossed her away," she continued. "You have no idea what a gift you gave up. I hated you for a long time. I thought nothing was more selfish than what you did that day. Now I just feel sorry for you. Thank you for bringing her into the world and into my life. She is my world. She could have been yours."

A SPASM RAKED THROUGH Iris' body as she fought with every fibre of her being to physically react to the words tearing a hole in her chest. She managed to raise her hand just slightly off the bed before it fell and a great sigh escaped from between her cracked lips.

"He'll find her," she whispered before going still.

Betty checked her pulse.

There wasn't one.

chapter twenty-three

Saturday, July 9, 1977

SHERWIN WOKE INTO A cloudy world, his brain numb and his vision fuzzy. Bright lights assaulted him from all angles. The smell of fresh flowers punctuated the air and though he could see their colours he couldn't focus enough to see what kinds were there.

"Sherwin?" Grace's voice came from the right side of the bed and she slipped her small hand into his. "Sherwin? Are you awake?"

He tried to speak but his mouth was dry. He could manage little more than a groan.

As his vision slowly cleared, a horrible pain spanned from his lower back to his feet and his face was suddenly on fire. He wished to fall back into the oblivion of sleep. Raising a hand weakly to his cheek, he felt a soft layer of gauze and tape.

"What…?"

"There was an accident," Grace said, rising from her chair to sit on the side of the bed. "At the race."

"A car," he said, the recollection of headlights coming straight for him weeding its way up through his foggy memory.

"Right," she said. "You were hurt bad, Sherwin. Real bad."

He tried to sit up but she placed a hand on his shoulder and pushed him back gently. "You have to rest."

"How long have I been here?"

"A week."

"*A week?* What's wrong with me?"

"It's your leg. It was broken horribly. And your foot. The car crushed it. They've kept you sedated so your body can heal."

"Can I walk, Grace?" he asked. "Will I be able to run?"

Tears pooled in Grace's eyes and he knew.

"The doctors say prosthetics are getting better all the time," she said.

He squeezed his eyes shut tight, turning his face away from her. "It's gone?"

"Below your left knee."

"Who did this?" His left hand balled into a fist. "Who hit me?"

"They don't know."

Sherwin's fist hit the bed, its aggression lost in the tangle of white flannel sheets. Angry tears spilled down his face.

"I'm sorry," she said, her heart aching.

He didn't turn towards her, unwilling to let her see his tears. "Where's my mom?"

"She went home to shower. She's been sitting here with you since the first night."

Sherwin mumbled something she couldn't hear.

"I'll go get the doctor," she said. "He wanted to know when you woke up."

It wasn't until he heard her move towards the door that Sherwin turned to look at her again. She walked with a weakness that reminded him of a funeral march. He desperately wished to call her back. The thought of being alone frightened him. He wanted to tell her he was sorry but he couldn't form the words because he knew what he really wanted to say was "*how dare you*". He wanted to punish her for leaving him on two perfect legs.

Angry tears burned through the gauze on his cheek. He wondered if he was ugly now. He closed his eyes and tried to remember that car in the fog but all he could see were the lights and all he could feel was the place on the mattress where his leg should have been.

GRACE WANDERED OUT into the hallway, leaning back against the wall and closing her eyes for a moment.

"I know who hit him."

Grace turned to see Joseph Carver standing a little ways down the hall, mimicking her posture, his face reflecting the same regret and sorrow she knew her own wore. "You!" she said. "What do you mean? Who?"

"Reverend Greene," he said, pushing off from the wall and meeting her by Sherwin's door. "He was driving my mother here. It was an accident. But he did it. I'm sure of it."

"He didn't even stop," Grace said, swallowing against a lump that rose in her throat.

"We didn't know what it was," Joseph said. "It was so foggy and Momma was having a seizure and we didn't even see him…"

"He didn't even stop." Anger bubbled up inside her. "It should be *him* in there without a foot."

Joseph stuck his hands in his pockets and looked down at the white floor tiles, rocking back on his heels. "I'm sorry."

"How's your mother?" Grace asked, wiping her face and smoothing her blouse.

"She died."

From Iris' Journal

January 10, 1969

I feel Samuel in every part of me and there is nothing more frightening in the world. We can't sustain this forever. He won't leave his church and I won't leave mine even though he is all the church I think I'll ever need.

To have a heart that is owned is like learning how to walk without a teacher. I am always stumbling and all he does is catch me when I fall.

It's ridiculous, the fool I am.

Saturday, July 9, 1977

SAMUEL KNEW BEFORE the call came. He knew before Joseph's voice cracked through the receiver with those two hard words. "*It's over.*"

He felt it in a cool breeze through the open window by his desk. He heard it in the sudden absence of sound outside—in the way the birds stopped singing and the leaves stopped rustling and even the power lines stopped their humming.

It was only a moment but that was all it took for a soul to leave a body.

Sweat dripped cool reminders of his own existence down his side and he was already reaching for the phone when it rang.

He passed Joseph and Grace in the hospital hall as he rushed to the side of his only love. They stared at him with a coldness that made him pause. He watched as Mrs. Colt carried a steaming Styrofoam cup through the door beside the children and he thought of Sherwin. Realization crushed into him with the violent suddenness of a hit-and-run—the memory of the drive to the hospital, the crunch of striking something, Grace with her blood-stained t-shirt. He might have collapsed with the truth of it had a nurse not come by at that moment, pushing a wheelchair, bumping him from his whirling thoughts.

He reached a hand towards Grace, a weak gesture of apology, but she only shook her head, teeth chewing her bottom lip and eyes beaming judgement on him. "I don't…I don't…" he said, but he couldn't find the right words. His heart couldn't stand more tragedy.

He rushed to Iris' room and collapsed at the side of her bed. His knees burned against the hard floor. Tears ran fire down his cheeks and he clasped his chest, trying to hold in his heart—

broken like glass—pieces that would have reflected a rainbow across his dead lover had there been any light left in his world.

He had witnessed death countless times in his role as a minister. He'd watched peaceful passings and pain-raked torture. He'd prayed over final breaths and held the hands of family members as they said goodbye.

Death was an event—the greatest moment of loneliness that should never be faced alone. He gazed at her body, calm now without the pain that had tortured her, her face thin but beautiful in sleep.

I should have been there for her!

She had been his blue sky. In this new world of constant grey he wanted only to cling to her. He lay his head on her shoulder—awkward over the side of the bed. He took her wounded hand and placed it on his head as he wept into her nightgown.

JOSPEH STOOD JUST OUTSIDE the door. The sounds of the Reverend's sobs washed over him in a kind of hateful baptism. The worst of it was that it all seemed very honest. Joseph was much happier to despise the man then lend him any pity. He clenched his jaw against the sympathy pooling in his heart.

No! He would not—could not—condone the relationship between his mother and this man. *This man. A man of God? Ha! A fraud. A man of flesh.*

He longed for the sanctuary of the woods. He longed for the truth his mother found there. He wanted it for himself. He thought of her sitting in her stone circle, how she'd smile, how it made her soft and young, how nothing was more beautiful than when she was lost in worship beneath that green canopy.

Can you feel Him, Joseph? He remembered the sound of her voice like it had taken residence in his head. He closed his eyes to listen as it whispered. *Can you feel the peace that passes through this place? Grab it and never let it go. Someday it will save your life.*

He finally stepped inside the door and cleared his throat.

Samuel stiffened and wiped his nose on his sleeve before standing slowly to face Joseph.

"I'd like to be with her now," Joseph said. No apology. No gesture of camaraderie. He refused to even make eye contact, gazing beyond the man as if his presence was inconsequential.

Samuel nodded and wandered away silently, hair dishevelled from the dead hand that had tried to comfort him in his grief.

THEY LET JOSEPH SIT with her body long into the day. He sensed the absence of her spirit in every moment of her silence. Her skin was chalky grey. It felt like plastic beneath his fingers. Her vibrant beauty had disappeared with the rest of her. He felt like he was in a vacuum, like something had sucked everything from the room and though life continued as normal just beyond the doors—though nurses and doctors hurried here and there and patients took walks along the corridors—within the walls of her dying there wasn't even sound.

"A social worker will be along soon, I imagine," one of the nurses told him gently when she stopped by the open door.

"Why?"

"A child your age can't live alone."

A prickle of fear iced up Joseph's back and he straightened in his chair, looking her in the eye and lying as if it was easy.

"But I'm eighteen."

She frowned, looking down the hall like there might be someone there to vouch for him. "Oh," she stammered. "Oh, I guess our papers were wrong then."

"Yes."

He watched her study him, felt the trail of her gaze as she took in his broad shoulders and farm-thick arms, the shadow of a moustache lingering over his lip and the maturity of his face. He bit down, clenching his jaw so he would appear hardened.

"Sorry to disturb you," she said, finally slipping away as quietly as she had appeared.

Joseph let out a long breath and relaxed in his seat. He'd be damned if he would ever leave his father's land.

"They won't take me," he whispered to the body.

He didn't cry for Iris. He couldn't find the tears to mark her passing. A strange emptiness consumed him, reminding him of hunger as he played with the buttons on his shirt until he roused the courage to leave the room.

When Reverend Greene approached him again it was all Joseph could do to keep from vomiting.

"I will do the service for you, Joseph," Samuel said, catching him in the hallway as he was making his way to the main entrance, his eyes swollen and red. "No charge. It would be my gift."

But Joseph didn't want a service. He couldn't bear the thought of putting her on display in the church of a man who *'knew her'*. He couldn't bear the thought of standing by a box that held the shell of her history, to hear the echo of his breathing bouncing off those massive pipes. He couldn't bear to look out at the empty pews and be reminded that they had lived a life removed from the world; separate from the town that should have felt like home. No one would come. Not one person in all of Fallmoore would set aside their lives to say goodbye to a woman they only knew through her quiet weekly stops at the supermarket and the ugly rumours that plagued them since the death of his father.

"What *did* you think of her, Reverend?" Joseph asked him, his sharp question stabbing at Samuel's heartache.

"I thought the world of her," Samuel replied, his eyes swimming with grief—grief that seemed genuine but Joseph wanted nothing more than to slap it from his face. No one loved Momma like he did. No one deserved to mourn her with more heart than him.

"I hope you paid her what she was worth." He practically spat the words before pushing past Samuel and rushing outdoors, the satisfaction of his outburst leaving him empty and sick.

He drew in great breaths of fresh air, bent in half with his arms pressed against his thighs as he fought to calm himself down. The hate he felt for Reverend Greene consumed him so completely that he was dizzy with it. He slowly recited the lyrics to Momma's song, eyes squeezed shut, body folded in on itself like he was trying to form a cocoon of protection from the truth of the day.

When he righted himself, he was pleased to find he was alone. He straightened his shirt and climbed onto his bicycle, blowing out an exasperated breath when he saw Samuel come through the double front doors to stand beneath the covered landing to silently watch him.

Reverend Greene had brought his bike to the hospital the day after Iris had been admitted. Joseph refused his offer of a ride home but the Reverend had insisted he escape every day or two to shower and get a proper rest.

"Not with you," Joseph had said.

He shot one final glance at the Reverend who stood there broken, arms loose and pointless at his side, before pushing off and pedalling from the parking lot.

The cool air hit his face, kneading his pain, working to calm the fire in his belly. Nothing was real and yet everything seemed sharpened and more apparent than ever before; like somehow, in her absence, the world was allowed to brighten after seeming dim in her light.

The road stretched before him, an impossible path he was loathe to travel because he had only ever travelled it with her. There she was in the Queen Anne's Lace and the puddle that showed the reflection of the sun; in the grass that fought its way through the gravel shoulder; in the birds that flew overhead, their songs an anthem to a life without worry. Her fingers slid through his hair as the wind whipped his weary body, and he heard her voice, forever and always, whispering the Psalms as the road passed beneath him. Her death became farther behind him but ever closer as he approached the home she'd made for them on her back.

His legs trembled as he finally pushed through the door into the empty house. The heavy silence was painful and he began clicking his tongue against it in his familiar heartbeat pattern as he brought an armload of wood from the porch and set about lighting the fire to scare away the chill in his bones as outside, night descended.

JOSEPH WAS RESTLESS. His body would not settle and his mind spun with the impossible task of facing life alone. He kicked off his sheets, his feet becoming tangled and his body going cold as the night air moved over his sweaty skin. He couldn't comprehend a life without his mother. She had been his whole world. Everything seemed suddenly hollow and meaningless. He felt lost and terrified. A deep part of him had wished for this—for freedom—but reality harshly enlightened him to the horror of such a thought. Now it was too late. He couldn't take it back.

It was midnight before he let himself cry as he wandered from his bed to stand before the stranger in the bathroom mirror. He didn't cry for her—she had made her choices. He cried for himself. For all he had lost and this new empty existence he had gained.

When he returned to his room, having left a broken vanity mirror in his wake, he ignored the bed and lay down on his closet floor, pulling the door closed to create perfect, familiar, *familial* darkness. His head pressed against one wall and his feet the other. Silence surrounded him. He found himself longing for the disgusting sound of her groaning bed springs.

His body relaxed slowly, settling down against the hard floor as darkness wrapped him in a comforting embrace.

This is my heritage. He sighed against the blackness and fell asleep.

EVEN IN THE DREAM he knew he was dreaming. Joseph was in a large room, empty except for a full-length mirror on a cherrywood stand against the far wall. He walked towards it, his footfalls sounding like a shovel breaking ground, cracking hard against stones and soil and bones.

He stood before the mirror, looking into his own eyes, realizing they were looking back at him, roaming over his face like he was a stranger. His reflection moved towards him and he couldn't help but back up. The reflection stepped out from the frame, the mirror behind trembling and turning to black.

He was frozen, staring at himself.

But it wasn't himself.

Tentatively he moved closer, raising a hand to match the raising hand of the reflection. They froze, palm to palm. He was looking into the bold eyes of the girl from the bonfire, the girl from his kitchen window, the girl from the hospital, the girl he couldn't shake from his mind.

Grace.

He watched the lips form the name but no sound permeated his dream.

IN THE HOSPITAL, Grace jolted awake, the tendrils of a strange dream chasing themselves down the hall and out of her reach before she could alert herself enough to catch them. She glanced at Sherwin. His face seemed hard, his jaw tight and angry as if, even in sleep, he couldn't escape his new reality.

Light spilled across him from a street lamp beyond the window, hitting him in such a way as to make the swelling on his cheek more pronounced. She'd spent an hour earlier that day, while he tore small pieces from a crossword book and tossed them about the room, trying to convince him he was as handsome as he'd ever been. She longed for the days of his easy happiness, his quick smile and gentle sparkle.

Grace stood, stretching her arms over her head and yawning. Dawn was still an hour away.

She slipped through the door and navigated the quiet hallways to the room where Iris Carver died. The bed was cast in a soft glow, freshly made, its pillow without a dent, its sheets without sweat or tangle. No scent but a violent antiseptic bouquet that made her slightly nauseous.

She put her hand on the bed, startled by its chill, thrilled somehow that a life had ended there only hours before. She let her fingers trace the length of the mattress. When she reached the pillow she lowered her face and sniffed the linens thinking, perhaps, some remnant of life would be there, but she found nothing.

She thought of Joseph. She thought of how *she* would feel, walking away from the death-room of her own mother. She thought of Sherwin and the harsh set of his face.

"You died anyway," she whispered to the pillow, the great tragedy of it all descending on her spirit like a suffocating cloud. "He lost his foot so you could die anyway."

She stepped back from the bed, her heart breaking, anger churning a hurricane within her. She closed her eyes and conjured the face of Reverend Samuel Greene. "For nothing," she whispered before slipping out of the room as quietly as she had entered.

IN THE FAR CORNER, Samuel leaned forward in his chair, hands pressed together against his lips as if in prayer. "Forgive me," he said to the empty room. He righted himself and slipped out the doorway, his feet plodding the familiar path along cracked sidewalks. His shoes heavy, his blood thick, his face stained with too many tears, drying on his cheeks in the cruel morning wind.

As the sun broke over the edge of town, he entered his church and rang the bell, its rich notes momentarily filling a space within him she had left impossibly empty.

He rang it for his congregation.

He rang it for his own forgiveness.

He rang it for his Iris.

chapter twenty-four

Sunday, July 10, 1977

AS JOSEPH BROKE THROUGH THE TREES into the clearing, he was shocked by the amount of colour there. It was as if he was seeing the space for the very first time. Tall pines stretched their branches high above him, their needles a rich green, smelling of Christmas. The massive oak was dressed in a heavy blanket of rustling leaves, and the wind-chimes tinkled as a mid-summer breeze danced through the clearing.

He put his hand against the tree trunk, feeling the rough texture of wood beneath his palm, sensing the history of the glade—of the Carver generations who had come before.

His father's branch stretched out towards the stone circle like a finger pointing blame. Joseph pulled himself up, wanting to be in the place of his father's final moments. He sat in the crotch where branch met trunk, looking out over the ground beneath, seeing it through the eyes of the man whose death he still didn't fully understand.

The twelve stones stood, stoic and proud, and he immediately knew they would be the first thing he got rid of. He jumped from the branch, tucking himself into a neat roll as he hit the ground before straightening up at the first rock.

They were placed in the earth by at least four inches all around and he had to retrieve the shovel from behind the hanging tree to loosen them from the soil.

One by one he dug up the rocks, placing them in a pile beside Paisley's cross.

As he removed the last rock the wind shifted and the trees bowed back to allow the sun to break through in a strong shaft of warm light, pointing straight to the place the rocks once circled. Joseph stood in the middle of the light, letting its warmth kiss his face, a sense of freedom and affirmation washing over him.

His mother had often spoken of signs but this was the first time he ever believed in one.

"Break ground there, Joseph," his mother had told him. "You'll find answers."

He slammed the shovel into the dirt, the shock going all the way up his arms as the head hit against something beneath the surface. A strange need overcame him and he got on his hands and knees, pulling at the dirt with his fingers until he uncovered a small wooden box buried just below the centre of their gathering place.

He sat back on his haunches, overwhelmed with déjà vu as he stared at the scarred top of the box. He pried it open with dirty fingernails and settled on his bottom as he gazed down on the contents.

A doll lay on a little blanket at the base of the box, her eyes closed, her features delicate. She had long eyelashes that looked plastic and they rested softly against her pink cheeks. The baptismal gown was stained but beautiful, and the sun gleamed against something in the folds of the dress. He reached in to retrieve a small gold ring, spinning it in his fingers, knowing it had been his mother's though unsure why he felt so certain. He slipped it onto his pinkie finger before pulling out a small stack of letters tied together with twine and lifting the doll so her gown straightened—long and pretty—and her eyes opened to reveal a rich green that matched the forest and reminded him of his mother.

He held the doll on his lap like a child and opened the first envelope.

October 19, 1964

My dear Joseph,

If I could capture the pride I have for you and turn it into gold you would want for nothing throughout your entire life. I see greatness in your eyes and a strength that far exceeds my own. I would like to give you the world but it isn't in me to give. You are my greatest accomplishment and though I fail you every day my prayer is that you would overcome the sins of your father and rise above the eccentricities of your mother. Love her and protect her.

I should have found it in myself to be the father you deserved but I find myself unable to properly love you without the presence of your sister.

She is alive. Find her and share our land with her.

There is a key beneath the second stone on the west side of the living room hearth. It is for a safety deposit box. The deed for the land. The truth about your sister. It's all there.

I would ask for your forgiveness but I don't think myself worthy.

Forgive your mother. She is just a broken bird.

Papa

The world is a fine place and worth fighting for and I hate very much to leave it. E.H.

Sunday, July 10, 1977

THE WORDS OF HIS DEAD FATHER permeated his soul. They moved through his veins and burned behind his vision. Joseph crushed the letter against his chest and raised his eyes to the heavens, the heat of the sun warm against his face. Momma's wind-chimes called out to him, their song a hymn of sorrow as fresh tears leaked from behind his eyes.

He lay the doll and letters on the forest floor and picked up a large branch from the edge of the clearing. He stood beneath one of his mother's chimes, glaring at its happy dance of colour and song as it moved with the breeze before he swung the branch as hard as he could, knocking it violently from its perch.

"I hate you!" he said as it fell, a rainbow of glass scattering across the dirt. "I hate you!" He moved about the clearing, delivering judgement.

His hands ached, his knuckles white as he held the branch like a baseball bat. It whooshed through the air as he swung, a near invisible blur of emotional ferocity as one by one, wind-chimes crashed from the trees; years of Momma's creative therapy crushed in one painful, selfish tantrum. He continued until he had knocked every one to the ground and he stood panting with the exertion, his skin glowing with sweat that dripped from his forehead and shared trails with his tears.

Forgive your mother. She is just a broken bird.

He fell back to the earth, abandoning the branch, the coolness of the soil calming him through his shirt. He picked up a large piece of green, broken glass and held it over his head. The sun caught it and shone through. He felt the warmth on his forehead like a kiss from God.

He closed his eyes and let the heat filter out across his face and down through his body.

The song came from deep within him and he felt the presence of his mother as the words floated from his lips and drifted up to the sky.

"*Ring out the grief that saps the mind;*
For those that here we see no more..."

He wept as he sang. He went through every verse just as his mother did when she used to sing it in that very spot every Sunday morning.

He sang until a sharp heat caused him to whip the piece of glass away. It hit the front door of the hunting cabin, falling before the entrance with a light clunk.

Joseph rubbed his forehead, smarting against the searing pain of a burn where the sun had concentrated its heat through the glass and onto his skin.

He wiped his face and stood up, walking to where the glass had fallen.

The old wooden porch groaned beneath his feet as he bent to pick up the offending piece.

He turned it in his hand and touched his forehead again as a strange conviction came over him.

He pushed the door open, letting it creep wide. Dust danced in the stream from a grimy window, disturbed by the fresh blast of air. The single room was interrupted by two support posts holding the floor of the loft area, and he saw the wicked shadow of a small creature scurry out of view into a dark corner.

Dirt and neglect was everywhere. Joseph set the glass on the windowsill and turned in a slow circle in the centre of the room. Peace descended on him.

He didn't need to build a church.

He already had one.

chapter twenty-five

Sunday, July 10, 1977

JOSEPH COULDN'T BRING HIMself to rebury the doll but the thought of it staring at him in the house made him uncomfortable—those eyes watching his every move like a ghost lingered behind them. He tucked it back into the box, her eyes closing in a jilted way—first the left, then the right. He placed the lid on top and set it beneath the hanging tree, covering it with leaves before stuffing the letters into his jacket pocket and heading back to the house.

The heavy content of the letters rested against his chest like a burden. He didn't know how to process them.

She is alive. She is alive. She is alive.

It echoed back inside his head over and over and he didn't know if he felt angry or deliriously happy. Or both.

His eyes burned as he fell to his knees in front of the cold fireplace. He placed his hand on the second stone on the west side and felt it shift beneath his weight. What if the truth ruined him? What if it destroyed any last shred of respect he held for his dear mother?

He hesitated, moving his hand back and forth just enough to make the stone click against the adjoining ones, replicating the rhythm he made with his tongue while he waited for sleep at night.

He knew he would look. He knew he couldn't continue without knowing. But fear held him there for a long lonely moment before he tried to flip the stone over with his fingers. There wasn't enough give. He grabbed the fireplace poker and dug it around the edge that seemed most open, prying it up just high enough to get his fingers underneath. He lifted the stone out and set it aside.

In the small gap left by the missing stone lay a little drawstring sack. He pulled the top open and dumped a brass key into his hand, still dirty from the woods. The number 472 was engraved across the top.

He stared at the number, convinced it was another sign.

He grabbed the old King James Bible from his mother's little desk and flipped to the fourth book. Numbers 7:2. '*Heads of the house of their fathers…*'

"I am," he said.

In context it talked of men bringing offerings to the new tabernacle Moses had built. He sat back, Bible on his lap and key crushed into his palm.

"I am Moses," he whispered before slipping the key onto a piece of string and hanging it around his neck so it rested beside the nail that killed his mother—hung by a string, much like his father.

Tuesday, July 12, 1977

THE PHONE RANG, sounding shrill in the quiet house. Joseph emerged from the closet, still fully dressed after a fitful night of little sleep. He rushed down the stairs and grabbed the receiver.

It was the funeral home. "Your mother is ready."

"I was coming into town anyway," he said.

Joseph took a wad of cash from his mother's ledger book and an old duffle bag that once belonged to his father, and he left the house to start up the old Chevette.

Joseph had driven since he was twelve years old but it felt strange to sit alone in the worn leather interior. His mother had told him he had to learn just in case anything ever happened to her and he needed to go for help. He felt powerful and strong behind the wheel and she'd let him race down their backroads, but never into town for fear of being caught.

He drove carefully, hoping to avoid the consequences of being pulled over without a license, but he knew his mother would want to come home in her own car, not strapped to the back of his old bicycle.

The funeral director was sombre when he opened the door to Joseph's persistent knocking. He led him back to an office where a plain grey urn rested on the desk.

Joseph handed him the money and the man counted it slowly as he spoke. "There are counselling services I can connect you to. They will help you with the grieving process."

Joseph stood awkwardly, hands in his pockets, staring at the urn and shaking his head. "I don't want any of that. I'm fine."

The man studied him through squinted eyes, judgement rolling off him in great waves. "You're a child," he said.

Joseph straightened himself up and looked the man in the eye. "I am the head of my father's house," he said. "I've been a man for a long time now."

Satisfied the agreed upon amount had been paid, the man lifted the urn and placed it in Joseph's hands. He slipped a white card into Joseph's breast pocket. "If you change your mind," he said. "There's a number to call on there."

Joseph nodded and turned his back, heading out to the car where he strapped his mother into the front seat. He threw the card out the window to land in a small puddle beside the front tire.

HE THOUGHT THE BANK would question him—a boy who wanted to get into a safety deposit box—but all he had to do was pull the string from around his neck and the lady in a blue pantsuit led him behind the desk to a long narrow room in the back. She helped him unlock the box, then she pulled it out and set it on the narrow table in the centre.

"Take all the time you need, son," she said, backing out of the room.

"Thank you." He waited until she had closed the door behind her before he flipped the lid open.

It was full of papers, all neatly folded into a tight little package, the top of which was an envelope stamped with the seal of a local law office. He unwound the yellow string holding it closed in the back and slipped out the papers it contained.

A small note was affixed to the front document with a piece of tape:

For my son, Joseph Carver
and
For my daughter, whose name I never knew

Joseph peeled it off and stuck it to the front of the envelope before sifting through the documents.

He found the deed to the Carver land with accompanying papers that left it to the children of Paisley and Iris Carver. There were life insurance papers taken out by his father for his mother, only days before he had died, listing Joseph as the sole beneficiary. A final paper gave instructions for Joseph to present himself with the papers at the office of Theodore Swift, SJD to collect his inheritance and insurance payout.

He was taken care of.

He sat with that thought for a moment before moving on to the pile of documents that had rested beneath the lawyer's package. There was a small leather-bound journal and when he opened it he recognized his father's tight, pointed handwriting. It was full of dates and observations and statements, but Joseph didn't want to take the time in that little room to read it.

He sifted through the other papers but soon realized he wouldn't be close to figuring out what it all meant in a short period of time. There were newspaper cut-outs about a strange cult near Harridan Point. There were articles about a doctor who used to live in Fallmoore. There was a photograph of a little white house with iron railings leading up to the screen door with an address written on the back: 46 Pinewood Row, Raylea.

None of it meant anything to him, so he gathered it into the duffle bag and left the bank, crossing the road and pushing through the door with *Theodore Swift, SJD, Attorney at Law* etched on the glass. A small bell jingled as he entered and a pretty lady with very red lips looked up from a small desk.

"Morning, hon," she said. "What can I do for you?"

Joseph passed her the paper naming Mr. Swift and she pointed him to an uncomfortable chair in the corner beside a table covered in old magazines and an overflowing ashtray.

She walked down a short hallway and knocked on a door marked with a brass nameplate.

She was probably only five years older than him but she seemed much more worldly and womanly than his mother had ever seemed. He was mesmerized by the shape of her legs, by the long spike of her shiny black heels, by the hem of her skirt that seemed far too short and far too suggestive—though what she was suggesting, Joseph couldn't quite put his finger on.

"He'll see you," she said, walking back towards him with a sway to her hips that made him almost dizzy.

He nodded, "Thank you, ma'am."

"Oh no," she said, taking her seat behind the desk and crossing her legs. "Miss will do just fine. I'm a long way from a ma'am I hope."

He didn't laugh or apologize. He felt embarrassed and stupid as he clutched the duffle bag against his chest and walked into the lawyer's office.

"Mr. Carver," Theodore Swift said, holding out his hand. "I've been expecting you."

chapter twenty-six

Tuesday, July 12, 1977

JOSEPH SET THE URN DOWN ON the hearth when he returned home. The envelope from the lawyer rested on the table in front of him but he found it hard to look at. He had learned the house and property were his, free and clear. Taxes were being paid out of a trust his father had set up before he died, built on the small fortune the Carver legacy had left from their years as the county's major alfalfa supply. His was now the only name on a bank account, holding the insurance payout that would make it possible for him to continue his life in the humble manner he was used to for many years to come.

The father he never really knew had cared enough to make things okay for him.

But things were not okay. The hollowness in his chest hurt more than anything he'd ever known. He was empty and alone.

He loved his mother. Her death hadn't changed that. He didn't know who he was in the wake of her absence.

Joseph didn't move when there was a knock at the door. He turned his body towards the fireplace and fiddled with the corner of the manilla envelope.

The door opened and he heard the sound of boots on the floorboards. "Joseph?"

He didn't respond as footsteps crossed the distance from the door to the table, stopping in front of him.

"Joseph?"

He finally raised his eyes to the sad face of Reverend Greene. "What are you doing here?"

Samuel pulled off his hat and worried over its brim with his fingers. "She deserves a service, Joseph."

"Why?" asked Joseph. "No one would come."

"You need it, son, for closure." Samuel laid a heavy hand on his shoulder.

Joseph pulled away and went to stand by the window. "Don't call me son."

"You used to call me 'Apple Man'," Reverend Greene said, not moving. "The first time I met your mother you were just a little guy—the cutest wee thing—shopping for apples. You took one right out of my hand."

"How long before you started screwing her?" Joseph asked.

"I loved your mother, Joseph. I loved her more than anything. I would have given her the world."

"How long before you started screwing her?"

Reverend Greene sucked in his breath and his body hitched like he was swallowing a sob. "Joseph…"

Joseph walked to the small desk and flipped open his mother's ledger book. "Samuel Greene, Saturday, March 19,

1977, $45," he read. "Samuel Greene, Saturday, March, 26, 1977, $45. It goes on and on."

Samuel reached around from behind him and shut the book. "It wasn't like that."

"Yes it was, Reverend." Joseph pushed Samuel's hand away and opened the book closer to the beginning, running his finger down the left column. "It was like that for Darcy Monahan and Theodore Swift too."

Once again, Samuel closed the book on him. "You don't understand."

Joseph was frozen on the lawyer's name, heat rushing through his body as he pictured the little tailor-suited man who had handed off his inheritance. "I think I'm going to be sick."

"You don't understand," Samuel said, thinking Joseph was still talking about him.

"You're right, I don't." Joseph pushed past him and went out to stand in the garden where he stared down at the irises, fighting to control his breath.

"They were her favourite," Samuel said as he came to stand beside him. "She once told me that it was her father—your grandfather—who named her. She said when she felt shattered and insignificant she would come and look at the strange shape of the iris." He picked one and stroked its petals tenderly. "They taught her that even broken things can be beautiful and have a purpose."

Joseph sat on the grass at the edge of the flowerbed, refusing to speak or move until Samuel had left with his flower.

chapter twenty-seven

Wednesday, July 13, 1977

JOSEPH'S MOTHER KEPT A fat roll of newsprint in the downstairs closet. She bought it from the Gazette office years earlier and would cut off pieces for everything from grocery lists to Christmas wrapping.

Joseph laid it on the ground and stepped on the raw end, pushing the cylinder with his foot. He let it roll across the floor, from the dining room to the living room on the other side of the house, before he sat down with his pencil and started to draw.

It was well before noon when he started but the shadows were long when he finally sat back to look at what he had done. He had worked along the paper as far as the staircase, its surface filled with shapes and angles, measurements and supply lists—plans for converting the old cabin into his church.

A knock on the door startled him and his body protested

after hours on the floor when he stood to answer it.

Grace waited on the stoop. "Hi," she said.

"Hi."

"I just wanted to say I'm sorry about your mother." A blush crept into her cheeks and she averted her gaze, chewing her cheek and staring at the porch swing like it held some rare fascination.

"Okay." Joseph's discomfort matched hers. He didn't know how to talk to a girl.

She scuffed her foot against the wooden porch floor.

Joseph studied her face, her little bow of a mouth and her slender nose. "You kind of look like her," he said, a strange warmth moving through his body.

"I guess I'll go…" Grace said, starting to turn away.

"You want to come in?" he asked, surprising himself.

She raised an eyebrow and tilted her head to the side. "Really?"

He shrugged and stepped out of the way so she could come through the door.

"What is this?" Grace knelt down by the long paper, touching her finger to some of his sketches. "Is it a church?"

"I'm going to build it," he said.

"Why?"

"I don't know. For my mother, I guess. For her memory."

"Hmmm." Grace traced the line of a tall steeple. "Most people just get a tombstone."

"I'm not most people," he said, walking to where the paper roll had stopped by the old sofa and starting to roll it up.

"So I gathered," she said, grabbing the pencil off the paper before it got rolled up with the rest. She stood. "What do you know about building?"

Joseph shrugged and leaned the roll against the wall by the door. He took the pencil from her hand and set it on his mother's desk. "It can't be that hard."

"I helped my neighbour build his deck," she told him. "Maybe I could help you build your church."

"Why?" he asked, taking a seat on the bottom stair.

"I don't know." Grace leaned back against the door, resting one foot up against the chipped paint. "I'm looking for a distraction, I guess. Sherwin can't really do anything right now while he's still healing."

"How is he?" Joseph asked. "Is he okay?"

"No," she said, dropping her gaze to the floor.

"Oh."

Joseph wanted to ask more, to dig into the story, to find more reasons to hate Reverend Greene, but the way she avoided his eyes caused him to bite his tongue on the matter.

"I'm starting tomorrow," he finally said when Grace turned to leave. "I'm going to clear the space. In the woods where you were with those kids in June—where they told that story…"

"Why there?" Grace asked. "Won't it be hard to get all the wood and stuff out there?"

Joseph shrugged. He didn't care. "It was Momma's favourite place. That old hunting cabin? It's empty. I'm going to convert it."

"Will it have a church bell?" Grace asked as she stepped back out onto the porch.

"Yes," Joseph said. "I'm going to steal it from Reverend Greene's church."

Grace laughed and waved as she picked up her bike from where she'd dropped it. She didn't know he was completely serious.

He stood at the door, watching her pedal out of sight. A strange wholeness settled his spirit, something he'd never known but had always searched for, even when his mother had been alive.

GRACE ARRIVED EARLY the next day and helped him carry the broom, dustpan, and two buckets of soapy water to the cabin.

"What's all this?" Grace asked when they entered the clearing. She kicked a piece of coloured glass with her toe and it clanked against another fragment before settling again in the dirt.

"Momma made wind-chimes out of them," he told her.

Grace remembered the sound of their haunting tinkle from that night with her friends. She started gathering the pieces, collecting them in the turned-up hem of her shirt. "What happened to them?" she asked.

Joseph shrugged and picked up a small blue piece that fit nicely in the palm of his hand. Its edges had been worn smooth from the long years hanging from a tree. "I came out here right after she died. I kind of took it out on them…" He rubbed at the scab on his forehead where he'd been burned through one of the pieces.

"Oh." She dumped the glass in a pile at the base of a tree.

"What are you doing?"

"I'm going to make some stained-glass for your church," she said, bending to pick up more. "Every church needs its own stained-glass, right?"

"You sure you're not just avoiding the mess we have to clean up in there?" Joseph asked.

"Of course not," she said. "Just help me and it'll be done

quickly.

THEY BEGAN THEIR CLEANING in the loft, sweeping every corner and wall—even the ceiling that rose up to a peak in the centre of the small cabin. With every window open and the door propped wide, they propelled the dust outside in great clouds of promise.

They worked mostly in silence. Grace wanted to ask about Iris but Joseph was tight-lipped, focusing the pain of his loss into his work.

"Where will you put the bell?" she finally asked, craning her neck back. "Don't you need a bell tower?"

Joseph pointed to the centre of the ceiling over the loft. "I'm going to bust through there and build one."

"But what do you *really* know about building?" she asked.

"I've read a lot."

THE NEXT DAY, Grace brought a large rectangular piece of plexiglass and a tube of clear epoxy. She lay out the glass from the wind-chimes first, not creating an intentional picture but an organic pattern seemed to bloom out of the placement. "How's this?" she asked when she'd filled the plexiglass with colourful pieces.

Joseph dropped his rag in the wash bucket and came over.

He stood above it silently until Grace got up to stand beside him. "You don't like it?"

He nudged her with his shoulder and grinned at her, strangely moved. "It's perfect!"

Careful not to ruin her design, Grace attached the pieces one at a time until her art was complete. She left it to dry while she helped Joseph cut a 2x2 foot hole at the peak in the ceiling, leaving all the leftover glass pieces in a basket against the wall.

Fallmoore Gazette
Friday, July 15, 1977
Local Reverend To Fork Over 'Greene' After Amputating Track Star's Future
by Mickey Slater

Rescue services responded to a desperate call on the foggy evening of the *Race For Relief* fundraiser when organizer, runner and local track star, Sherwin Colt, was struck down by a vehicle on Douglas Street.

The late model Toyota was driven by Reverend Samuel Greene, pastor of the First Presbyterian Church in Fallmoore. The Reverend was rushing Iris Carver, widow of the late Paisley Carver of Carver Alfalfa, to the hospital. She was experiencing violent seizures as a result of an infection. She later succumbed to her illness, leaving behind a teenaged son.

Sherwin Colt suffered indelible harm to his body and future, losing his foot as a result of the injury. He is to be fitted for a prosthetic but doctors say he will never run again. Colt was being wooed by various universities as a valuable addition to their track teams. His future, at this point, remains unclear.

Greene has been charged with reckless driving resulting in bodily harm. He will pay a hefty fine and complete 40 hours of community service. He has demonstrated great remorse and humility and, in a formal statement he says, "I will regret this accident all of my life. Not only have I stolen the hopes of a promising young man but I fear I have lost the trust of my entire community. The Lord works in mysterious ways and I can only have faith that somehow good might come of all this."

"It was an accident," says Mirium Colt, single mother of the injured senior, "and I'm trying very hard not to be angry but that's my baby. It's insulting to think that's all my son's foot is worth."

When asked how he will spend his 40 hours, Reverend Greene said he will go where he is led.

Sunday, July 17, 1977

THE ACCIDENT SITE didn't look like anything special. It was just a piece of road on which something unfortunate had happened. The road didn't remember. It held no sign of trauma. There wasn't even a mark on the pavement. All the scarring was on Sherwin.

Neal and Cam Darvey drove them there. They parked on the side of the road and Cam pulled a homemade cross out of the hatchback, handing it to his brother before slamming the trunk closed.

Grace helped Sherwin climb from the car and hobble to the crash site. He was getting used to the crutches but he hated them because they represented his new weakness. A thick woollen sock covered his stump. He stood on the side of the road, his leg swinging uselessly, his face clouded by the shadow hanging over his spirit.

"Here?" Neal asked. Grace and Sherwin both nodded. Neal held the cross upright while Cam drove it into the ground with a mallet. "It's kind of morbid, buddy," he said. "I mean, no offence, but you're not dead or anything." He landed the last blow and stepped back from the cross.

"Part of me is," Sherwin said.

With Grace at his side, he hobbled across the gravel to the cross. He had his sneakers in his hand—the beautiful shoes Grace had given him right before the race—their laces tied together. One looked nearly brand new but the other was slightly misshapen and, though Grace had tried her hardest, the blood stains wouldn't come out of the canvas. Sherwin hung the shoes over the cross and stood staring at them. Grace wrapped her arms around his waist.

“They were supposed to be my saving grace,” he said sadly, his face pinched and focused as he fought to control his emotions.

“Let me be that for you,” Grace said, trying to lighten the mood.

“Can’t believe that bastard just got a fine,” Neal said.

“That’s ‘cause he had God on his side,” Cam joked. “Probably prayed some stupidity demon into the judge and then hallelujah, amen, he works a little judicial miracle out for himself.”

“Bastard!” Neal said.

“He brought a gift basket to the house,” Sherwin told them. “Cheese and fruit cake and crap—like that would fix things.”

“It was an accident,” Grace said.

“I don’t want cheese,” Sherwin said. “I want his freaking foot!”

“What would you do with it?” she asked.

“I'd kick him!” He was trying to be funny but he couldn't find it in himself to let the humour reflect in his dark tone.

Neal and Cam climbed back into the car but Grace and Sherwin stood by the cross, staring at the deathbed of Sherwin’s dreams. “What now?” he finally asked.

Grace tightened her grip around his waist. “You keep getting better and you keep getting stronger.”

“I have nothing,” he said bitterly.

“You have me.”

Sherwin looked down at her, studying the flecks of gold in her eyes. “What do you want with a gimp?”

“You’re the same person, Sherwin.”

“Am I?” He kicked his stump out in front of him. It swung back like a pendulum.

"He'll pay for what he did," Grace said.

"Will he? Will he really? How?"

"I don't know how, but the universe has a way of working these things out. You ready to go?"

"Wait," he said, pulling a piece of paper from his pocket and hobbling to the cross. A nailhead stuck out from the crosspiece and he jammed the paper onto it, stabbing it through a university logo.

"What's that?" Grace asked.

"My track scholarship," he said, before turning back to the car.

chapter twenty-eight

Monday, July 18, 1977

THE WOOD AND PAINT CAME FROM Ernie's Hardware, delivered on a flatbed truck along with a box of nails and a package of paint rollers. It took an entire morning to haul everything to the clearing.

Joseph rigged up a system with plywood, two old tires, and a rope that allowed him to pile on a few hundred pounds of weight, throw the rope over his shoulders, and pull it along the path.

Grace was doing something for her mother and he missed her quiet presence.

He cut the 2x4's to size and fed them through the hole in the roof before climbing through himself and securing the four corners so they stood up square. He added the base pieces and perpendicular slats all around the outside, placing a frame at the top where he planned to attach the bell. He created a little pitched roof with plywood, hinged on the north side so he would have access to the beam, and then he faced both sides with a plywood triangle.

It was a simple project and he hadn't expected it to take the whole day but the sun was starting to set as he drove in the last nail.

"It looks great!" Grace called from below.

He grinned down at her. "It'll look better when it's painted to match the cabin."

"It looks like a church now!" she said

He climbed down the ladder to join her in looking up. "It *does* look like a church," he said. "Sort of, I guess."

She punched him on the arm. "Come on," she said. "I want to put up the stained-glass before all the sunlight's gone." She pulled on his sleeve, dragging him with her into the cabin.

Her glass project waited on the floor where it had been left to dry so none of the pieces would shift.

Grace squeezed a small dot of the epoxy in each corner of the main window before she bent to pick up a side of the stained-glass. "Help me," she said, waiting for Joseph to grab the other side before they lifted it into the window.

Together they pressed it against the epoxy, waiting a full minute before stepping back to admire it in the fading light.

"It really is perfect," Joseph said.

It was raw and rudimentary but it possessed a beauty of its own in the colour and design that cast swirls and lines across the wooden floor.

"What should we call it?" Grace asked. "All the windows in the town church have plaques with names for their pictures."

"It doesn't need a name," Joseph said. "It just is."

"It's a rainbow," Grace said.

"A rainbow means the world ended," Joseph said.

"Or that it's beginning." She slipped her hand into his and Joseph froze.

Her grip was soft, her skin warm, and he thought of the blisters on the pads of his hand and wondered how they felt to her. He remembered holding Momma's hand when they prayed together, her palms bearing the same softness as Grace's, the same promise of companionship. *You don't have to be alone.* He blinked against the familiar voice that whispered in his head.

"How's Sherwin?" Joseph asked, pulling away and grabbing the broom from against the wall to take care of the mess his project had made in the loft.

"Angry," Grace said. "He says he wants to take Reverend Greene's foot."

"That sounds fair."

"Maybe," she shrugged

"Or we could just steal his church bell."

Grace stared at him, testing his resolution with her steady gaze. "You really are serious, aren't you?"

Joseph walked passed her with a dust pan full of wood shavings to dump outside. "As the grave," he said.

chapter twenty-nine

Friday, July 22, 1977

AFTER GOING THROUGH ALL the papers from the safety deposit box, Joseph decided to take a day off from his project to chase down the clues about his sister. If she was alive, he needed to know her.

He parked the car against a curb two blocks off the main street of Raylea and fingered the old polaroid he'd stuck in his visor.

The house at 46 Pinewood Row looked just like the photograph except for the evidence of more than a decade of seeming neglect. The white paint had peeled back from the wooden siding and large chips had broken off the iron railings, dusting the steps and stoop like dandruff. The screen door had a long tear in it that someone had frankensteined together with black embroidery thread. He touched the scar in the screen, wondering if it said anything about the lost sister he hoped to find there.

Joseph pulled the screen open and knocked on the inside door but he could hear no movement inside. He waited only a minute before letting the screen slam shut and wandering around to the back of the house where he found another door. He knocked again but still heard nothing.

"You looking for Mrs. Mulligan?" a voice asked.

Joseph saw a woman leaning on a spade at the edge of her garden in the yard next door.

"Is that who lives here?" he asked her.

"Not any more," she said, shaking her head. "Her sons came and put her in a home last week. Said she couldn't take care of herself any more."

"Have you lived here long?" he asked. "I'm trying to find someone who used to live here."

"Been here well on twenty years, son. It was always Mrs. Mulligan who lived here as long as I've been here."

"Maybe someone rented a room then?"

"Well, yes," the woman said. "There were a few over the years. The basement has a full apartment in it."

"Was there ever a baby?"

"There was." She paused to think. "That must be ten years ago now though…"

"Fifteen," he said. "Since she would have come here."

"Time's not the same as it used to be, you know?"

He didn't know. "Do you remember a baby?"

"A girl," she said. "Pretty wee thing with big wide eyes. Her mother's name was Betty, I think. Betty Belle. She was French. Smoked those long cigarettes, you know the ones in the magazines? Such a pretty baby she was. They didn't stay here long. Maybe three years or so? Why are you looking for them?"

"She's my sister."

The woman took a good long look at him. "Where were you back then? Why weren't you with your momma?"

"I was," he said. "I was with my momma the whole time. My sister was missing. Betty Belle stole her—my twin sister—right from the hospital where she was working as a nurse…"

"Goodness!" the woman said, putting a hand against her cheek. "She did say she was a nurse. Now that I think about it, that's why they left. She got a job at the hospital in Fallmoore."

"Betty Belle is in Fallmoore?" he asked, shocked at his luck.

The woman shrugged. "Last I knew of her, but that was a long time ago. If what you're saying is true, I'm very sorry. For what it's worth, she really seemed to love that little girl. She was always good to her and loving on her."

"Good," said Joseph. "I'm glad. I just really want to know my sister, you know?"

"'Course you do," she said. "And you should. There's nothing better than family."

He nodded, taking one last look up at the house. "So I've heard. Thanks for your help."

"Good luck," she called after him as he made his way back to the front yard. "I hope you find her."

THE PHONEBOOK HUNG in a plastic binding from a chain in the dimly lit booth on the main corner of town. Joseph flipped through the pages to Fallmoore. He ran his finger down the column of B names, landing on Belle. Pulling a pen from his inside jacket pocket, he wrote the address on his palm before driving all the way back to his hometown.

The house it took him to was much nicer than the one he'd visited in Raylea. It was still small but it was well kept with pretty gardens and a brightly painted door. The idea that all this time he had been so close to his family killed him. Years wasted when, instead of existing in a world of guilt and loneliness, he could have had a sister by his side. He ached at the thought of it.

Nerves made his heart race as he stood at the front door, eyes closed, trying to calm his breathing and slow his pulse before knocking.

Betty opened the door, dressed in her nursing uniform, either just getting home or just ready to head out for a shift. "Yes?" she asked.

"Hello, Mrs. Belle." He held out his hand for her to shake. "My name is Joseph Carver."

She dropped his hand and took a slow step backwards, recognizing him as the boy she'd seen in Iris' hospital room. She made a move to shut the door but Joseph took a step towards her, placing his foot just inside the ledge.

"You know who I am," he said. "And I know who you are."

"What do you want?" She looked over her right shoulder towards the staircase.

"I want to meet my sister."

"Mom?" a voice called down from the top of the stairs. "Is that Jenna?"

"It's nobody, Grace," Betty called up the stairs. "Stay up there!"

Joseph felt the name slam against him and he took a step back again. "Grace?" he whispered. The dream from the night of his mother's death floated in front of his consciousness.

"No," Betty said, seizing the opportunity of his back-step

and following him over the threshold and out onto the stoop, pulling the door closed on them both. "Don't you say her name," she hissed, pointing her finger in his face. "And don't you ever come back here, you hear me? She is my daughter as sure as heaven, and there's no way I'm going to let you break her heart with the truth about the monster your mother was."

"My mother is dead," Joseph said.

"May she rot in hell!"

Joseph slapped her across the face, the sound of it like a gunshot. Betty gasped and pressed her hand against her stinging cheek.

"How dare you," she said through clenched teeth.

"You don't talk about my mother," he said, his face only inches from hers. "She was not a monster. You *stole* my baby sister from the hospital when she was born!"

"No one would ever believe you," she said, pushing hair back from her eyes. "Your mother *abandoned* her. She didn't want her. She threw her away. What kind of person does that to a baby? I didn't kidnap her, I rescued her!"

"She looks a little like me, doesn't she?" Joseph asked.

Betty shook her head but he could see fear written all over her face.

"Be sure your sin will find you out," he said as he backed down the steps to the street. "Everything is brought into the light at some point."

Betty didn't go back into the house until Joseph had climbed into a car at the end of the street. Her face stung and her heart pounded in her chest. She thought she might be sick.

Slowly, she closed the door and leaned back against it, trying to still her breathing. She knew it would only be a matter of time before everything was revealed. Joseph was right. Some secrets couldn't be kept forever.

And her time was almost up.

chapter thirty

Friday, July 22, 1977

GRACE SAT BENEATH HER OPEN window, her back to the wall, trying to make sense of what she had just heard. It couldn't be true. Pressure built in her chest and the words in the novel she was trying to read blurred. She shook her head, trying to clear it, and pulled herself up to the window to see a boy going down the street from her house, marching to an old car parked near the stop sign. He glanced back once, catching her gaze in the window, pausing mid-stride to show his whole face before carrying on down the street. He didn't smile. He didn't blink. He didn't wave, but his eyes held a ferocious determination that startled her.

Grace gasped and turned back around, sitting again, trying desperately to understand why Joseph Carver would say such things.

The front door closed and her mother soon stuck her head into her room, her face flushed and sweaty, a wicked red mark showing the blurry shape of three fingers on her cheek. "I'm heading in to the hospital now, Grace," she said.

"Who was that?" Grace asked.

"Nobody. Jehovah's Witnesses. I sent them away."

Grace nodded and picked up the book she'd set on the floor.

"I'll see you tomorrow then," her mother said. "Love you."

"Yeah, night mom," Grace said to the pages, holding her position on the floor until she heard the door close again and the car pull away.

She waited until the sound of the engine faded before she stood and approached the mirror on the back of her door. She studied her face as if she'd never seen it before. She didn't see her mother there and it terrified her to think she'd never recognized that. She touched her cheeks, exploring their plumpness, tracing her little turned up nose. Her mother's face was angular and stern, harsh lines reminiscent of her French heritage.

Joseph Carver.

Could it be true? Could she really have a brother?

She thought of their moment in the woods; their brief frozen exchange at the kitchen window; the way he'd occupied her thoughts since she'd first set eyes on him; the way he felt safe—like he belonged in her life without any invitation or explanation.

There had never been a moment in her fifteen years when she hadn't felt loved. Her mother raised her with tenderness and care, and Grace couldn't believe she hadn't grown beneath her heart—that she was the product of lies.

Kidnapped?

No, she thought. *No.*

And yet, as she stared at herself in the mirror, she thought she could see the answers staring right back at her.

No!

Flinging her door open, she rushed to the den where they piled old newspaper for the fireplace. Finding the latest edition, she flipped to the obituaries near the back and pulled the page loose that had Iris' photo on it.

Grace had never known her when she was alive. Her only living connection to her had been that night when she'd spied on Iris and Joseph through their kitchen window. In the paper she was reduced to a thousand tiny grey dots. Grace touched the face of the stranger. Touched the little nose that looked so much like her own. "No," she whispered, touching her own face again. She tore the photo from the paper and stuffed it into her bra before stopping by the door long enough to grab her jacket and slip into her sneakers. She dashed outside and hopped on her bike.

Her legs burned as she bent over the handlebars, pedalling as hard as she could, hair flopping over her eyes so she had to throw her head back every so often. She didn't even know she was crying until she slowed down and turned into Joseph's driveway.

The car was there and a light was on inside though she saw no one through the window.

She wiped her face on her sleeve and climbed the steps to knock on the door. Her body vibrated with confusion and she didn't know what she was doing there or how it could possibly help.

Joseph opened the door a crack and peaked out before pulling it wide and standing in front of her. "Grace," he said.

She stared at him, slowly shaking her head and biting the

nail on her left ring finger. "It was just a joke, right?" she asked around her finger, her voice shaky.

"No."

"But..."

"No."

"The story in the forest," she said. "It's true?"

"Parts of it."

"Which parts?"

"I'm still working that out."

"Who am I?"

"My sister," he said. "My twin."

A sob grabbed her body and she cupped her hand over her mouth to catch the sound, her brow furrowed as the pain in her eyes shot out at him accusingly. "Why aren't you more upset?" she asked. "Or more surprised?"

"I've been looking for you my whole life," he said. "And since I met you, even though I didn't know...I think part of me actually did...somewhere deep down...I don't know...I just felt connected...My mother told me I killed you." He paused to let her absorb the words. Her eyes were wide. "She told me that when we were being born I flipped over you and my cord wrapped around your neck. She said you were strangled before you even came out."

Grace stumbled forward into the house and leaned back against the wall beside the coat tree, slowly sliding down until she sat on the floor while Joseph closed the door.

Joseph sat down in front of her, their crossed legs almost touching. He didn't speak. Her face was flushed, her eyes red and shadowed with a pain he knew too well. The house groaned around them as outside the wind shifted and moaned. The scent of a coming storm lingered on the air. The clock ticked through minutes on the kitchen wall and Grace shuttered, wrapping her arms around herself, squeezing her upper arms and rocking back and forth as she fought through layers of terror and grief.

"My mother told me I was born on a cool day in September," she said, finally breaking the silence. "When is your birthday?"

"September 8," he said. "When's yours?"

"September 8," she whispered, letting her head fall back against the wall, breathing out a painful sigh. "My mother is a good woman."

Joseph nodded slowly.

"She told me my father was dead."

"He is."

"Paisley Carver?" The name slid from her lips in a smooth whisper like it had always been part of her.

Joseph nodded.

"Did he really kill himself because of me?"

"No," Joseph said. "Not because of you—because of the people keeping you from him."

"So, your mother?"

"And yours—ours."

"It's a lie," she said quietly.

Joseph looked down at the scar on her arm as he absentmindedly scratched at his own. "I never had chicken pox," he said.

"What?"

"Your scar. It's from chicken pox, right?"

She rubbed her hand over it and looked at his matching scar. "Yes."

"Do you remember getting it?"

"No, you?"

"No. That night in the woods…? Did you hurt yourself? When you ran away, I mean?"

She stared at him stupidly for a moment, her face blank without understanding. "What?"

"I got a terrible pain in my leg as you were running away."

She sucked in her breath, confusion spilling across her face in a furrowed brow. "I tripped. I sprained my ankle."

Joseph reached over and lifted the fringe of bangs from her forehead, not surprised to find a red mark near her temple. "And how did you get that?" he asked.

She pulled back, pushing her hair down, eyes rising to the burn on his own forehead. "Maybe a week or two ago," she said. "I don't know…it just felt hot and that mark appeared."

Joseph couldn't tear his eyes from her's. "We've always been connected," he said. "I've always felt you there, somehow. I mean, I didn't know it was you but I always felt something… someone…have you?"

"No," she said, rubbing her scar. "Maybe. I don't know. I don't know about any of this."

Joseph rose and went to the kitchen. He filled a drinking glass with water and brought it back out to her, setting it on the floor beside her.

Grace cried quietly against the wall, struggling to grasp what this new truth meant for her and her future.

August 17, 1974

Today is my birthday. Today I am 30. Today I am old. Today I am sad.

Have I wasted my life?

I have a son who loves me. I have a beautiful man who loves me. I have a God who loves me.

I am held in a trinity of love.

So no, I suppose it's not been wasted and no, I suppose I should not be sad.

And yet...

Shadows haunt me even as Joseph sings birthday wishes from beyond the wax candle we use twice a year to mark our time here.

I've never seen the sea. I think perhaps this is the greatest tragedy of all. Perhaps salt water is the truest kind of baptism— the kind that might cleanse me and make me whole again — but I suppose it's not meant to be. And so I seek salvation in the trinity that holds me closest.

chapter thirty-one

Saturday, July 23, 1977

GRACE FOUND HER MOTHER IN the hospital cafeteria, staring at a bowl of untouched tapioca pudding while a cigarette sent a grey stream of smoke into the air from where she left it balanced on the edge of an ashtray.

Grace slid in across from her. She lifted the cigarette and ground it out, swiping at the air to dispel the smoke before finally meeting her mother's eyes.

"It's after midnight, Grace," Betty said. "What are you doing here?"

Grace pulled the crumpled newspaper clipping from her shirt and smoothed it out on the table in front of her mother. "You know why I'm here."

Betty shook her head slowly, pushing away the newspaper, chewing on her lip. She looked terrible—her eyes red rimmed and shifty.

"You know," Grace said again.

"Grace…sweetheart. I don't…"

"You *stole* me?" Grace leaned forward, her voice low. "You stole me from *this* hospital?"

"I saved you, Grace."

"You lied to me, Mom. You lied to me!"

Betty was still shaking her head. "I saved you."

"No," said Grace. "No."

Betty reached across the table and tried to touch her daughter but Grace pulled back, her chair screeching across the floor.

"I won't be there when you get home." Grace backed away from the table.

"But Grace, where will you go?"

"Families should be together," Grace said, walking towards the exit, her body tense and expectant, like at any second her mother's hand would fall on her shoulder and pull her back.

"You can't go, Grace, please—I'm your mother!"

The desperation in Betty's voice almost caused Grace to pause. She stopped at the door, her hand on the panic bar as she looked back over her shoulder to see her mother still sitting at the table, her face pale. "Enjoy your tapioca, Betty," she said before leaving the hospital and getting back on her bike.

GRACE'S EYES WERE SWOLLEN when Joseph opened the door to find her standing on his porch again. She held a backpack in front of her, its seams straining against the load spilling out the top—flowery hints of blouses and the tips of socks.

"It's 2 a.m.," Joseph said, yawning and rubbing a hand over his face.

"I know," she said. "I'm sorry. Can I stay here?"

Joseph stepped aside to let her in. "You can have Momma's room."

He showed her up the stairs, carrying her bag for her, pushing through his mother's door and setting it on the quilt.

Grace stood just outside the bedroom, her hand on the doorframe, looking around the space with a nervous uncertainty.

"She's not here," Joseph said softly. "There are no ghosts here."

Grace nodded and let him exit the room before she allowed her own foot to cross the threshold.

"I'll be right down the hall," Joseph said. "If you need anything, just…"

"I will," Grace said. "Thank you."

"Aw, what are brothers for?" He was trying to tease but his efforts fell flat.

Grace shook her head slightly, frowning.

"Sorry," Joseph whispered. "Get some rest." He clicked the door shut.

Grace took in the simple furnishings. She opened the small closet and let her fingers run through the modest collection of dresses hanging there. A faint citrus scent floated in the air as she disturbed the material, and she thought it nearly perfect her secret mother would smell like lemons. There was something rather sour about suddenly knowing the truth. She heard bedsprings creak in the other room and thought perhaps there was something sweet about it too.

The covers were cool when she finally slipped beneath them, her mind and body weary from the emotions of the night.

A small alarm clock ticked from the table on the right side of the bed and she stared up at the whitewashed ceiling, watching the shadows of the trees dance in the pale light of the moon.

Her mind spun. She squeezed her eyes shut. Finally she grabbed the ticking clock, slammed it into the top drawer on the bedside table and flipped the pillow over her head.

She didn't notice the book that fell to the other side of the bed until sunrise.

THERE WAS NO ANSWER when Grace tapped on Joseph's door the next morning. "Joseph?" she called as she cracked the door open. The bed was empty. "Joseph?" She called again, pushing into the room.

A shuffling sound came from the closet. "Joseph? Are you in there?" She pressed her palm against the painted wood. "Joseph?"

"I couldn't sleep," he said, his voice leaking out from the crack at the floor.

"So you went into the closet?"

She heard the sound of his body changing position. "It's a long story," he said.

Grace let herself slide down the wall beside the closet door until she was sitting on the floor. She fingered the leather book she'd nearly tripped over when she climbed out of bed that morning. "I found something," she said. "I think maybe it's your mom's journal."

"What does it say?"

"I don't know. I didn't know if I should open it."

"Read it," Joseph said.

Grace unwound the thin leather strip that was wrapped

around a wooden button on the front. The smell of the leather was strong and masculine, creating a strange paradox with the beautiful cursive on the first page.

"*My daughter is dead,*" Grace read aloud. "*I didn't even look at her. I didn't name her. It's easier that way. She is dead. She doesn't need my love. Love is for the living. Paisley judges me but I know he'll keep loving me because we're both alive. Joseph just stares at me with lonely eyes. A baby can't love, can they? A baby can only take. Even when I'm nursing him, he stares at me. Sometimes I think his eyes are the colour of God. I think God mourned when his only son died just like I think Joseph mourns for his only sister. My daughter is dead. I wonder if I'll ever be sorry...*"

"Stop!" Joseph said, pushing the closet door open and reaching out to close the book and take it from her hands. "It can't help."

Grace's eyes swam and she turned her head to try and fight the tears. "She really didn't want me."

Joseph took her hands and helped her stand. Grace smoothed out the skirt of her dress.

"That was hers," Joseph said, recognizing the embroidery along the hem.

"Sorry," Grace said, wiping her eyes. "I just thought..."

"It's fine. It's good. You should wear it." He set the journal on his bed and turned back to Grace. "You look like her," he said. "She would have liked that you were wearing it."

Grace shook her head and nodded towards the book laying on his quilt. "Would it make her sorry?" she asked quietly.

"She wouldn't have written that if she wasn't sorry already."

Grace looked down at the white cotton and her bare feet sticking out the bottom and she felt like an imposter. "I'm going to change," she said. "This doesn't feel right."

Joseph nodded and held the door open for her. "You'll want to be wearing pants later anyway," he said.

"For what?" Grace asked, going back into the hallway.

"For stealing the church bell."

chapter thirty-two

Saturday, July 23, 1977

THE GRASS WAS WET WITH DEW AS Joseph and Grace snuck around the side of the church, keeping away from the street lamps and the big white spotlight that lit up the stained-glass at the front. Rain fell in steady streams, its constant rhythm against the rooftops of the surrounding buildings masking any noise their footsteps made.

Joseph had been careful to flip off the headlights as they approached the parking lot from the top of the hill, coasting in neutral to the darkest spot of the lot beneath an overhanging walnut tree—as far as he could be from Reverend Greene's parsonage at the back of the property, while also being hidden from the main street.

The window wells were deep caves of corrugated metal, their floors a thin layer of gravel over concrete beneath a thick carpet of old leaves. Joseph jumped down into the one closest to the rear of the church and pushed the window open, the long dead leaves crunching beneath his sneakers.

He turned over and slipped through the window on his belly, dropping heavily to the basement floor four feet down.

"Pass the bag."

Grace fed the duffle bag of tools down to him before slipping through herself, stumbling clumsily to her knees before regaining her footing and brushing off her jeans.

Joseph pulled a flashlight from the bag and clicked it on. "Follow me," he whispered, leading her across the basement floor, past the wooden nativity that sat out front every Christmas season, past the rack of mouldering choir robes, past a metal shelf of canned food kept for needy families, and up the stairs to the main level.

"Are you sure?" Grace asked, her voice laced with fear.

"He deserves a lot worse," Joseph said, moving to a stairwell that curved around a column running all the way to the belfry. The stairs creaked beneath their feet and they were both breathing heavily by the time they reached the top.

"This way," Joseph said as he stepped carefully across a wide gap, open all the way down to the main floor, to a thin ledge on the other side. From there he was able to shimmy up, supporting himself by planting his feet parallel to the studs making up the wall. "Careful," he warned Grace as she began to climb behind him.

The bell was encased in a metal, box-like contraption that rested on a wooden square in the centre of the belfry. The bell-frame was attached to the square by large bolts that were fed down through the wood and secured with nuts beneath.

When he reached the beam holding the bell, Joseph hopped the short distance back to the opposite side and sat, straddling the beam.

"Rope?" he asked Grace and she rifled through the duffle bag, pulling out the yellow coil and handing it across the beam to him. He ran one end through the bell-frame and passed the end to Grace who took it and tied it around her waist, leaving little slack.

"Good," he said, doing the same with his end of the rope. "This is just in case it shifts when the bolts come out. Duct tape," he prompted and Grace pulled the grey spool from the bag. "Make some long strips for me, okay?"

She nodded. The sound of the tape pulling free echoed around the enclosed space and she winced against the noise.

Joseph lay flat on the beam, reaching down and up into the belly of the bell to grab the clapper. When he pushed it against the side it made a pitiful metallic sound—nothing like the strength it boasted on a Sunday morning.

"Tape," he requested, holding out his hand for Grace to stick a strip to his finger.

He used it to secure the clapper, adding two more pieces for good measure. The last thing they needed was to accidentally ring the bell and alert the whole town.

"I need you to hold the light on it here, Grace." Joseph pointed to the first bolt that fastened the bell to the wood. She directed the flashlight and he fit the wrench around the nut underneath.

Joseph fought through years of rust as he braced his feet against the opposite side, pulling with all his might until he finally felt it give. Four times he had to wrestle the rust and resistance until all the nuts were unscrewed. As he got to the last bolt he looked up at Grace. Sweat dripped down her temple. "Ready?"

She shook her head, nervousness dancing in her eyes.

"When this final one comes out the bell might shift. You have to brace yourself, okay? Just in case."

Grace nodded and wiped at a bead of sweat.

"We can handle it—don't worry. Reverend Greene told me it was only around a hundred pounds."

Grace adjusted her position, getting onto her stomach and reaching out across the expanse to grip the rope right near the top of the bell.

"Yeah, that's good," Joseph said. He gave the bolt its final turn and pulled it out from the top. It dropped, spinning slightly on the beam before plummeting down the belfry shaft, hitting the walls twice before pinging against the floor far below. The bell shifted but didn't drop. Joseph slid down on his stomach to match Grace's position, holding the rope with one hand.

Dust and bits of rust rained down as the bell gave way from its comfortable place against the wood.

"You got it," Joseph said, willing Grace to remain calm. "We got it. You stay right there." He was able to pull himself back into a sitting position, wrapping any slack from the rope around his arm as he slowly shimmied himself back across the beam to Grace.

Together they lifted the bell. Using the rope for leverage, they set it on the ledge, sitting back beside it on either side as they caught their breath.

"Now what?" Grace peered down over the edge to the top landing. It looked an impossible distance away. "We can't just carry it down."

"Right," Joseph agreed and started to untie the rope from his waist. "We'll lower it. We know we can handle the weight, right?"

Grace nodded but didn't make a move to undo her end of the rope.

"Momma once told me that the bell was the call for all the sinners to gather together so they could receive God's forgiveness and leave changed," Joseph said, tracing his finger through the dust on the bell.

"You don't believe that?"

Joseph shook his head, "Of course not. A bell is arrogant." He sat back again and wiped his finger on his trousers.

Grace leaned over to see what he'd scratched in the dust. *LIAR* screamed up at her from the bell. "Then why do you want it?" she asked

"So he doesn't have it."

"This is just revenge?"

"Isn't it, Grace?" he asked. "For what he did to Sherwin?"

"But that was an accident."

"Was it? Was it an accident that he pretended to be such a godly man while he was paying my momma to sleep with him?"

"My mother told me the bell was to let the dead know we hadn't forgotten them," Grace said.

Joseph looked her square in the face. "Your mother is a liar too."

Grace chewed her bottom lip and her eyes swam with shiny tears. "I know," she whispered and she untied the rope from her waist.

"Sorry," Joseph said, swallowing a lump of guilt.

Grace wiped her sleeve across her eyes and shrugged at him. "It's true."

Joseph took a bolt and began to scratch it against the wooden wall.

"What are you doing?" Grace asked.

“I’m writing his sins,” he said, moving on the to second ‘I’ in his mother’s name.

“Good,” Grace said, picking up the wrench and carving her boyfriend’s name deep into the wall too. “He needs to know why.”

Their vandalism worked like therapy, calming them both enough so they could lower the bell over the edge of the ledge, feeding out new rope slowly as they gingerly let it down the eight feet to the landing below.

“There,” Joseph said as it came to rest on the wooden platform. He dropped his rope and quickly climbed down the wall, waiting at the bottom to spot Grace as she did the same after him.

They used the rope again, pulled tight, as they descended the wooden staircase to the main level.

“This will never fit out the basement window,” Grace said.

“I know,” said Joseph, marching straight for the front doors.

“But then it’ll be left unlocked.”

“If it’s really God’s house then it should never be locked.” Joseph flipped the deadbolt. He pulled the door open and it sang a long low note as it groaned against its hinges. “Come on,” he said and they began a jagged half-run, the weight of the stolen bell between them, to Iris’ Chevette.

They put the bell in the backseat and climbed into the front, breathing heavily. Joseph let his head fall back against the headrest and he let out a big sigh. “We did it,” he whispered, turning his head to grin at Grace. “We did it,” he said a little louder, slapping a palm against the steering wheel. “You were amazing! We were amazing! We did it!”

Grace hunkered down in her seat. “Let’s get out of here,” she said, her voice trembling slightly.

"You okay?" Joseph asked as he put the car into drive and headed for the street.

"I'm fine," she said. "We just can't get caught. I just want us to be away from here." She crossed her arms over her chest and kept low as they made their way through town and out to the Carver house.

"Belle stole a bell," Joseph said as he parked the car.

"What?" Grace sat up in her seat and opened her door.

"Grace Belle, right?"

"Yeah."

"It's a little bit funny," he said. "That's all."

Grace glanced in the backseat before she climbed out. She could still read *LIAR* though the R was smudged. "That's not funny."

"Ironic then."

She slammed her door shut and headed for her bike that leaned against the porch, pausing with her hands on the handlebars. "Thank you for taking me," she said, not turning around.

"You mean that?" Joseph asked.

"Well, it scared me," she began. "*You* scare me. This whole situation with my mom scares me. But it felt good to do something. Even if maybe it was wrong." She looked back over her shoulder, a small grin playing at the corners of her mouth though she still looked close to tears.

"You can stay here again tonight you know," Joseph told her. "You don't have to go back to her."

"Yes, I do," Grace said. "I can't just leave her like that."

"Why not?"

"I don't know. I at least need to give her a real chance to explain herself. And she hates going to church alone. I don't want to do that to her. Not now. Not yet." She wheeled her bike over to him, pausing at his side and leaning over to kiss him on the cheek. "Thank you for finding me."

Joseph shrugged. "Thank you for being found."

"You're weird," she said, climbing onto the bike.

"I know." He watched her leave, the faint sound of her clinking chain still audible though she disappeared into the night shadows nearly as soon as she pulled away.

chapter thirty-three

Sunday, July 24, 1977

THE CHURCH DOORS WERE UNLOCKED when Samuel arrived early on Sunday morning. His feet felt heavy as he pushed through them. He was concerned about the door, but he took a quick sweep of the sanctuary and everything seemed in order. He thought it possible, in his distracted state, he'd just forgotten to lock it the day before on his way out.

His heart hurt as he wandered the empty pews, setting hymnals right and straightening the Bibles. He stopped at the front pew and sat, gazing up at the face of Jesus in the stained-glass. Grief gripped his soul in a vice and he found it hard to even breathe. He missed Iris with a ferocity that frightened him and he mourned her every moment. His grief felt as intense as his love for her and that frightened him too.

In the calm quiet of the church he asked the shepherd,

"Would you take this cup from me?" The whispered prayer slipped from his lips like a ghost.

No answer came.

"I am weak," he said. "I need your guidance." He shifted on the pew and the old building groaned aloud with an echo of his pain.

He finally put his hands on his knees and forced himself to stand. He took one last glance at the stained-glass, feeling judgement from it. "Where are you?" he asked before heading back down the aisle towards the main foyer again, kicking a metal bolt that was lying on the floor. "Where did *you* come from?" He picked it up, sticking it in his pocket before heading up the stairs towards the belfry.

He uncoiled the rope from where it waited on a large hook and pulled down hard to announce the beginning of the day and the call to worship. The normal resistance was gone. No sound punctuated the morning. He pulled again. Still nothing. Tipping his head back, he leaned over the edge of the landing and looked straight up. He should have been looking into the belly of the bell, eight feet above him. Instead he saw nothing but the old wooden frame it used to rest on.

A lump of fear rose in his throat. He reached across to the far wall, stepping over the opening to place his foot on a cross-stud in the frame, and he pulled himself up to the small ledge by the beam.

The dust had been disturbed. There were long smears and it looked like more than one person had been in the space. A metal nut lay on the beam and he reached across to grab it. It was cold in his hand and he stared at it with a kind of dumbfounded wonderment before he pulled the bolt from his pocket and slowly wound the nut onto it. He spun the piece between his fingers, seeing the fresh tool marks on the bolt and wondering why anyone would ever steal a church bell.

Then he saw her name carved roughly in the wood on the wall. He traced the letters, remembering the feeling of her skin beneath his fingers.

This hadn't been theft.

It was revenge.

And he knew, without a doubt, who was responsible.

As he climbed back down to the main floor of the church, the organist and her husband—one of the elders—came through the doors.

"No bell today, Reverend?" she asked, unbuttoning her jacket.

"It's been stolen," he said, still fingering the bolt in his pocket.

"Heavens! Who would steal a church bell?"

"I haven't any idea." He swallowed against the lie and blinked his eyes against their burning.

Samuel wandered to the men's room where he splashed cold water on his face and did his best to brush the dust from his suit. He stared at himself in the mirror, loathing the liar who gazed back at him.

When he finally emerged, congregants had begun to arrive and the organist was playing through the first notes of the opening hymn.

Great Is Thy Faithfulness floated on the air, its message powerful but its lyrics resting like judgement on Reverend Samuel Greene as he greeted those arriving with a quick nod and tight smile.

He walked up the aisle and took his spot behind the pulpit, facing his congregation as the song finished. "Morning by morning, new mercies I see," he said, quoting a line from the song. "What if that isn't true? What if your morning is all grief—is all 'mourning'? What then? How do we sing such things if our heart is telling us something different? New mercies? Where?" He gazed out at the faces and felt the weight of their expectation. "There was no bell this morning. Did you notice?"

Several heads nodded.

"I arrived to find it stolen. That little bell we worked so hard to be able to afford, stolen right out of the church—out of God's house."

Gasps spread across the room.

"The Lord Jesus Christ doesn't afford us more than we can handle. He also promises that in all things there is a purpose. I ask him now, what is the purpose of this? Where is the lesson? I am hurt by this." He twisted his neck and pulled on his collar, deeply disturbed and uncomfortable. He looped his finger in his tie and pulled it down to loosen it. He turned to indicate the stained-glass behind him. "There was a shepherd," he said, "a shepherd who tended one hundred sheep. One day, as he counted them, he realized he had only ninety-nine. 'Where is my sheep?' he asked and the ninety-nine could only '*baa*' as sheep do. So he left them. He left all ninety-nine to go in search of the one who'd gone astray. And he did find it. Caught in a briar patch, bleating with fear, and he rescued it gently and returned it to the flock." He paused and ran his hand back over his head. "You are my flock, yes?" There were some nodding heads. "I am your shepherd, yes? Called to lead you in the pathway of the Lord. Well, I ask you this…what if the shepherd is really that one lost sheep? What then? What happens to the ninety-nine?" He braced his arms against the pulpit and implored the sea of faces with his eyes. They stared back at him expectantly but offered no answer to his question. "You expect me to be above reproach, yet I am mired so deep in the briars I don't know that there is a way out."

"Everyone has bad weeks, Reverend," a middle-aged Deacon called out from the third pew. Mumbled agreements filtered across the sanctuary.

"Yes, they do," Samuel agreed. "And how much of that is our own fault? We make our beds and we lie in them, yes? And who do we lie down with? Our earthly flesh or the cross?" He raised his hands high, "Behold," he cried, "He makes all things new again. He separates the wheat from the chaff and he returns what has been lost to those who are faithful. Are you being faithful? Am I?"

"It's just a bell, Reverend." This time the voice came from a woman sitting beneath a window on the right side. "It means nothing and if God wills it, it will be returned."

Samuel nodded slowly, his head bowed so they were only looking at his crown. "I climbed into the belfry this morning," he said. "It's dirty up there. Dust everywhere and there was just an empty frame where the bell should have been and I think isn't that just how Jesus feels about us—when we take all his blessings and do nothing with them—aren't we just an empty belfry? He climbs up and looks around and sees that we've done nothing with his promises and the pain that must cause him..." He lifted his head and looked up to the ceiling. "Such a betrayal." He lowered his gaze to make eye contact with various congregants. He saw their concern, the way their frowns tilted their brows and the way they looked around at one another as if to say, *'what do we do?'* or *'how can we help?'*

"My heart is burdened," he went on. "I didn't mean to bring you such heaviness this morning. I had a sermon prepared and I was ready to share with you about steps of faith. I had a lovely little story about a lion and a mouse but it feels wrong not to share what's pressing on my heart." A few more nodding heads. "We might dwell under the wing of the Father and though he promised not to give us more than we can handle, we are not immune to the sorrows of the world." He flipped open his Bible and read to the people from Ecclesiastes 9. "So I reflected on all this and concluded that the righteous and the wise and what they do are in God's hands, but no one knows whether love or hate awaits them. All share a common destiny—the righteous and the wicked, the good and the bad, the clean and the unclean, those who offer sacrifices and those who do not. As it is with the good, so with the sinful; as it is with those who take oaths, so with those who are afraid to take them. This is the evil in everything that happens under the sun: The same destiny overtakes all. The hearts of people, moreover are full of evil and there is madness in their hearts while they live, and afterward they join the dead. Anyone who is among the living has hope—even a live dog is better off than a dead lion! For the living know that they will die, but the dead know nothing; they have no further reward, and even their name is forgotten. Their love, their hate and their jealousy have long since vanished; never again will they have a part in anything that happens under the sun. Go, eat your food with gladness, and drink your wine with a joyful heart, for God has already approved what you do. Always be clothed in white, and always anoint your head with oil. Enjoy life with your wife, whom you love, all the days of this meaningless life that God has given you under the sun—all your meaningless days. For this is your lot in life and in your toilsome labor under the sun. Whatever your hand finds to do, do it with all your might, for in the realm of the dead, where you are going, there is neither working nor planning for knowledge nor wisdom."

He closed the Bible and gazed out at the people. "God's Word is infallible," he said. "We are allowed our sorrow and our mourning and our griping so long as we cling to The Rock of our salvation. In our weakness he is made strong. In my weakness he is made ever strong!" He laughed pitifully. "Perhaps you find yourself feeling much the same way. We are human. We are made in the image of God and so are our emotions. May we honour him with them despite our human ways. Let us pray." He raised his hand again, stretching it out over the congregation in a gesture of blessing while he prayed the 119th Psalm over them. "May my cry come before you, Lord; give me understanding according to your word. May my supplication come before you; deliver me according to your promise. May my lips overflow with praise, for you teach me your decrees. May my tongue sing of your word, for all your commands are righteous. May your hand be ready to help me, for I have chosen your precepts. I long for your salvation, Lord, and your law gives me delight. Let me live that I may praise you, and may your laws sustain me. I have strayed like a lost sheep. Seek your servant, for I have not forgotten your commands. Amen."

"Amen," the congregation murmured.

The organist had barely begun to play the postlude and he hadn't even gathered his Bible from the pulpit before an older woman climbed up on the stage and wrapped her arms around his waist. He stood awkwardly for a moment, before he felt himself melt into her embrace. "You don't have to be perfect, Reverend," she said to him. "No one expects that. But we do expect you to be honest, so thank you."

He pulled back from the hug and felt overwhelmed with emotions. He swallowed them down enough to thank her.

"I'm bringing you a pot of soup later," she said, clinging to his hand.

"You don't have to do that, Ethel."

"Pish posh," she said, her face lit with a genuine smile. "Sad days call for warm soup."

"Thank you," he said again, retreating into his office where he dissolved into gut-wrenching sobs.

GRACE LEFT THE CHURCH with her mother, riddled with guilt but also disturbingly satisfied to have witnessed a glimpse of Reverend Samuel Greene's undoing. It didn't heal Sherwin—she wasn't so foolish to think that—but it *was* a small bit of comeuppance. *He deserved it,* she thought, the pain in the Reverend's voice echoing in her mind as she chewed her lip against a wave of shame that washed over her.

She smoothed her skirt as she slid into the car. Her mother smiled at her from the driver's seat but Grace offered nothing in return.

"That was…interesting," her mother said.

"Yes."

"The Reverend was not himself at all. I've never seen him like that…so emotional…and over a bell."

Grace leaned her head against the window to gaze up at the belfry as they pulled from the parking lot. "Perhaps it's more than a bell."

"What do you mean?"

"Maybe he has a life we know nothing about. Maybe he's been scorned by a secret lover."

"Grace!"

"Maybe he's been caught in a lie."

"Grace…?"

"Lies destroy people, Mother."

"If you're talking about the other day…about Iris Carver…I did what I thought was best."

Grace crossed her arms and turned her body towards the door. "Lies destroy people."

She thought the courtesy of coming home the night before and facing her mother again would have helped with the gaping wound in her heart, but it only served to burrow the hole deeper.

"We'll get through this, Grace." They pulled into the driveway and her mother put the car into park, turning off the ignition and sitting with her hands still on wheel. "We will."

"I'm going back over there," Grace said.

"Where?"

"You know where."

Grace picked up her bike from where she'd dropped it on the lawn the night before and pushed off onto the street, pedalling away in her Sunday clothes.

"Grace!" Betty stood beside the car, watching her daughter move farther and farther away from her.

"I'm not ready," Grace called back. She wasn't sure she ever would be.

chapter thirty-four

Monday, July 25, 1977

JOSEPH FOLLOWED THE OLD trail, the wheelbarrow bouncing over roots as he fought to balance the bell. Grace followed behind him, the coil of rope draped over her shoulder.

"It won't be as easy putting it up," he said.

"Easy?" she said. "When was it ever easy?"

He laughed lightly and brought the wheelbarrow to rest outside the cabin door. "Ready?"

Grace handed him an end of the rope. "Sure."

Joseph fed the rope through the metal frame in the same way he'd done in town. They carried it around the side of the building together where a ladder rested against the lip of the roof.

"You go up first," he nodded towards the ladder.

Grace climbed to the roof and pulled up the slack from the

rope, keeping it tight as Joseph climbed up beside her, then they used the rope to lift the bell between them.

Flipping up the side of the bell tower roof, they hoisted the bell, grunting against its weight and grinning a kind of celebratory victory at each other before lowering it to rest on the wooden frame Joseph had built.

Back inside the cabin, they climbed into the loft and one by one Joseph fed the bolts down through the bell frame into the wood and secured them beneath with a nut while Grace waited below, playing with a little stone she'd dumped out of her shoe. He removed the duct tape that held the clapper dormant and threw the grey ball to the floor.

"We did it!" he said, climbing down, catching her eyes as he planted his feet back on the floor. He strung the clapper rope across the loft to where he hooked it over a nail beside the window, vowing to himself he wouldn't ring it until his little church was complete. "You're not happy?" he asked, looking back at Grace.

She shrugged.

"Are you angry?"

"I'm not anything," she said. "Sherwin still doesn't have a foot. Your momma—*our* mother—is still dead. That's just a piece of metal." She tossed the pebble against the bell. The sound it made was like something very faraway. "How does this hurt him? I want him to hurt for what he did."

"Really?" Joseph cocked his head to one side. "*Really* hurt him?"

Grace shrugged and went to sit on the edge of the loft. "I don't know. I just need someone to hate right now and I can't handle it being my mom. He took Sherwin's foot." She crossed her arms over the railing and rested her chin on them.

Joseph sat beside her, his feet dangling over the edge like hers. “Maybe we *should* take his foot then.”

They sat side by side, silently watching the dance of colour and light through Grace's stained-glass. Outside, a breeze whispered against the walls, brushing branches up against the wooden siding.

“You did a good job on this, Joseph.”

Joseph looked around with pride at the raw wood walls and thick plank floors. “It won’t be warm in winter.”

“Churches are always cold in winter.”

“I’m going to paint tomorrow if you want to help.”

Grace shook her head. “I’ve got work to do,” she said. “I told Sherwin's mom I'd help her with some things in her yard. He was always the one to cut the grass and trim the hedges.”

“Right. Real life. You going to tell anybody?”

“About this?” she asked.

“Yeah.”

“Of course not.”

chapter thirty-five

Tuesday, July 26, 1977

JOSEPH OPENED THE URN AND grabbed a pinch of his mother's ashes. He let them fall from his fingers into each of the four cans of white paint before resealing the lid and placing the urn on a small ledge built into the wall at the front of his little church. The grey ash sank slowly into the paint, becoming one with it before he tipped the bucket and let a large puddle form in the bottom of a plastic paint tray.

He attacked the walls with abandon, pushing against the paint-roller aggressively, feeling the strain of the work in his shoulders as he left long streaks of white against the wood. He wanted the room to be bright. He wanted it to be alive, a place of living. He glanced back at the urn and shook his head sadly.

He was on the third wall before he even realized he'd been singing his mother's song under his breath as he worked. He let his voice rise to the rafters, celebrating the isolation and freedom in letting loose.

"Ring out the grief that saps the mind,
For those that here we see no more
Ring out the feud of rich and poor
Ring in the redress to all mankind.
Ring out, wild bells, to the wild sky,
The flying cloud, the frosty light
The year is dying in the night;
Ring out, wild bells, and let him die."

He set down the roller and looked up to the bell. It was tired and shabby and perfect; its presence the very definition of a sigh. Its rope swung slightly from the breeze coming through the open windows. Joseph hadn't rung it yet. He knew if he had been able to hear it when it rang from town, then town people should be able to hear it if it rang from here. And he had wanted to save its christening ring for the final touch when his church was really finished.

"Ring out, wild bells," he murmured as he climbed the ladder to the loft and grasped the rope. One pull couldn't hurt.

He gave it a hard tug, his head bent back to watch the clapper hit the side with a deep resounding note that vibrated in his chest. It was different than the sound he'd heard from the big bell tower. It was more immediate and intimate and powerful and he was so lost in the moment of it he didn't hear the door open and footsteps fall on the wooden floor.

"It's funny how the size of a building changes the sound of a bell, isn't it?"

Joseph spun around. Reverend Samuel Greene stood in the

open doorway, holding his hat in front of him like a repenting schoolboy. “What are you doing here?” Joseph demanded, climbing back down to the main level.

Samuel pointed up to the ceiling with his hat. “I’d like to talk about taking my bell back.”

Joseph crossed his arms over his chest and started to speak but Reverend Greene didn’t seem interested in him anymore. He was taking painfully slow steps down the centre of the shed, walking like a sad bride to the shelf at the front. He stopped in front of the urn. “Is that Iris?” he finally asked.

“What’s left of her.”

“You can think whatever you want of me, son.” Samuel sank down to his knees, still staring up at the urn. “You can put whatever judgement you like on me. It won’t change the fact that I loved her. That I still love her. That I'm quite sure I will love her as long as I have any life left in me.”

It was as if a switch was flipped in Joseph’s head. Fury boiled to the top. When he swung the paint can he wasn’t expecting the impact to jar him so hard. The jolt of the metal can hitting the Reverend’s skull sent such shock waves up his arms that he stumbled back against the wall as Reverend Samuel Greene slowly toppled onto his side without making a sound.

Joseph stared at what he’d done, scared and elated all at once as he knelt down and gazed into the Reverend’s slack face. “You have no right,” he whispered, pulling off Samuel’s shoes and socks and tossing them into a back corner. “You have no authority here.”

THE POUNDING IN HIS HEAD was incredible. Samuel squeezed his eyes against the pain and tried to adjust his position but found he couldn’t really move. His arms were bound behind him and secured to one of the loft support posts. His shoes and socks were gone but there was a jar of water with a straw sitting beside him. He managed to twist his body enough to bend down and reach the straw. He took a long sip and sighed as he let his head fall back against the post.

Joseph was curled up, asleep against the far wall with his back to him, a nearby oil lamp projecting the only light, its flame flickering and casting long shadows across the wooden floor. The dark sky outside the windows refused to tell him if it was early night or close to morning.

Samuel fought against the bindings but the rope cut into his skin. He could feel something wrapped around his head and wondered if whatever he’d been hit with had caused him to bleed.

He shifted his eyes to the shelf at the front but in the dim light cast by the lamp he could see the urn was gone. “The Lord is my shepherd, I shall not want…” he whispered into the quiet building, quoting the scripture he hoped would calm his fears and still his rushing heart.

JOSEPH CURLED HIS BODY tighter around the urn, clinging to his mother, trying to eke her guidance from within the cool ceramic, unable to still the tears sliding down his cheek as he listened to Reverend Greene recite verses he'd heard in her voice a thousand times. It was calming and familiar.

As the Reverend finished his recitation, Joseph began his own, echoing his mother’s favourite promise. “There shall no evil befall thee, neither shall any plague come nigh thy dwelling. For he shall give his angels charge over thee, to keep thee in all thy ways. They shall bear thee up in their hands, lest thou dash thy foot against a stone. Thou shalt tread upon the lion and adder: the young lion and the dragon shalt thou trample under feet…"

Samuel picked up where his voice trailed off. "Because he hath set his love upon me, therefore will I deliver him: I will set him on high, because he hath known my name. He shall call upon me, and I will answer him: I will be with him in trouble; I will deliver him, and honour him. With long life will I satisfy him, and show him my salvation."

Joseph rolled over and looked at him across the room. Samuel was pitiful as he lifted his head and met his eyes. "Would you untie me, please?" he begged.

Joseph sat up and scooted over on his bottom, stopping in front of Reverend Greene and crossing his legs, resting his hands —formed into fists—at his sides. "Admit what you did," he demanded.

Samuel held his gaze sadly.

"Admit it!" Joseph said again, raising his voice.

Samuel still said nothing.

Joseph slapped him.

Samuel turned his head back slowly and licked a bead of blood from his lip where it had split. "I loved your mother, Joseph," he finally said. "Yes, I slept with her. But it wasn't about sex. I loved her. It was about love."

"No!" Joseph said and slapped him again but with less force. Tears burned his eyes and he wiped his nose against his shoulder.

"She did what she had to do after your father died. She brought men into her bed but it was only to make sure *you* were taken care of." He paused for a short moment. "I think I loved her from that first time I met her in the grocery store." He looked off into the distance as he remembered, realizing dawn was coming by the lightening of the sky outside the windows. "It will be morning soon. People will start looking for me. I have a meeting with the board today."

"I heard about your breakdown in church last Sunday," Joseph said. "That must have been embarrassing."

Samuel shrugged, cringing as the rope tightened with his movement. "Actually, it was quite freeing. It was nice to learn my congregation is such a gracious group."

"And if they knew the whole truth?"

"I was meeting with the board today to tender my resignation from the church."

Joseph sat back, surprised, his eyes widening in disbelief. "Why?"

"Because I don't want you to be able to take it from me."

They sat in silence while the sun rose and then Samuel finally asked, "Why did you build this church, Joseph?"

"For my mother," he replied. "For her memory. She said we were closer to God here in this clearing than anywhere else."

A small smile spilled across Samuel's swollen face. "That sounds like her."

Joseph stood and loomed over him. "Don't you talk about her!" he yelled.

"What are you going to do with me?"

Joseph started pacing. "I don't know."

"Let me go, Joseph. I will leave and never come back. I'll leave the town. I'll leave the county if you need me to."

"What will that do?" Joseph asked.

"Nothing maybe. Or it'll give you the space you need to heal."

Joseph sat down in front of him again. “Did you really love her?”

Reverend Greene nodded.

“Did you know I had a twin sister she just tossed away because she didn’t want a girl?”

Samuel considered him for a moment and then asked, “Did you know she was raised in a community that threw away their baby boys and groomed their girls to be child-brides at twelve years old?”

“You’re lying,” Joseph said.

“She escaped when she was seventeen and met your father. She made herself a promise that she would never bring a girl into the world to be treated as she had been treated.”

“You’re lying.”

“She thought if she ever had a daughter and the community she’d left found her, they would take her from her and rape her.”

“No.”

“She wanted a boy because she thought she needed a chance to redeem herself from all that was inflicted on her. She thought she could do that by raising a son who didn’t want to hurt little girls.”

Joseph clenched his jaw so hard it hurt.

“You were her one joy, Joseph. I wanted to be her second but she was too focused on providing a good life for you.”

“I hate you,” Joseph said.

“Okay.”

“I don’t know what to do.”

“Untie me.”

“I want to burn this church down with you inside it.”

“But this is your mother’s church. Isn’t that what you said? Isn’t that why you built it?”

"You can all be ashes together."

"And then what?" Reverend Greene asked. "Then what would you do?"

"Then I'll take the bell out of the ashes, tie it to my ankle, and jump off the bridge into the river."

"You don't want to do that. Not really."

Joseph nodded his head towards the oil lamp. "I just have to tip that over. It would be easy."

"It would be the hardest thing you've ever done," Reverend Green warned him, his eyes soft and his brows turned in to show a level of compassion that stirred up remorse in Joseph's chest.

"Watching my mother die was the hardest thing I've ever done."

"Me too," Reverend Greene said softly.

JOSEPH TRAVERSED THE SLIPPERY terrain between mourning and fury. He glared at Samuel but he refused to speak anymore. What words were left? The thought of this man and his mother; the hours lost; time she threw away; moments that should have been spent invested in her son, instead steeped in lust with a *Reverend.* And of course it was lust. More than once she's told him he was the only man her heart would ever need. Was she a liar? He wasn't ready to accept that. He thought her much too strong to be someone who would fall in love with a man so weak he gave his life to God rather than forge his own path.

Samuel met his glare with calm, glassy eyes. He didn't try to engage him. He seemed content to allow Joseph his own torture, accepting his situation, and eventually drifting back to sleep.

Joseph continued to stare at him until his eyes blurred and then focused instead on the dirty bare feet sticking out from beneath Samuel's trousers, splayed apart to form an awkward vee.

It should be him without a foot. Grace's angry voice floated back to him. He imagined her face, the hurt in her eyes.

Joseph hadn't seen Sherwin. Everything he knew, he knew because Grace had told him. He tried to imagine what it would be like to wake up to a world in which every dream had been crushed, to wake up missing a piece of himself. His throat grew thick and a sob built up from deep in his chest when he thought of Samuel crashing into him. He curled his hands into fists as he realized it only happened because Momma was sick.

And that only happened because he had pulled out the nail.

No!

Sherwin lost his foot because Reverend Samuel Greene was humping his mother.

With a despairing cry he stumbled over to his toolbox and grabbed the handsaw, his entire body shaking as he approached the sleeping Reverend.

He lay the blade against Samuel's ankle, seeing the pressure points of white appear on his bare flesh beneath the teeth of the saw. With his other hand he clasped the leg tightly as he gritted his jaw and applied a little pressure.

SAMUEL MOANED AND HIS HEAD rolled on his shoulders. Pain radiated from his shoulders and it slowly registered again that his hands were tied behind his back. He wiggled his fingers, the slight turning of his wrist causing the rope to dig in where his skin was already raw. He groaned and let his head rest back against the pole to which he was tied. His eyes fluttered open, a headache pounding behind them, the world in front of him a blur.

There were fingers on his leg. He felt them, just above his ankle, squeezing with enough pressure to be uncomfortable.

And something else.

Something sharp.

His muddled brain cleared enough to see the saw pressed against his leg. He sucked in his breath and his eyes grew wide with understanding but he didn't make another sound. He listened to Joseph's ragged breathing, recognizing the boys fear as it radiated through his trembling grip, his clenched teeth, the sweat that rolled off his face and onto the floor.

Samuel did the only thing he knew to do.

He prayed.

IT WAS AS IF AN EARTHQUAKE moved through Joseph's body. He felt it beginning in the tips of his fingers and he stood by helplessly as it journeyed the pathways of his skeleton, causing a shift of will and focus.

He saw the hand holding the saw, the blade poised to harm in a way he could not take back. His whole body hitched in protest, leaning forward suddenly so as to scrape along the Reverend's ankle with a sound like tearing fabric.

Joseph threw the saw to the ground, shaking his hand like he'd been stung, staring at beads of blood that rose along the rough cut the blade had made.

"I didn't mean…" but he choked on the lie because he *had* meant it. In the moment, before he lost his nerve, he had meant it right down to his broken core.

He stumbled from the building while he tried to swallow a sob. Outside, he bent over double and retched in the weeds beside his little church—vomiting until he was nothing but a shell.

chapter thirty-six

Thursday, July 28, 1977

IT HAD BEEN THREE DAYS SINCE THEY raised the bell and Grace was anxious to go back and see the progress Joseph had made on the painting. Night had begun to fall when she bounced up the church steps, knocking quickly on the door before pushing her way through. "Joseph?" she called, her voice echoing up to the rafters.

A low groan came from the far corner and a foul smell assaulted her nostrils. She raised her sleeve up to her nose and walked over to investigate.

A man was tied to a support post with the same rope she and Joseph had used to lift the bell. He raised bloodshot eyes to her and she immediately recognized him.

"Reverend Greene?"

"Help me," he begged, his words as cracked as his lips. The floor around him was stained with urine. A handsaw lay discarded just beyond his reach.

She thought of all the angry words she'd said, all the things she'd imagined doing to the Reverend after she learned his part in Sherwin's accident, and suddenly none of them meant anything in the light of what real suffering looked like. "Joseph did this?" she asked, her voice shaking.

The Reverend nodded. "He believes I wronged him. I don't know where he is. He was gone when I woke up again."

"How long have you been here?"

"I don't know," he said. "Please help me."

She steeled herself against the smell, kneeling down at his side to work the knots behind him.

"He believes I misused his mother," he explained hoarsely.

"She was my mother too," Grace said.

He paused to look her square in the face, nodding slowly after a moment. "You look like him," he said, pulling his hands forward as the knots gave way, rubbing his wrists that were raw from the rope.

"Did you?" Grace asked. "Misuse our mother?"

"I loved her more than my own life," he said. "I would have given anything to trade spots with her in that hospital bed—to take that nail through my own hand. I would have been crucified for her."

"Looks like you were," Grace said, standing back from him as he struggled to his feet on shaky legs.

"Thank you," he said, shuffling to the door. "Grace?" He turned back towards her. "Tell him I understand. Tell him I forgive him. Tell him I deserved it for a hundred reasons but that I'll never stop loving Iris."

Grace remained silent but gave him a small nod. She watched as he pulled the cloth from around his head and wiped his face. An angry cut glared out from his temple but no new blood was there.

"He's a good boy," Reverend Samuel said as he left through the open door. "He's just a little lost. Will you help him?"

Grace nodded, standing dumbfounded as he hobbled down the stairs and along the path in bare feet, his clothing stained beyond saving and his smell lingering long after he disappeared into the woods.

The small window in the loft offered a beautiful breeze and so she climbed the ladder, feeling shaken after the exchange with the Reverend, wanting to separate herself from the mess and stench he'd left behind.

When she got to the top she found Joseph curled up in a tight ball against the back corner. His body was shaking but no sound escaped him.

"Joseph?" she called to him. "Joseph!"

He didn't turn.

She rushed toward him and wrapped her arms around him. He resisted at first, keeping his tight fetal shape, but he soon dissolved, clinging to her like he was drowning, sobbing against her denim jacket.

It was a long time before he could form words.

HE WAS FREE. Samuel had never smelled air more fresh and he pulled it into his lungs in huge draws that made him heady after being cooped up for so long.

His whole body hurt but he was free. He half stumbled, half ran down the pathway, shoving branches out of his way and kicking fallen twigs before emerging from the woods near the Carver house.

He paused, letting his eyes travel the facade of the home that would never again hold her laughter. Such love he'd found in those walls! He licked his lips, tasting her herb garden, its scent lingering on the air.

He dropped to his knees beside the flower garden, brushing aside untrimmed grass to reveal the woody roots of the iris plant. He traced their wild tangle, trying to decipher the puzzle of their existence as tears splashed down his face. "Iris!" he cried out, his voice catching on a summer breeze and disappearing back into the woods just as she had disappeared from his world. With a sorrowful moan that shook his soul, he got back to his feet and navigated the driveway, stumbling on the gravel.

The rocks cut into his flesh and each step seemed more torture than his time trapped in Joseph's church. Sobs wrenched through his body and he fought through the pain, focused only on getting home.

Each step grew heavier and heavier and the pain from his head-wound made him dizzy. He forced one foot after the other. *Left, right. Left, right. I - ris. I - ris.*

He was half a mile down the road when his foot caught on a sharp stone and he fell forward.

He lay, spread out on the edge of the pavement, arms reaching towards home though all he felt in his heart was hopelessness. "Where are you?" he sobbed into the night, praying to the God who'd gone silent. "Where are you?" He pounded his fist on the road in an angry tantrum against heaven, screaming at the empty road and his quiet God and the world around him that did nothing but ignore his pain.

With great effort he raised himself up to a seated position. He picked gravel from his palms, pressing them against his shirt to catch the blood that rose to the surface. His heart pulsed in his foot where the left nail on his big toe had torn when he tripped. It hung against the side of his foot, hanging on only by a thin strip of skin. He ripped it off, crying out as the fresh pain sent a new shock through him.

He tossed the nail towards the ditch.

A wooden cross was there, rising up out of the tall grass like sweet salvation. A pair of running shoes hung from the cross-piece by their laces. "Thank you," he whispered to the night. "Thank you." New sobs possessed him as his confused mind began to fully understand what such a find meant to his mission of getting home. "Thank you!" he yelled-sobbed-laughed. It was an ugly sound but there was nothing sweeter as he crawled into the ditch and tugged the shoes from the cross.

He inspected his feet as well as he could in the darkness and picked out a splinter that had become embedded in his flesh. Pulling large leaves from a plant in the ditch, he wrapped both feet as best he could, then slipped them into the shoes. They were too big and they were damp from being left outside but they were like dipping his feet into a cool stream. They were like heaven.

Using the cross like a crutch he managed to pull himself into a standing position. Tears trailed down his cheeks as he took his first step. His feet still hurt, his head still pounded, his palms pulsed with their fresh wounds, and his body ached from the long hours on the floor of the church, but as he looked down at the shoes and took step after step, all he felt was hope.

"Thank you," he said, once more, this time as a prayer.

May 4, 1977

For twelve years I've let one man love me. I wonder if this makes me a monster or him a fool? I looked through my book. 618 nights he's called on me — gazed on me with affection — adored me — waited for me. He makes me feel like every part of me is loveable.

Why?

For twelve years my life was pretty good. For seven it was hell. Why should anyone give me anything? Am I due for another painful seven or shall I risk all and dream of doubling my happiness?

Last time as we lay in bed, he stroked my palm and told me he'd wait forever. I asked him why and he told me he has nothing else to wait for. I am it. I am his whether I'll have him or not.

But I do have him. And I want him. With every beat of my heart and every breath I take. He is my first thought every morning when I wake.

He is my everything.

But so is Joseph.

I wonder if I can trust him with my heart as I've trusted Samuel?

chapter thirty-seven

Friday, July 29, 1977

JOSEPH LET THE DIARY FALL closed. Her words moved through him, a warm eraser attacking every bit of hate he still clung to. He wished for many things but above all he wished for one more moment with her—one moment in which he could say yes.

Yes, Momma, you can trust me.

He had spent the night in his little church again, seeking forgiveness for the terrible things he'd done, finding understanding in words that spanned his entire lifetime.

Grace had stayed until he settled back to normal breathing. She'd cleaned the area where Samuel had laid and she'd stacked the paint cans in a corner.

"You should sleep in your own bed tonight, Joseph," she'd said. "You need to rest."

He'd shaken his head. "I have to find my own way back."

She'd nodded and kissed his forehead before shutting the wooden door behind her, a basket of colourful glass tucked beneath her arm.

He groaned as his body protested the hard floor and he stretched, rolling his neck until it cracked, gazing up into the belly of the bell.

It had hung there less than a week but instead of victory, its presence was ringing shame. He closed his eyes and thought of Samuel.

Tell Joseph I forgive him.

How? Joseph wondered. Memories of what he'd done—of what he had learned he was capable of—sent a chill through his body.

Forgive?

How could Samuel forgive him if Joseph wasn't able to forgive himself?

And what of Momma? She would have looked upon him the same way she did when he was a small boy and he'd stabbed a frog with a sharp stick; her gaze thickened with pain and disappointment, her hand resting over the heart he'd broken.

"We never hurt one of God's creatures," she had told him. "We are their keepers. We care for them as God cares for us."

She helped him make a box with pieces of bark and they had buried the frog by the pond while its family sang a low funeral song.

"Is God angry with me, Momma?" he asked as they stood by the little mound in the mud.

"He is not angry, love. He is hurt."

Joseph wasn't sure why but he knew that was worse. He had cried into her apron until she wiped his tears and said, "we must never do things to hurt another who would never hurt us."

Pressing against his knees, he forced himself to stand. His head nearly brushed the underside of the bell where it hung in the low ceiling over the loft. He reached up to touch the clapper with his fingertips, the metal cold against his skin. With a flick, he sent it swinging against the side—the resulting *dong* sounding low and weak.

Regret clouded his vision as tears swelled in his eyes. He plopped to his bottom, his sigh seeming to hold more substance than the sad sound of the bell.

Yes, Momma, you can trust me.

Sunday, July 31, 1977

SAMUEL STOOD IN THE CENTRE of the sanctuary, halfway down the middle aisle, in a direct stream of light from the stained-glass window. Particles of dust moved before his eyes as his heavy sighs caused them to dance against the backdrop of what would be his last service in this church.

Who would he be without this place?

A sinner? A martyr? A joke?

The board had accepted his resignation with grace. They didn't want to know his reasonings—they only needed to know he no longer felt called to this place.

"He makes all things beautiful in His own time," one of the elders told him. "Go where He leads you."

He felt led to damnation.

He didn't tell them that.

He thought of all the good he'd done there and wondered if it mattered under the shadow of the lies he had lived.

Sherwin Colt had told him to go to hell when he delivered a peace offering fruit basket.

Funny. He was already there.

His body ached as he limped down the aisle towards the wall that held the bell rope, knowing it would be fruitless but unable to stop himself. His tortured feet cried for relief from within his Sunday loafers but he considered the pain a penance.

I'm paying the price. This is what I deserve.

The cross and shoes that rescued him from his agonizing walk rested beside his desk as a reminder that, through it all, he still had a holy teammate—even in the silences and misery; after all, could love really be a sin if it was actually the greatest commandment?

He touched each pew, soaking history into his skin as he left his fingerprints on the memory of his own narrative within those walls. He imagined her there, her white dress making everything seem shabby, her eyes their own stained-glass, her smile all the light he would ever need.

The shadow around his soul hugged tighter and her image faded like fog from his vision.

A folded paper lay on the church floor beneath the bell rope. His heart raced as he read the two words scrawled across it and he stumbled back to look up into the belfry—into the belly of their precious bell.

"*I'm sorry,*" was all it said but in those two words it said everything.

A sob built in his throat as he unwound the rope and hot tears trailed his cheeks as he pulled twelve times, the resounding glory of its peal shattering every last bit of reverential decorum until he was nothing but a weeping mess on the floor of this church that was no longer his own.

chapter thirty-eight

Sunday, July 31, 1977

JOSEPH STOOD BENEATH THE belfry, gazing up at the beautiful wind-chime Grace had hung to surprise him. "How did you know I'd take the bell back?" he asked.

She nudged him with her shoulder and he could hear the smile in her voice. "I knew," she said.

"How did you even make it?" he asked. "It's beautiful."

"The same way Iris used to make them, I suppose," she said. "I just put it all together instead of making separate ones."

It hung in layers, branches lashed together to form triangles from which hung rows and rows of the shiny glass on fishing line. There were four tiers, the largest at the top, and it formed as much a chandelier as a wind-chime.

Joseph reached up and held the large green piece hanging from the very centre. It hung on a cord strung with heavy glass beads to give it enough weight to pendulum. "Is this the piece from the windowsill?" he asked.

Grace nodded. "It was one of the biggest," she said. "I hope you weren't saving it for something else…"

"No," Joseph rubbed the spot on his forehead where he'd been burnt through that very same piece. "I mean yes, it *is* special, but this is perfect."

He told her the story of the burning and the overwhelming sense of purpose he found through that piece of glass.

"God's voice," Grace said.

"What?"

"God's voice, right here in the middle of your church." She smiled as she took it from his hand and swung it so it pulsed back and forth between all the strands, causing colours to dance along the walls and floors and a tinkling melody to fill the air.

"Ring out the false, ring in the true," Joseph said softly, his voice thick, his eyes misty.

"Her song?" Grace asked.

"Yeah," he said. "This is better than a bell."

"How did you do it?" Grace asked. "Take the bell back, I mean. How did you do it on your own?"

Joseph shrugged, still gazing up at the chime. "I don't know. I just did it. Adrenaline maybe? Strength by guilt?" he smiled sadly. "One person can manage a lot if what they're doing means a lot, I guess."

"I think it meant a lot," she said, giving the centrepiece another good swing.

June 26, 1977

My Dearest Joseph,

I feel you slipping and I'm desperate to hold on because I'm not sure who I am without you. You are as much a part of me as any limb.

I crave your love even more than I crave Samuel's.

I have his.

I am unsure of yours and nothing frightens me more than the possibility of a life in which you leave me.

Please don't leave me.

I need you beside me. You're the only thing that makes your father's death bearable.

Someday you will know the truth.
Someday you might hate me.

I pray your love is stronger.

I've tried to raise you well. I've tried to instill in you a sense of conscience, confidence, and conviction. Perhaps my methods are strange — it's okay if you question them — but I pray the one thing you never question is the capacity I have to love you because that is vaster than the skies and deeper than the ocean. I hope there is never a night that you fall asleep without knowing unequivocally that I love you more than life and that I have placed you — as I always say — as a seal upon my heart.

I am proud of you. I am proud of the boy you've been and the man you nearly are. The world is wide open to you and a million times better with you in it.

You are in and of my soul. I take you with me everywhere. I will never let you go.

My love is as strong as death.

Momma

Sunday, July 31, 1977

"THANK YOU FOR BRINGING the bell back," Samuel said. He stood in the doorway of Joseph's little church, watching the boy who sat quietly on the floor, his back pressed up against the half-painted wall.

Joseph nodded but didn't speak, nervously turning Iris' gold ring on his pinkie finger as sunbeams blazed through the scattered stained-glass, just hitting the toe of his sneakers. Grace sat beside him and offered Samuel a weak smile.

He entered, leaving the door open to let in a hint of the warm breeze that blew through the clearing.

"The parishioners think it was a miracle," he said as he made his way across the wooden floor. He sat opposite Joseph, the expanse between them a yawning chasm both were afraid to bridge. "They were so full of gratitude."

"Did you tell them the truth?" Joseph asked.

"No." Samuel stretched out his legs to catch the full beam of sun. "Sometimes it's better to let people believe in miracles. They *are* real, you know. Sometimes. But whatever faith is built upon, it's still faith, right? Why did you return it?"

Joseph turned his mother's diary over in his hands, touching the worn cover with tender reverence before sliding it across the planks to Samuel. "She loved you."

Samuel picked up the book and held it against his lips, breathing in the musky leather scent as if he was inhaling the last little bit of her that clung to the world.

"It's all there," Joseph said. "Her story of you." He was quiet for a long moment before adding, "I have to believe in something."

"We all do," Samuel said, turning the pages as if they held

something holy, tracing his fingertips over the words without actually reading them, as if by leaving his fingerprints on the markings he was imprinting her heart onto his skin. "It's strange," he said. "My grief feels exactly like love. It hurts the same. Like I can't breathe and there's so many more colours but not nearly enough all at once."

"Did she go to heaven?" Joseph asked.

Samuel wiped a hand across his nose. "There has never been another woman with such an aptitude for love. Do you know what God's greatest commandment was?"

"Love," Grace said softly.

"Love," Samuel repeated.

Joseph pulled the gold band from his finger and spun it, appreciating the moments it caught the sun and threw shots of light around his church.

"She thought what happened with Paisley made her a terrible person," Samuel said, watching the ring turn, blinking every time it flashed reflected sun into his eyes. "What she couldn't understand was that her whole life was informed by the horrible way in which she grew up. The fact that she rose above it, that she found reasons for moments of happiness and that she raised a child—all of it speaks to her strength. Did you know anyone stronger than your mother?"

Joseph didn't. He'd finally read through all the files his father had left him in the safety deposit box and had pieced her story together like a tragic puzzle. His heart ached with his newfound understanding. He put the ring back on his finger. "Was it really so bad?" he asked. "How she was raised?"

"Worse."

"I should have forgiven her," Joseph said.

"You loved her. That was enough."

Joseph shook his head. “No. Not enough. If it was enough she wouldn’t have needed you.”

Samuel sighed and let his head fall back. “She didn’t need me,” he said, gazing up at the wind-chime. “I was the one who needed her. Maybe I tricked her. Maybe I just took her.”

“No,” Joseph pointed to the diary. “No, you didn’t.”

“I miss her,” Samuel said, one fat tear rolling down his cheek. The chime tinkled softly in the breeze from the open door. “I feel her here.”

“Me too,” Joseph said.

They wept together then, tears tracing a million colours through the window Iris would have loved so much, spanning the gap between them somehow.

For a brief moment they were almost connected.

GRACE SLIPPED HER HAND into Joseph’s and leaned her head on his shoulder, mourning with them but not for Iris—not really. Iris was a stranger to her. Instead, Grace mourned for the missing pieces, the lies of the only mother she really knew; the lost years with the brother she’d always missed; for the broken man who sat across from them who, for all his faults, had played an important role in bringing them all together.

“So,” she said, lifting her head and wiping her eyes with her sleeve. “Does this mean we’re like a family now or something?”

Joseph stiffened beside her and locked eyes with Samuel before a shaky, “No,” slipped from his lips.

Samuel observed them both with sad eyes. “I don’t expect anything from either of you,” he said. “Not now. Not ever, if that’s what you want.”

Joseph dropped his gaze to the floor. “I just…I just don’t

know how…"

"Nobody does, Joseph. I don't know if we're even meant to."

"She knew."

"Yeah," Samuel agreed, getting to his feet. "She did. She would have loved this, Joseph. What you did here. She would have been proud."

"I'm sorry," Joseph whispered, cramming every terrible thought and action into three simple syllables because he didn't have words for more.

"I don't need you to be sorry, Joseph," Samuel said. "I understand why things happened the way they did. Both of us made choices that hurt the other. It's about picking up the pieces now. It's about trying to find a way to be happy again. Maybe. Someday."

Joseph choked on a sob and leaned on Grace while Samuel nodded a goodbye and left through the open door.

"He's not a bad man," Grace said.

"I know," Joseph agreed. "I just…"

"I know. I get it. You ready to go?"

"In a minute. Wait for me outside?"

Grace nodded, giving his hand a final squeeze before stepping beyond the door and leaving him alone in his little church.

JOSEPH SAT QUIETLY while the light danced across the floor and the walls. She really *would* have loved it. He held that truth tightly to his core. There was sanctuary in this place and he knew that though there were tears today, sometime soon it would become a space of peace. Maybe even laughter.

There were still walls to finish painting and he had ideas for building at least one bench out of wood from the surrounding forest. It just didn't feel right to call it a real church without a pew to rest on.

Shadows began to grow against the floor, chasing the happy light away as he climbed into the loft and stood beneath the wind-chime.

He lifted the string of leather from around his neck and held the nail he had worn since that fateful day. He traced the word '*relic*' he'd carved into the rusty surface and he remembered the promise he made to his mother.

"Don't make a relic of me, Joseph."

He spit on his thumb and tried to erase the carving but it remained, gazing up at him with glaring clarity. "I'm sorry, Momma," he whispered, untying the ends that had completed the necklace and reaching up above him to knot them into one of the lines holding the centrepiece of the chime.

He let go of the nail, sending it knocking against the large green piece of glass. It tinkled merrily and it sounded like forgiveness.

"Not a relic, Momma," he said softly. "Just a memory."

JOSEPH STEPPED OUT onto the front stoop. Grace sat on the step, peeling the bark from a twig she'd found on the ground. She smiled up at him—the kind of smile that spoke the exact comfort you need in a moment of particular grief.

Joseph pulled the door closed behind him and looked up to gaze on the bell tower before turning towards the path that would lead them back to the house.

Grace jumped up, brushed bark from her pants and slipped

her arm through his as they started down the forest trail. "*Oh, come, come, come, come, come to the church by the wildwood,*" she started to sing, her sweet voice lifting through the trees like a hallelujah chorus, but she stopped when she saw his face.

"I've never really liked that song," Joseph said.

"Me neither," Grace said. "I just thought…I don't know...like we needed a postlude or something to guide us home."

"Why are you so weird?" Joseph asked, unable to stop a grin from splitting his face.

"It's a family thing," Grace said, her playful smile matching his despite their tear-stained faces and swollen red eyes.

When they laughed together it was much like weeping together—a powerful shared expression that sealed them to one another in a way nothing else could have.

Behind them, the wind-chime sang, its notes floating on the breeze like a whispered vow, and somewhere faraway—in a place made of light and promise—Iris smiled.

SOUNDTRACK

Music is powerful. It holds a million stories within its lyrics and countless emotions in its melodies. *The Church in the Wildwood* was not written to music, but music did play a role in inspiring, in setting moods, and in expressing sentiments that lay just beneath the surface of the words you read on the page.

The following is a list of songs that encompass the mood of *The Church in the Wildwood.* If you felt the emotion of the narrative, you're sure to feel it again as you listen to these songs.

1. Bedroom Hymns *by Florence + The Machine*
2. In A Week *by Hozier (with Karen Cowley)*
3. Slumber My Darling *by Sarah Sample*
4. Cinder and Smoke *by Iron and Wine*
5. Young Pilgrims *by The Shins*
6. Photograph *by Ed Sheeran*
7. Mama Says *by Billy Pilgrim*
8. The Outsiders *by NEEDTOBREATHE*
9. Lost In My Mind *by The Head and The Heart*
10. Who By Fire *by Leonard Cohen*
11. The Promise *by Tracy Chapman*
12. Just Breathe *by Pearl Jam*
13. If I Should Go Before You *by City and Colour*
14. Need It *by Half Moon Run*
15. I Will Follow You Into The Dark *by Death Cab For Cutie*

AUTHOR'S NOTE

There are so many people I need to thank for helping me make this project a reality: the members of my Monday night 'Writers Jam'—your encouragement is invigorating and my dining room table has never been more motivating; Marie Bezeau for introducing me to the old song and Margaret Terry for telling a story about her uncle's sanctuary in the woods; the founders and staff of NaNoWriMo who pulled this story out of me and kept me motivated with witty speeches and ridiculous merit badges; the tireless beta-readers who helped me bring this story to a place of strength and endurance: Bill Aicher, Brian Austin, Carolyn Austin, Heidi Eastman, Susan Gowing, Aidan Hennebry, Larry Kozlof, Michelle McLaughlin, Luke McLaughlin, Margaret Edington, and Rollan Wengert; all the readers of my blog who have rooted for me over the years and kept me going with their encouraging voices; my parents who have never stopped encouraging my imagination—even when it got weird; Mr. Abel, my high school English teacher, who forced me to try harder and dig deeper than I wanted to; Anne Rice, for making me want to be a writer; Leonard Cohen for teaching me there's no such thing as perfect; my children for allowing me moments of closed-door silence; and finally my husband Scott, for saying things like *'you look pretty'* even when I hadn't washed my hair in two days and was cross-eyed from hours in front of my MacBook Pro.

Alanna Rusnak lives on a small patch of untamable land in mid-western Ontario with her three children, husband, and an over-weight cat. Fueled by copious amounts of tea and chocolate, she writes fiction and creative non-fiction from within her tiny study.

Facebook *facebook.com/alannarusnakauthor*
Goodreads *goodreads.com/alannarusnak*
Instagram *@alannarusnak*
Twitter *@alannarusnak*

Subscribe for updates at **alannarusnak.com** for news of upcoming releases, press events, and the status of various projects.

Also by Alanna Rusnak

Eve Undone

Kissing Johnny

and watch for
The Ghost of Iris Carver
a Wildwood companion novella

Manufactured by Amazon.ca
Bolton, ON

17631877R00173